Let The Dead Bury The Dead

Joan King

Published 2016 by Beating Windward Press LLC

For contact information, please visit:
www.BeatingWindward.com

First Edition
ISBN: 978-1-940761-29-9

Dedication

To Uncle Jimmy, Private, 1st Armored Force, US Army

Captured December, 1942 by Rommel's Afrika Korps, North African Theatre, Tunisia

Interned in Stalag 3B Furstenberg.

Forced marched to Stalag 3A Luckenwalde, February 1945.

Fled Stalag 3A after Russian advance on Germans. Crossed the Elbe River to freedom and waiting Americans, May, 1945

Always my hero, a kind and loving man.

Prologue
The Philippines—1943

The shouting of the Japanese guards awakened Sergeant Aaron Timmons, but his survey of the prison yard revealed nothing.

"Everybody here?" he whispered.

"What's going on?" a voice from the bunk above him asked.

Aaron ignored the question while the men in his group murmured their names. They were one short.

"Where's Whitehead?" Aaron asked.

A young private from New Mexico kicked the still form beside him. "Dead, I think."

Aaron shrugged. Whether the man died or not made little difference to him—the body was accounted for. If one man escaped, the other nine in his group would face execution. Tonight, they would live.

The guards dragged a prisoner across the muddy yard. Sweat pouring off the man's face glinted in the light of the full moon. The constant creak of the bunks ceased as those who remained human enough to care heard the pleas for mercy. They waited for the screams to begin. In the morning, another body would be added to the fifty or sixty who died of disease and despair during the night. Aaron and his men would dig the shallow pit for their emaciated remains.

Aaron rolled over and dozed until an agonizing wail chilled the sultry air.

"Let the dead bury the dead," he chanted in his attempt to block the sound.

He was not a religious man, yet the words he had read that afternoon in Corporal Lowell's New Testament echoed in his mind. *Let the dead bury the dead.*

The screaming intensified.

Between malaria and dysentery, Aaron felt as dead as the prisoners he buried. Perhaps that was why he and his men, the sickest and most wasted of the walking, were chosen for the detail. What other disease could they catch?

Let the dead bury the dead.

The man screaming was lucky. A few hours of torture, a shot to the back of the head and his suffering would end. The living had no hope, no relief from the fevers, the diarrhea, the toil, the beatings. Some men gave up and refused to eat the handful of worm-infested rice given them. Within days they became a meal for feral dogs and the stench of rotting flesh in Aaron's nostrils.

Aaron clamped his palms over his ears. Why fight death? What had he to go home to? He had walked out on his wife and never answered her letter telling him he had a baby daughter.

Let the dead bury the dead.

He was as lifeless as Corporal Lowell. Yesterday, he rolled his friend's body into a swampy burial pit with no more thought or care than if he had removed a dead animal from the road. Lowell died for him—executed for stealing quinine from a Japanese officer, quinine for Aaron's malaria.

The cries became unbearable.

"Let the dead bury the dead," Aaron murmured.

He prayed for his body to grow cold like those he buried. Let the dogs drag his body from the burial pit. Better to die than try to make up for the pain he had caused. Better to die than see the disappointment in the eyes of his child he had never held or acknowledged. His wife named the baby Grace.

Grace. The fragrant flower of hope. Where had the phrase come from? He banged his head against the edge of his bunk to stop the thought. In this hell, hope drove men mad. Yet, the words flowed. *I came upon a flow'r with petals pale and dewy leaf. The flower God christened Grace.*

"No," he moaned. Better to die than go insane. "Let the dead bury the dead. Let the dead bury the dead."

A cloud slipped over the moon. Across the compound, a shot ended the screaming. A man whimpered somewhere in the barracks. Another coughed. Aaron drew his legs to his chest and in the moonlight, rocked to his chant.

"Let the dead bury the dead."

Chapter 1

Every spring and fall when I was a child, Gypsies passed through our county and camped in an area known then as the Cottonwood Flats. They came with their rusted cars and trailers, lit their fires on the banks of the river and stayed until they ran out of work or were run off. On the Gypsies' arrival, the small children of Iron Mound, Oklahoma hovered near their mothers, while the young men, itching to be free from toiling in the fields, sneaked away at night to hear their fortunes told by exotic women in long black skirts.

How much of that time is actual memory and how much I absorbed from stories told during holiday gatherings and late night reflections, I'm not certain, but I remember early March of 1945 when I first met Sam. It was the day I learned about my father. The day my grandpa found the moonshiners' still.

I was six. And a half. At that age, those half years were as important as the number itself. Grandpa had kept me home from school because I woke up that morning with a cough. Since Mama's tuberculosis, he fussed over every little tickle in my chest. His closet became a refuge where my sadness and loneliness couldn't find me in the months following her death. The opening where he hung his clothes wasn't much wider than a regular door, but the closet went deeper and was filled with the treasure of suitcases and boxes of dresses, hats and shoes that once belonged to my grandmother. I loved to poke through her things.

Grandpa told me to stay in bed, but by midafternoon I was fidgety and sneaked into his closet. At the time, I didn't realize finding the snapshot of my parent's wedding day would spark a longing for a father. I'd never met him. Nor had I been particularly curious. I simply grabbed the photograph from the bottom of a shoe box, stuffed it into the bib of my overalls and scrambled out into the blustery afternoon before my grandfather caught me and sent me back to my room.

His front yard had a sprawling elm tree. I settled onto the rickety floor of a tree house built by my best friend John Caleb Parker. I pulled the photograph from my overalls. In the fuzzy image caught forever in black and white, Mama was dressed in a wedding gown, laughing, and dancing with my father. He was darker, his black hair shining. Because of his soldier's uniform, I imagined him a hero, which was why I'd never seen him. He had gone to war. Someday he'd march down our driveway, his medals sparkling. Someday he would wave to me and call, "Gracie Timmons, come here and give me a hug." By then the lady from the county would have confessed she made a huge mistake—my mother was alive, pretty like she was before she became sick. Just as in the snapshot, my father would take Mama in his arms, and they would dance to the buzz of locusts until sunset.

My eyes stung with tears. Everything around me became as out of focus as the photograph. Praying was new to me, something Grandpa taught me, and until that day my prayers were the *Now, I lay me down to sleep* sort. This one was different, specific. I prayed my father would be standing in front of me once I finished with the all important 'Amen,' such prayers a silly idea only to grownups.

I cracked open my eyelids and blinked. At the end of the driveway, a man stood inspecting our mailbox. He had the same black hair and dark eyes as in the picture. No medals. He probably had those in his pocket. When he saw me and waved, I shyly raised my hand. That was when I noticed the patterned scarf around his neck.

A Gypsy! I ducked behind a branch. I had waved to a Gypsy.

I'd never seen one this close, but John Caleb had told me enough to give me delightful shivers. Not that I believed his tales of Gypsies kidnapping children and concocting hexes, but neither did I feel the need to prove him wrong. I skidded down the trunk and sprinted to the backdoor where I pressed my face into the dusty screen.

"Grandpa." I looked over my shoulder in terror. The Gypsy had followed me. "Grandpa, hurry!" Because of my sore throat, the plea came out more of a squeak than the scream I hoped it to be.

I let the screen door slam, breaking my grandfather's most hallowed rule, and scrambled through the kitchen into his bedroom. He wasn't there. The backdoor creaked. The Gypsy was inside. I flailed past the clothes in Grandpa's closet and piled cardboard cartons atop an old suitcase to build a wobbly fort. Afraid to breathe, I slumped to the floor. My feet banged to the rhythm of my pumping heart. Grandpa had told me this practice was a bad habit. Until then, I thought him fussy. No more. I grabbed my feet in horror as his line of suits and shirts were swept away.

The wall of boxes collapsed. A hand reached through the gloom. Cold fingers wrapped around my ankle and pulled me toward the opening. I rolled onto my back to kick blindly with my free leg forcing the Gypsy to release me with a yowl that got Grandpa's hound dog to barking. In the commotion, I crabbed deeper into the closet, only to have the Gypsy grab the back of my overalls. I shrieked and thrashed until one of my shoes flew off and bounced against the wall.

"Dadgummit, girl. Now stop that. What's got into you?"

I caught a whiff of pipe tobacco and twisted around. "Grandpa?"

"Who'd you think it'd be?"

"The Gypsy?"

"Gypsy? Where?"

I pointed a shaky finger in the direction of the yard.

"You go back to bed," he said.

He bolted from the room. I wasn't about to miss out on a fight. I scrambled for my misplaced shoe. By the time I caught up, Grandpa had the Gypsy backed against the chicken yard fence. The hens had fled to the other side of their pen in a cloud of dust and feathers. Above their squawking, I heard Grandpa threatening to call the sheriff.

The Gypsy held out his empty hands to prove his innocence. "May I be trampled by my father's horses if one of your chickens disappears into one of my pots."

"I've heard that one before," Grandpa said.

"And I hear you are the big man at school."

"I'm president of the school board, so?"

"You have a hole in your water tank."

"What's that got to do with it?"

"I can fix it."

Grandpa rubbed his forehead as if the Gypsy had given him a headache. He did the same thing with me whenever I asked him too many questions. Grandpas could have bad habits as much as anyone.

"What do you want for it?" he asked.

The Gypsy removed his hat. "Teach me to read."

"What?" Grandpa's laugh erupted through his nose. "Never heard of a Gypsy wanting to do an honest day's work, let alone read."

I tugged at Grandpa's overalls in warning and whispered, "John Caleb said the Gypsies'll put a hex on you."

"I want to learn for my poor babies' sake," the Gypsy said. "That is good, no?"

It wasn't much of a hex. Nothing happened that I could see except Grandpa's face softened a bit.

"I can read," I said. "Mama taught me. If she was here, she could teach you, but she died."

The Gypsy's gaze flicked from Grandpa over to me for less than a second and no more, but in that moment I saw a sadness that reflected mine. I missed Mama, her smile, the way she hugged me just tight enough. She hadn't died of tuberculosis like the lady from the county said. She died of a broken heart, a cliché, I know, but she did. She said those very words as she was taken away.

I leaned against Grandpa for comfort and let his arm find its way around my shoulder. The warmth of the day faded quickly this time of March, along with the fun of sneaking out of bed. My throat felt raw as if I had swallowed a handful of sandburs.

Grandpa nodded at me. "I got my hands full trying to find a teacher for this girl. The dang Parker twins ran off the one we had. Tied her up in the outhouse."

The rest of our class watched in horror. John Caleb's brothers were too big for any of us to stop them.

"A nice hen would fill my babies' bellies tonight," the Gypsy said. "They're sick and hungry."

"You come back tomorrow and fix my tank, then you can have your chicken."

"That is good. I will go now and come back tomorrow."

Like the hex, the fight was a disappointment. I should have stayed in bed.

After the Gypsy left, Grandpa felt my forehead. "We'll go see Young Doc MacKay in the morning if you're not any better."

"I'm better, already."

He smiled at my lie as he bundled me into a blanket in his car. His milk cans were loaded in back. Twice a day he delivered our milk to the Iron Mound Children's Home, a dark stately building atop a hill scoured by prairie wind and children's feet. I loved riding with Grandpa, but the fear of being left at the orphanage hung over me. I stayed in the car while he hauled the milk into the orphanage's kitchen. After Mama died, I was left in such a place where there were too many children and too little affection. In the manner of bureaucracy, no one told me my mother had disclosed the name of my father's father until I was brought before a stranger with a weathered face and a clinging sweet aroma of pipe tobacco which, for some reason, assured me I would be loved.

On the way home, we took the bone-rattling river road, a short cut which usually added thirty minutes due to the route's neglect by the county. Grandpa preferred to have the bolts shaken from his car rather than contend with the traffic on the main highway. His idea of traffic was anything more than three vehicles.

We passed an abandoned tarpaper shack before our car clattered across a rickety wood-planked bridge. I raised my feet off the floor in hopes of making our car lighter. On the other side, a circle of trailers were parked in the Cottonwood Flats. Gypsy women in long black skirts looked up from their fires to shout unintelligible words to their offspring who, like other children, pretended not to hear. Men smoking cigarettes squatted near a string of horses. None of them was the Gypsy who came to our house.

"What's his name?" I asked.

"Who?"

"Our Gypsy. They got names like ordinary folks?"

"They've got more names than Carter's got liver pills, but yours didn't say."

A fit of coughing overtook me to which Grandpa responded by ordering me back under the blanket. I pulled the photograph from the bib of my overalls to hold in front of his face.

"What's my daddy's name?"

"Where'd you find that?"

"The closet."

"Thought I told you to play somewhere else. Someplace not so dark and musty."

"You told me it was too cold outside."

"Aaron," Grandpa said, giving up. "Your mama ever talk about him?"

"Nope."

"Not surprised." The car meandered toward the ditch. Grandpa whipped the steering wheel to the left, taking us back to the middle of the road. He said nothing more and drove past our house to the orchard on the hill where he stopped to pull me from my cocoon. He set me on the ground beside a peach tree and snapped a twig from a branch.

"See this? Looks dead. There's nothing here but gray trunks and branches. No blooms, no leaves, nothing."

I wiped my nose and studied the twig.

"That's how life is," he said, handing me the twig. "Sometimes it's pretty darn dreary and lonely. I know that for a fact. There'll be times you don't think you can make it through the winter 'cause it hurts so bad, but eventually spring comes and the orchard blooms. There's nothing we can change about any of it, except keep believing and waiting. But I promise you I will. Spring'll come."

I couldn't see how this had much to do with my father so I asked, "Where's my daddy?"

Grandpa let out one of those long breaths meant to put me off.

"Where is he?" I asked.

"He got all mixed up and forgot who he was supposed to love. It hurt your mama awful bad."

Remembering to love Mama came as easily as remembering my name. And I was only six. And a half. "How can a grownup forget something like that?"

"Don't know, but he took off."

"Did he forget me, too?" Afraid of the answer, I asked another question. "Are you mad at him?"

"Doesn't have anything to do with mad. More to do with disappointment. I love my boys. Always will." He fiddled with his pipe and eventually lit it. "No use getting into it." He took a couple of puffs and patted me on my head. "It all happened before you were born. Do you remember living here?" He swung an arm in the direction of a house over the hill.

"Nope."

He'd asked me before and shown me the place. I thought it a sad house and hid my eyes whenever we passed it.

"You did," he said, "until about a year and a half ago. Then one day your mama up and left. Didn't take much more than you and a few clothes. Left a note saying she had a job in Dallas and she'd write as soon as she got settled, but she never did. How did ya'll end up in St. Louis?"

The memories of why my mother and I had been living in a place haven to rats and cockroaches and people abandoned to sorrow were too murky to answer. Each time I shrugged away his questions. I remembered little before Mama became sick.

I jammed my hands on my hips. Grandpa was weaseling again. "Where's my daddy?"

"Last I heard, the Philippines when the Japanese invaded."

"Where's that?"

"Clear on the other side of the world."

"Farther than St. Louis?"

"Yep. A lot."

"Will he ever remember me?"

Grandpa sighed. "The army don't know if he's alive. Nobody knows. They say he's probably dead. I'm praying he's not."

Dead was an ugly word. I had yet to get past the loneliness of my mother's abandonment for that was what death meant to me.

He meant to help me understand my loss. Yet winter seemed to have settled over him as well. He shrank inside his denim coat. As he helped me into his car, he nodded at the photo in my hand.

"One thing about your daddy, he's a good looking man with those brown eyes and black hair. He got that from his mama. She was Shawnee." He patted me on the head. "Tell you what. Brownie didn't come up this evening. I bet you she's got a new calf. Let's go find her."

He steered us away from my daddy as surely as he steered us away from the ditch.

"Okay."

"Promise you'll let me take you to Young Doc MacKay and you won't fuss."

He'd caught me fair and square. I gave up without an argument and crawled back into my blanket to watch the sun set the sky above the horizon on fire. Could my father see the sunset halfway round the world, the same as me? I wouldn't forget him.

"What you gonna name your calf?" Grandpa asked. He'd given me my own milk cow for Christmas.

I didn't have to think long. "Peaches."

He laughed. "What if it's a bull calf?"

I smiled up at him, pleased I had made him happy again. "It won't be."

I must have gone to sleep after that. When I woke, it was dark outside. I was alone. Grandpa had gone to find Brownie without me. Condensation fogged the windshield. I cleared a spot with my sleeve to see his lantern twinkling through the trees.

I scrambled from the car. "Grandpa?" The night swallowed my voice.

A bitter wind whipped the tree branches into an eerie dance. I followed a cattle trail by moonlight until the path unraveled like a frayed piece of yarn. Each strand ended in a tangle of brambles where only rabbits or possums could go. All the straggly blackjacks looked alike, crooked and bare.

I was lost. My attempt at praying hadn't worked out too well, yet I tried again.

In answer to my plea, a voice cut through the darkness.

"How could you do this to me? On my own land." It was Grandpa and he was angry.

"You're flat stupid if you think I'm planning on milking cows for the rest of my life."

"It's that or jail, again."

"Go home Dad. This isn't any of your concern."

He called Grandpa *Dad.* My father? He had come home.

I sprinted in their direction. As I neared a ring of lanterns and several trucks, I stopped dead. Grandpa was arguing with my uncle Rag and three other men standing by a fire with barrels and big pots.

Uncle Rag looked nothing like the photo of my father. He had curly hair and something was wrong with one of his eyes. He didn't live with us, and I only saw him once, which was fine with me. He'd wanted to borrow Grandpa's car. Grandpa wouldn't let him, told him now that he was out of jail he needed to get a job. Rag yelled and stomped around. I headed for Grandpa's closet and stayed there until my uncle left.

"I was hoping you'd learned your lesson," Grandpa said.

One of the other men pointed a gun at Grandpa's chest. "Nobody's going to jail, old man."

"I'll take care of him," Uncle Rag said, easing the barrel to the side. "Go home, Dad."

"I want all of you out of here by morning," Grandpa said, his voice fading.

"All right. Now, go."

If I had known which direction Grandpa's car was, I would have flown to it. The last thing I wanted was for Uncle Rag to catch me. I picked my way through the low buck brush until I came to a fallen tree where I dropped to my knees. From there I hoped to follow Grandpa back to the car.

Grandpa stopped a few yards from me to wrap his arms around his chest. As he did so, his flashlight illuminated his pinched face and his struggling to catch his breath.

"Grandpa?" I whispered.

"Gracie?"

I raised my head.

"Stay down," he said.

I ducked behind the log. He staggered over to the tree and sat beside me.

"You all right?" I asked.

"Brownie has a heifer." A diversion even I could detect, but I let him get by with it for a moment. I wanted to make him feel better and my questioning wasn't going to do that.

"I told you Peaches was gonna be a girl," I said.

He moaned and grabbed at his chest. "Go to the car."

"But I don't know which way."

"Go." His grip on his chest loosened.

I tugged on his sleeve. "My throat hurts."

When he didn't move, I buried my face in his chest the way I did when I wanted to listen to his heart. I heard nothing but my own. The awareness that something terrible happened seeped under my skin like the cold. What was I to do? Go to the strangers or try to find the car?

My hands and feet grew numb while I contemplated the question. The beam of Grandpa's flashlight grew dimmer.

"Hey, old man, you spying on us?"

I drew my shivering legs into my jacket and huddled closer to Grandpa. The man who had the rifle poked Grandpa with the barrel.

"Don't hurt him," I whispered.

Grandpa fell to one side. The man stumbled backwards.

"I'll be," he muttered, then shouted, "Hey, the old man's dead, there's a kid here." No one answered him. He pointed a finger at me. "You stay here."

Where could I go? I was lost and too cold to run.

His calling to the others echoed in the clear night air as he sprinted back toward the fire.

I clung to Grandpa's jacket, hoping he'd wake up. A pebble landed next to me. At the light's edge, a hand waved me toward the darkness.

"Little one," a voice whispered. "Come here." The hand motioned again.

I moved to stand, but it signaled me to stay low. I hesitated—what if I followed and got into more trouble? Someone from the camp approached. As I watched his shadowy form, a cold terror paralyzed my breathing. I scrambled toward the waiting hands. They pulled me into a thicket and covered my mouth. If my sore throat would have let me scream, I would have pierced the night.

"Hey, kid?" the shadowy man called.

The man carrying me didn't answer, but jumped into a blackness that looked as if it had no bottom. He landed softly, tightened his grip on me and scrambled along a gully. His breathing coarsened, but he continued to hurdle logs and circle foggy sloughs until a horse snorted quietly.

"Shhh," he whispered to the animal.

As he lifted me onto the horse's back, I caught a glimpse of his sweaty face in the moonlight.

My Gypsy.

He wrapped his coat around me and swung himself up behind me.

"You have your Mama's heart," he said. He gently clucked to his horse.

"You remember my mama?"

He soothed my cheek with the back of his fingers. "Yes."

"She died of a broken heart, but nobody believes me."

"I do."

His remark struck the sorrow of my mother's death, and I buried my face in the crook of his elbow to sob.

I kept it there as I asked, "What's your name?"

He leaned over and whispered into my ear. "Sam."

Sam? A common, ordinary name? There were three Sams at our church alone. They were everywhere.

"Grandpa says Gypsies got more names than somebody's got pills."

"Ah. . . You call him Grandpa?"

"Uh huh."

"And to some he's known as Mr. Timmons, to others Henry, to his son, perhaps, Papa? See? One man and many names. So I'm Stefan to him, Sven to someone else. Eli to another."

"I get it," I said. "But I don't know what my daddy called him. He forgot me. I thought you were my daddy when I saw you. Are you going to be my daddy?"

"We must be quiet."

The shadowy man. I'd forgotten him. I leaned against Sam's chest as we rode in silence, Sam humming a strange tune to the rhythm of his horse's gait. Before I gave in to my exhaustion and fever, I wondered if I had been kidnapped by a Gypsy.

Then I remembered my grandpa, growing cold, and knew it no longer mattered.

Chapter 2

In murky dreams, I smelled horse's sweat. A woman's dark eyes reflected flames of a fire. She forced a bitter liquid between my lips and cooed words I couldn't understand. The dreams ended abruptly with the sensation of cold. I forced open my eyes. Miss Louise, the tiny spinster who owned Iron Mound's general store, tried to lay an icy cloth on my forehead. I turned my face away. For my trouble, I ended up with a cold wet ear.

After the lady from the county took me away from Mama, I was wary of older women. With Miss Louise, I made the mistake of placing my cheek against the cool display glass of her meat counter the first time I was in her store one hot September afternoon. No one warned me she took great pride in the case, that no child touched it and walked away unscathed by her tongue. Since then she tried to woo me out from behind Grandpa with a handful of candy corn, something hard to come by with the war on. I accepted her bribes, only to dart back to the safety of his worn overalls.

Lately, Miss Louise had been complaining of young men leering through her lace curtains as she undressed for bed. No one believed her tale. She was as withered as last year's apple forgotten on the tree. The county sheriff grew tired of taking her nightly calls and dodged her, but most people overlooked this and her other peculiarities to patronize her store because they had nowhere else to go.

Miss Louise caught a cold dribble of water running down my neck as she sat beside me on the bed. "Don't worry, dear. You're here with me. Upstairs above my store."

On the nightstand beside the bed was the twig Grandpa gave me and the photo of my parent's wedding day.

"Grandpa," I croaked with what little voice I had left. I wanted his reassuring hand resting on the back of my head. I wanted to smell the aroma of his pipe, to hear his assurance the orchard would bloom again.

"I know," Miss Louise said. "I've sent Young Doc MacKay out to find him. Tell me what happened last night." She squeezed my hand as if that would help free the memories of the night's terrors.

They came back slowly. Grandpa, my cow Brownie, the men and the Gypsy.

"Did you know any of them?"

I twisted the sheet into a rope. "No." I left out Uncle Rag. I hoped never to see him again.

Miss Louise closed her eyes. Tears gathered. One fell on my cheek as she leaned over to kiss my forehead. It helped absolve a little of my fear of her, but not the aching inside me.

She abandoned me to sit in a rocking chair. The chair and the floor creaked in protest of her movement until she planted both feet on the floor with a thump, startling me.

"No wonder that Gypsy wanted to get out of here so fast," she said. "They know when there's something afoot."

"Sam," I whispered. He had not been a dream. The thought brought both comfort and sadness.

"Is he the Gypsy who found you?"

I nodded and added, "Kidnapped."

"No, dear, Gypsies don't kidnap children." She rocked another minute. "But yours could be in big trouble for other reasons. Listen to me. Don't say a word to anybody about him. Promise?"

The same with all the rest of the men, especially Rag with his droopy eyelid. I nodded, then drifted back into strange and frightening dreams.

The next time I woke, Young Doc MacKay was sliding his stethoscope across my chest. There was nothing young about him. He had silver hair and a face as deeply wrinkled as the bark of a timeworn cottonwood. The town had given him the label to distinguish him from his father, Old Doc MacKay, who died at ninety-three after delivering a set of triplets. The description stuck.

Once he finished, he had me sit up so he could thump me on my back like a watermelon. Miss Louise offered him a cup of coffee which he turned down with an order to open my mouth wide. He stuck a tongue depressor down my throat to make me gag. The funny little sound he made worried me. When he finally accepted the coffee, I swallowed and blinked back the tears.

"Hurts, doesn't it?" he said, patting me on the head. He looked up at Miss Louise. "What was it you gave her?"

"I believe it was elderberry tea?" Miss Louise said.

"You believe? You don't know?"

Her twinkling eyes were the only reply.

The doctor sighed and stared at the ceiling like an exasperated teacher. "Miss Louise. . . Oh, never mind." He put his stethoscope away. "Whatever it was, her fever's gone."

He pulled a sucker from his pocket, the only reason I ever put up with his doctoring. He handed out the reward for not squirming or bawling. I didn't bother to unwrap it. My confusion and sadness were too much for a lollipop to fix, even a coveted cherry one.

He led Miss Louise to the far corner of the room where they had a whispered conversation while glancing at me. Children know nothing good comes from one of these discussions. I slipped below the blankets, wishing I could hide in Grandpa's closet where it was dark and safe.

"I'll tell her," Miss Louise whispered.

I felt her hand on my head.

"Dearie?" she said, tucking the blanket under my chin. "Doctor MacKay found your grandpa. He brought his body back. He thinks it was a heart attack. That means something in your grandpa's heart broke."

"Mama died of a broken heart," I said.

She blinked back tears. "I'm sorry."

"There wasn't a finer man than your grandpa," Doctor MacKay said.

Their words were perplexing. What did I care if they were sorry or if my grandpa was a fine man? I wanted him to come and take me home. I'd promise him I'd never hide in his closet again or try on my grandma's hats and shoes. I'd never snoop in boxes and find a photograph of my parents. If I'd never found the snapshot of my father or wanted Grandpa to find Brownie's calf, Grandpa's heart never would have broke.

The doctor peered over his glasses at Miss Louise. "While I was there, I couldn't help but notice an abandoned still. The fire was smoldering. Didn't look like your typical good ol' boy operation." He took a sip of coffee. "Which brings up a point. How did my little patient end up here?"

"I found her on my doorstep," Miss Louise said, giggling, though she eyed me as a reminder to keep my promise. "There was a knock on the door downstairs and there she was."

"I can swallow that if you want me to," Doctor MacKay said, "but I'm not so sure Sheriff Lundy will. Just to let you know, he was tromping around the site when I got there."

Miss Louise's hands fluttered to her face, their skin as fragile and translucent as the tissue paper she wrapped ladies underwear in.

"Oh, Lordy, this day, the next one, then the briar patch," she said.

"I don't think you need to worry about the briar patch quite yet. But Lundy'll be here before you know it. What's going on?"

"Most bootleggers around here are just out for a good time and a little pocket change. They wouldn't hurt a fly, but let's say this *somebody* who left a little girl on my doorstep thought different or he wouldn't have got in the middle of it."

"I can understand that, but why not tell the sheriff?"

"Because Lundy's a lazy idiot who might go blabbing this over town."

I thought it best to disappear beneath the covers, again.

I knew little about Sheriff Lundy other than he disliked Miss Louise's pestering him with stories of young men peeking in her windows. Like most children around, I stayed away from him. He was a huge man with jowls as floppy as a hound dog's. His uniform was comprised of a wrinkled khaki shirt and a sweaty Stetson. My view of him that morning consisted mostly of his belly overflowing his trousers and a pistol nearly as long as my arm. Though snuggled under the blanket and pretending to sleep, I had left a small opening in which to peer through.

Lundy had a blustery voice and demanded Miss Louise tell him how I ended up at her house when my grandpa died near a moonshine still. She repeated the story she gave the doctor minus the giggles. Sheriff Lundy snorted his skepticism and hitched his gun belt to his waist only to have it slide over the rolling hill of his stomach down to his hips.

"She remember anything?" he asked.

At the question, a chill crept down my arms and legs.

"Not a thing," Miss Louise said. "Young Doc MacKay's not sure if it's because she's sick or in shock, but she'll be all right. Children are quick healers."

"How would you know? You're an old maid." The sheriff laughed so hard his gun belt fell. He caught it and squirmed it back into place. "Maybe you're right, let's see." He sauntered across the room and whipped the blanket from my face. "She's awake." He winked at me.

I gasped, setting off a hacking spasm. Between coughs, I heard him mumble how I ought to be sent to the Children's Home and Young Doc MacKay arguing I didn't belong there with my infection. I was about to let loose a wail when Miss Louise hurried over to the bed and nudged the sheriff aside.

"Doc thinks it could be tuberculosis," she said. "Her mother died of it, you know."

Lundy moved back a step and licked his chapped lips. "No, I didn't. You think she's got it, Doc?"

"Maybe you ought to go," Dr. MacKay said.

"If she remembers anything, let me know."

"Most certainly." Dr. MacKay shut the door behind the sheriff. When he turned around, his face glowed red. "Miss Louise, you're the most exasperating woman I know. This child does not have tuberculosis. What gave you that idea?"

She looked puzzled at his outburst. "I didn't say she had tuberculosis, did I?"

"Worse. You said that I said."

They went down the hall to argue. Without them there, a gloom settled over the room, echoing the question I had been too terrified to voice, *What's going to happen to me?*

Mrs. Ponder, the preacher's wife, came to sit with me while Miss Louise worked in the store. I slept most of the day. When Miss Louise returned that evening, she looked at my eyes and throat before asking if I felt well enough to go to Grandpa's house for my clothes and things.

Miss Louise drove an old Model A coupe with bouncy springs in the seat. She'd tried to make them behave by covering them with a scratchy wool blanket. Despite her efforts, they persisted in popping up like turtle heads in a pond. By the time, we arrived at Grandpa's house, I had curled up in a fit of giggles.

"Can we feed Beau?" I asked. "He's grandpa's hound dog."

"I want you to wait for me. Don't go in the house by yourself."

I felt too happy to listen. I was home. Against her advice, I jumped from the car before she could follow me. As usual, I skipped to the house. As usual, I let the screen door slam. Part of me expected to find Grandpa in his favorite chair, wearing his glasses to read the newspaper, or in the kitchen fixing supper. I sniffed the air for the sweet aroma of his pipe tobacco. It was gone, as he was.

I retreated to his closet where I sat on the floor and tapped my shoes together while watching, praying for him to peer into the door. Miss Louise called my name, her voice growing and fading as she walked through the house. When she discovered my hiding place, I jumped up and ran outside to sit next to Beau on the back step.

Spread across the hill were the bare peach trees. Where were their blooms? Where was the spring Grandpa promised?

Miss Louise handed me one of my grandfather's faded blue handkerchiefs she must have found in his bedroom. I stopped scratching Beau's ears long enough to wipe my eyes.

"Grandpa's not here."

"I know," Miss Louise said.

"Where is he?"

"I thought you understood." She sat beside me and cupped my face in her spidery fingers. "I've never had children, you see."

What that had to do with my question, I didn't know. "Is he in heaven with my mama?"

"Yes, of course."

"Then why did the doctor bring his body to town?"

She explained about souls and bodies, funerals and cemeteries. I laid my head on her lap. Some things I remembered Grandpa telling me. My mother was buried in St. Louis. Someday he wanted to bring her "home." I hadn't understood it then. Together with Grandpa's lecture about orchards and winter, I had learned two hard lessons in two hard days. I hoped there wouldn't be another one tomorrow.

"I think your grandpa knew he wasn't well," Miss Louise said. "A few weeks ago, he asked me to take care of you if anything happened to him. At least until we hear something about your father."

I didn't tell her the Army thought my father dead. It was best to leave such things alone and not stir up talk of the Children's Home.

"Who's gonna take care of Beau?"

"Your Uncle Rag will milk and feed until we can get things settled."

I was able to follow her back into the house. While she gathered my clothes, I found the small cardboard suitcase the orphanage in St. Louis gave me and placed in it my most prized possessions—my Raggedy Ann doll and the A-B-C book my mother made me. There were other things to add when I got back to Miss Louise's, things to keep alive the memory of my Grandpa— his faded blue hanky, hope in the form of a peach twig and the snapshot of my father.

Chapter 3

Miss Louise moved me into a bedroom toward the back with blue flowery wallpaper. I added my new treasures to the suitcase and slipped it beneath the bed covered with a patchwork quilt. The room had a dresser and a closet. I never had a closet of my own before. Grandpa nailed pegs on the wall for my school dresses. This closet wasn't much good. Except for a tiny place for my dresses, every inch was piled high with boxes of what Miss Louise said were her business papers. But the window overlooked the backyard with the biggest oak tree in town.

Mrs. Ponder stayed with me the next morning. She brought a half a dozen books that once belonged to her children who had grown and moved away. I suspected it was to keep me too busy to mope. She read one aloud to me. Though it was a Tuesday, Miss Louise and Young Doc MacKay thought I shouldn't return to school until next week, especially since I would have to attend a different school in town, my old one being too far away.

When Miss Louise brought me lunch, Mrs. Ponder went home.

"She's playing the organ for the funeral service this afternoon," Miss Louise said. "Do you feel well enough to stay by yourself?"

I nodded as I leafed through another one of the books.

"I've closed the store," she said. "Most folks are going to the funeral, but if you don't want to stay by yourself, I'll find someone."

"Can I go outside and play?"

"Not yet, but go ahead and get dressed."

By midafternoon, I had grown tired of reading. I found Grandpa's hanky in my cardboard suitcase and tied the blue bandana around my neck. I became a cowgirl galloping around the room, pretending to rope the bedposts with my nighty. A branch cracked in the backyard. I looked up to see my best friend

John Caleb Parker take his last practice swing before he let go of the limb. He landed on the sill with a grunt, his legs dangling out the window. Something plinked against the house to our left. I dragged John Caleb inside before he slid the wrong direction. He flopped onto the floor like a landed fish.

"Whew, that was close," he said. "Figured it was you when I heard the *yehawing*."

"Wanna play cowboys and Indians?" Now that I knew my father was Shawnee, I claimed dibs on the Indian.

There was another thump against the house. We peeked over the window sill.

One of his pimply-faced siblings sneered up at us. "Hey, skunk, get down here."

"I ain't no skunk, Riley Parker," John Caleb said.

"Maybe not, but you stink like one."

"Go 'way."

"Bring the pipsqueak with you." Riley launched a piece of gravel. He was so cross-eyed his aim was pathetic.

Another rock ricocheted through the limbs and nicked John Caleb's arm. He yelped. While Riley kept us distracted, his twin, Roland, had sneaked into the yard. Unlike Riley, Roland was a dead shot, but he wasn't as bright, which was equivalent to saying one turnip in the patch was dumber than the next. Both had failed the eighth grade so many times they had sprouted whiskers on their chins.

"I'll tell," John Caleb shouted. "Miss Louise'll come after you with Old Bluster."

Old Bluster was a double barrel shotgun which Miss Louise often bragged could turn thieves into tea strainers. Our threat was pure bluff. Not the shotgun, but Miss Louise. She was at the funeral.

Instead, I stuck my tongue out at the twins—once I'd ducked out of sight. A bit cowardly, but no two boys were meaner than the Parker twins. John Caleb and I sat beneath the sill, listening to the ping of gravel against the side of the house. As dumb as the twins were, they were smart enough to avoid breaking Miss Louise's window.

John Caleb sighed. "I'm sure gonna miss Mr. Henry." His name for my grandpa. "You want my arrowhead?" He showed me a piece of flint, his only true possession. Everything he had, including his overalls and boots, once belonged to someone else, probably several someones. "I promise you can keep it forever. I won't ask for it back, cross my heart and hope to die." He looked at me with teary eyes.

I pretended to study it until the shadow of sadness moved over me. It was enough, and I gave it back to John Caleb.

Once the plinking against the house ended, John Caleb peered out the window.

"Coast is clear. Come on. We gotta get out of here," he said, sitting on the sill.

I calculated how far the closest branch was from the house and came up with a long ways. "What for?"

"The sheriff's downstairs and yapping about how you belong in the Children's Home."

"But Miss Louise's at the funeral."

"Not anymore. She's here with a judge, and Pa's all hot under the collar 'cause she won't open the store for Ma to get groceries until they decide what to do with you."

"I'll play sick. The doctor said he wouldn't send me to the Children's Home as long as I'm sick."

John Caleb rolled his eyes at me. "You can't play sick your whole life."

I thought about asking him why not—his father had. The common opinion was you could come nigher to persuading a horse thief to hang himself than persuading George Parker to work.

"What am I gonna do?" I asked.

"We'll run away and join the Gypsies."

His revelation sucked the air from my lungs. "How did you know?" I asked. Nobody was supposed to have seen Sam kidnap me.

"Cause I'm really a Gypsy."

While I gawked at him in amazement, John Caleb rattled on about outlaws having kidnapped him from the Gypsies when he was a baby and selling him to the Parkers. Anybody with an eye in their head would know this was impossible because he shared the Parker family's bright red hair and freckles, not to mention their curse of being unable to read. On the other hand, Sam couldn't read either. That was why he wanted Grandpa to teach him.

I puffed up my chest. I couldn't let John Caleb get the better of me, not when I knew a *real* Gypsy.

"One kidnapped me and left me with Miss Louise," I said. "His name's *Sam.*" I added the extra emphasis to rile John Caleb even more.

"No foolin'?"

I placed my palm across my heart, our sign of honesty. "No foolin'." My excitement spoiled quicker than milk on a hot day. "I wasn't supposed to tell," I whispered. "Don't tell Miss Louise or anybody."

"Promise, cross my heart and hope to die." He slapped his chest.

His word was enough.

Upon meeting me, John Caleb swore we would be blood brothers for life, despite my insistence I was a girl. When Grandpa caught us about to consummate our vow with John Caleb's rusty broken-bladed knife, he suggested ketchup. We poured it on our palms and shook hands. John Caleb's allegiance puzzled me at first. Where I'd lived in St. Louis, my playmates tended to be evicted when the rent came due, but Grandpa said it was easier to get rid of a sandbur in your sock than John Caleb, especially if we fed him fried bologna, our favorite supper.

"Let's go find Sam," John Caleb said.

Now that I had broken my promise to Miss Louise, I decided I might as well.

"Wait a minute." I grabbed my cardboard suitcase with my treasures. "Okay." But when I peered out the window again, the distance from the second story to the ground seemed to have doubled.

"Maybe we ought to take the stairs," I said.

John Caleb eyed the ground. "Yeah, maybe."

We sneaked down the hallway. Miss Louise's house was twice as big as Grandpa's. At the front was the kitchen and dining room on one side and her parlor on the other. Her bedroom was in the middle overlooking the side porch. Across the hall was the bathroom and the door leading to the stockroom downstairs, the only way in or out.

The open tread stairs creaked and moaned at us. A string of bare bulbs hung from a high tongue and groove ceiling, making the stockroom a big dreary place. It took up the back third of the building and had tall shelves filled with cardboard boxes and wooden crates. There were three doors. I hadn't notice this when Miss Louise brought me through the day before.

"Which one?" John Caleb whispered. He glanced over his shoulder at my indecisiveness. "Don't worry, we'll find your Gypsy."

I wasn't so sure. Not when we couldn't find our way out of the general store.

"I think it's the one by the window," I said.

We trotted over to turn the knob.

"Shoot, locked," John Caleb said.

The door to the right swung open, sweeping us back against a crate.

Miss Louise grabbed me to hold me upright. "What are you doing down here?"

I wailed, "I don't want to go to the Children's Home. I got an infection."

John Caleb put his hands on his hips. "It ain't fair to send her there without her having a say so. It ain't."

"Are you through with your lecture?" Miss Louise asked. His head wobbled, which she must have taken for a yes. "And your name?"

"John Caleb Parker," he stuttered.

"Should have known you were a Parker."

The way she said it made John Caleb slump a couple of inches.

"Well Mr. John Caleb Parker, that's about the wisest thing that's ever come out of the mouth of a Parker and half the judges of the county. Are you Gracie's friend that Henry told me about?"

"Yessum."

"And what were you two planning?" she asked, eyeing my suitcase.

"Running away?" I said.

"Let me have that."

I handed over my suitcase.

"Did you forget your grandpa wanted me to take care of you?"

I nodded, without mentioning my broken promise of Sam.

"As a favor to me and your grandpa, the judge is here to make that formal," she said. "He came for the funeral. You are not going to the Children's Home. Understand?"

I nodded so hard my eyeballs hurt.

"Good, let's go say hello to the judge. Then John Caleb, I want a word with you."

I was sent outside to sit on the front porch of the store after Miss Louise introduced me to the judge. She kept John Caleb inside. His only hope, I figured, was with the judge around, she wouldn't use Old Bluster on him.

Miss Louise had put up a handwritten *Closed until 5* sign on the door. The lumber yard, hardware store and the filling station down the street were open and busy. The town of Iron Mound that gave the orphanage its name was supposed to have dried up with the departure of the railroad, but no one told the folks who lived there, and the town hung on. Sullivan's General Store was the hub—part grocery store, part dry goods, and more importantly, the weather bureau and rumor mill, which amounted to the same thing.

On the front porch, the hands of the RC Cola clock took their time going around the dial. Years ago someone had penciled beneath the clock, *Time spent on the front porch ought to run slower than that of the world.* Miss Louise liked it so much she never painted over it. Nobody knew who wrote it. It was the big mystery of the town.

The Parker truck was across the street. I recognized it by its rust, its general disrepair and the red-haired girl in back, John Caleb's oldest sister, Maggie. John Caleb came out to sit next to me. He waved at Maggie.

"What'd Miss Louise do to you?" I asked.

He stretched back his lips to show off his yellow, orange and white "false teeth" before giving me a few kernels of candy corn.

"Nothing." He spit out the candy corn. "Told me she'd come after us like a witch on broom, if we tried to run away. Then she asked how I got into the house. Said I was welcome anytime, but to come through the door." He grinned and popped one of his "teeth" back into his mouth.

With our attention on our candy, we didn't pay much heed to the man crossing the street until he was on the sidewalk in front of us. One look at his droopy eyelid, and I jumped to my feet, lost my balance and tumbled into his arms.

"Careful, Gracie," he said.

I had convinced myself he wouldn't come around again, that he couldn't, but there he was, his one good eye studying me from the top of my head to my banging shoes. I put one foot on top the other to stop their bad habit. Rag knelt in front of me and pressed a discolored quarter into my palm. "You need something, you just come to your old Uncle Rag. We're all we got, each other. I'll take care of you. You take care of me. See?"

I stared at the quarter glued to my sticky palm. Did he know I was there the night Grandpa died? I had been too worried about the Children's Home to consider the possibility of ending up with him. What if Miss Louise was wrong about my living with her?

Rag raised my chin with his finger. "I loved your mama. Everybody did. She was the prettiest, sweetest lady I ever set eyes on. What's more, I know what it's like to lose your mama. Mine died when I was a little boy. I missed her so much it hurt awful."

He tried to hug me. I wiggled from his grasp, wondering if the eye under his droopy lid was thinking the same thing as his good one.

John Caleb grabbed my hand to look at my quarter. "A whole two bits, Gracie."

Rag swept off his grimy hat to puzzle over John Caleb. "You gotta be one of George Parker's brats."

"I'm not a brat," John Caleb mumbled.

"Course not. You know what they say about a Parker, don't you?" He scrubbed John Caleb's scalp with his knuckles. "If he ever had two nickels to rub together, he'd be too lazy to do it."

John Caleb raised his upper lip like a growling dog. His candy colored teeth failed to make an impression. Rag laughed, but he reached into his pocket and tossed John Caleb a quarter.

"Here you go."

"Wow. Thanks," John Caleb said.

"And don't say I never gave you anything for your trouble."

John Caleb and I were comparing our coins when a wrinkled hand rested on my shoulder. I leaned into Miss Louise for comfort. My worries had worn me down.

"I missed seeing you at the funeral," Miss Louise said to Rag.

"I'm here now."

"Is that any way to treat your father's memory?"

He sighed. "I couldn't get his car started."

I figured it was because Grandpa didn't want him borrowing it, but knew better than to remind Rag. With Miss Louise beside me, my uncle seemed to forget me. He reached over to snap his fingers in front of John Caleb's face.

"Hey, boy? How many brats your daddy got these days?"

"Nine."

Rag hooted. "Never figured old George to have that much ambition."

"Pa says Ma's swallowed another watermelon seed. That's her over there coming down the sidewalk."

Mrs. Parker was a weary-looking woman dragging two toddlers along. She carried a younger one in her arms. From the looks of her, she had swallowed the whole watermelon and not just the seed. The way she held her round tummy freed a gauzy memory from wherever I kept forgotten times.

I pointed at Mrs. Parker. "Mama got fat like that." I glanced up at Miss Louise. She had raised her hands to her mouth. Rag leaned heavily against one of the porch posts. I stuck my finger in my mouth, wishing I could hide it. This was why teachers disapproved of pointing at another person. The simple gesture turned people cold.

"Did your mama have a baby?" Rag asked.

His paleness and the forcefulness of the question evaporated the moment's memory. I couldn't remember a baby. Sometimes, I barely remembered Mama.

"Did she? Tell me," Rag said.

"She wouldn't know." Miss Louise wrapped her thin arms around me. "She's no more than a baby, herself. I want to hear nothing more about it. Let's go inside. We have other business to tend to."

I followed her, but she circled her finger for me to turn around and sit on the step. I'd said something wrong, terribly wrong. To help me think, I banged my shoes together. John Caleb sat beside me and did his part by sharing the last of the candy corn. It didn't help me figure out the problem but made it less important.

We had the candy corn about finished when Rag stormed out of the store, slamming the door hard enough the glass in the large front windows rattled. He'd obviously forgotten Grandpa's rule about such things. Miss Louise probably had the same commandment. We turned to look at the door. Sure enough, here she came.

"Henry Timmons, Jr., come back here," she called, too late to stop Rag. He'd turned a corner and disappeared.

John Caleb doubled over in laughter at Rag's given name. Miss Louise huffed and went back inside. I slumped on the step, delighted Rag was gone. Maybe forever?

The thought pleased me, immensely.

Chapter 4

I didn't see John Caleb the next three days. I missed him. Every morning, he'd come by Grandpa's house and Grandpa would hoist us up on old Moonie, his draft horse. John Caleb and I would flail Moonie with our heels all the way to school while the poor horse twitched and shivered until he rid himself of his two annoying flies. Then he'd trot home for his oats, leaving John Caleb and me to sit at our desks, side by side. In our one-room school house there were twenty-eight children grades one through eight and one teacher. I was the only girl in the first grade, John Caleb the only boy. Starting Monday I would have to go to the school in town where Miss Louise said there was a dozen or more students in my grade alone. I would be lost without John Caleb. The only good I perceived in the new school was I might possibly give up the title of worst jacks player ever.

After breakfast, I sat on my bedroom floor sulking and bouncing my jacks ball. Miss Louise peered through the doorway to watch me for a minute.

"How would you like to help me in my store today?"

Despite her kindness and the judge's decree that I belonged to her, I felt as scattered as the jacks on the floor with no Grandpa or John Caleb to gather me up.

"Yes, Ma'am."

Before opening, she walked me along the six aisles. Groceries were at the front, with the produce along one wall opposite the meat counter. Hardware was located in back, close to the stove and table where the old men of the town gathered to play dominoes. She'd placed clothing between these two essentials. I stopped to sniff the new overalls because their deep blue smell reminded me of Grandpa.

One of my favorite places was her candy counter. Several times that morning I stood in front of it, hoping she'd give me a handful of candy corn. Instead, she'd send me after a can of green beans for a lady or ask me to show a man where the hammers were. Once I finished with whatever errand Miss Louise sent me on, I'd go to the checkout to watch her fingers fly across the keys of her cash register, a huge brass machine. It was her piano. Its ring made music to her ear.

The day almost passed before I gathered the courage to ask, "Can I punch one of the keys?"

She let me push *Sale* when she checked out the next customer, but warned me all other keys were off limits.

"Not until you learn to add, subtract, and multiply," she said.

I sighed with disappointment. It would take years to learn all those things. Arithmetic was my worst subject in school.

Feet pounded across the porch. The door banged open and a red-faced John Caleb ran into the room. I danced a little jig of delight as he grinned at me and collapsed against the counter, gasping for air.

Miss Louise waved him off. "You're getting everything sweaty. School out already?" She glanced up at the clock.

"Yessum."

"You didn't skip class, did you?"

"Nah, teacher got tired of putting up with us." He kicked off one of his over-sized shoes to rub his foot. "I ran the whole way."

"That's got to be a good five miles."

"I cut across. I got news. Lots of news."

"Let's hear it after you go back and close the door."

"Sorry," he said.

He had it halfway closed when Mr. Becker squeezed through. Mr. Becker looked as red-faced and winded as John Caleb.

"I found a teacher," he said, patting me on the head as he rushed past.

"Shoot, I was gonna tell," John Caleb said.

Mr. Becker was one of the school board members along with my grandpa. Mr. Becker's wife had volunteered to substitute until a new teacher was found. I liked Mrs. Becker. She played the piano and liked to sing, but the big boys weren't afraid of her and talked all the time.

"We've had a devil of a time finding one," Mr. Becker said. "The only two applicants we had turned us down. Then I got a call this morning from a lady. She sounds real good. University of Tulsa cum something or other."

John Caleb leaned closer to me. "Betcha she's old."

"How do you know?" I asked.

"She's a teacher."

He had a point. Miss Jewel was old. Grandpa had told me she was his teacher and came with the school's books, blackboard and desks fifty years ago.

Mr. Becker gave John Caleb a disapproving glance. "If we can only keep the Parker twins from running her off."

"That's my other news," John Caleb shouted. He grinned so wide two dimples appeared among his freckles.

"They're quitting. They told Pa last night they was through. So he loaded 'em up today and took 'em to Hampson's Egg Farm over by Stillwater to clean chicken houses."

"Sounds like a perfect match of talent and career," Miss Louise said.

John Caleb wasn't finished. He grinned even wider. "Best thing—it's too far for 'em to come home."

He did a whoop and a war dance until the look in Miss Louise's eyes froze him solid.

"I guess that problem's solved," she said.

"Partly," Mr. Becker said. "Her father's a big shot oilman over in Tulsa. We can't just give her a back room in some family's drafty old farmhouse. That's why I'm here. What would she think of that?" He took off his hat to scratch his head. "You've got to wonder why someone like her would want to come this far out in the sticks to teach at our school. Do you know of anybody here in town that'd have a room? She'll be here tomorrow."

"I do, as a matter of fact."

"Where?"

"Right here."

He hemmed and hawed a bit before he admitted, "I heard you've been having problems with Peeping Toms?"

"Oh, that. Don't you worry. If I catch anybody sneaking a look at your teacher, I'll pepper 'em with Old Bluster."

Her answer did little to reassure Mr. Becker. His smile slid sideways.

"This is the answer to my prayers," Miss Louise said. "Gracie won't have to go to a different school. She can ride out with her teacher."

John Caleb let out another whoop and I joined in.

The new teacher's name was Miss Redding. I repeated her name until I went to sleep so I wouldn't forget. John Caleb showed up at the store before it opened the next morning. Saturday was the busiest day of the week what with the shopping for Sunday dinner and farmers coming to town. The third time we asked Miss Louise when the new teacher would arrive, she shooed us to the door.

On the way out, I finally gathered my courage. "Can we have some candy corn?"

She waved at me as if I were silly for asking. "It'll give you cavities. And let me know when Miss Redding gets here."

"We'll be the first to see her," John Caleb said.

We waited an hour, playing jacks and discussing whether Miss Louise would let us build a tree house in her backyard. Our hope of being the first to see the new teacher crumbled when Mr. and Mrs. Becker showed up with their two girls. Soon several other parents arrived to welcome Miss Redding.

As I gathered my jacks, I noticed John Caleb gawking over my shoulder.

"What's the matter?" I asked. "Your freckles are twitching."

I turned around. He wasn't the only one staring. Everyone on the porch seemed mesmerized by the prettiest lady ever to get out of a car in Iron Mound. Her brown hair was put up with silver combs, but one curl had worked it way loose to hang across her forehead. She whisked it aside and smiled at us.

"Miss Redding?" Mr. Becker stuttered.

"Are you Mr. Becker? I'm so pleased you invited me," she said, extending her hand for Mr. Becker to help her up the steps. She wore a navy wool skirt with a waterfall blue blouse that shimmered in the sun.

John Caleb and I were so excited we forgot to tell Miss Louise the new teacher had arrived. She must have heard all the chattering and came outside on her own. Along with us she couldn't get close to Miss Redding for the crowd. John Caleb and I were able to wiggle past the grownups and pop up next to her. She smelled sweeter than honeysuckle. As she was talking with Mr. Becker, I surrendered to the temptation of running my hand down the silky sleeve of her blouse. She turned to me and smiled.

"And who have we here?" she asked.

When I told her my name, she squeezed her eyes closed for a moment and repeated it with a quivering voice.

"She's the little girl I told you about," Mr. Becker said.

She opened her summer blue eyes. "So you're going to help me get back and forth to school?"

Help her? I'd lock the Parker twins in the outhouse if they bothered her. Fortunately, that wouldn't happen now that they were gone.

"Are you one of my students, as well?" she asked John Caleb.

He nodded, his mouth sagging in wonder.

"You'll have to excuse John Caleb," Miss Louise said. The crowd parted to let her through. "I believe his heart's melted and run down into his shoes. And I doubt his will be the last. I'm Miss Louise."

Miss Louise fixed a big supper that evening. Of all the rooms I had seen in Miss Louise's house, her dining room was my favorite with its tall narrow windows, polished floor and the Blue Willow china that looked like a patch of spring flowers planted in the soft glow of the round oak table.

A scoop of mashed potatoes plopped onto my plate. I would have protested I was old enough to serve myself, but all the excitement of the day had taken its toll. A spoonful of carrots came next, and I sighed at another dilemma. I hated the vegetable. Grandpa had despised them as well. He said it was hereditary and never cooked them. I solved my problem by pushing the carrots to the far side where they wouldn't contaminate my potatoes.

Miss Louise made a poor attempt at suppressing a smile. "How'd you find things at school?" she asked Miss Redding.

"Fine. I went over the grade book," Miss Redding said. "Later, I'd like to ask you about some of the children."

"Oh?" Miss Louise said. "The Parkers?"

"Yes. How did you know?"

"There at the end, they wore Miss Jewell down. My advice is do the best you can for them, then go on."

Miss Louise turned to me as if talking about the Parkers was as distasteful as a tablespoon of cod liver oil. Not that I blamed her, but her change of subject was about as smelly.

"Your Uncle Rag called this afternoon," she said. "He's agreed to take over the farm and manage it."

I had a mouth full of potatoes, so I only nodded. She turned to Miss Redding and tried to explain Rag, as if that were possible.

"I figured if we dangled a big enough carrot in front of him he'd bite," Miss Louise said.

I looked at my untouched carrots. If Rag liked them, then it was another sign he really wasn't my uncle.

"We just had to make it worth his while," Miss Louise said. "He knows the milking and the orchard better than anyone." She tapped my plate. "Eat your carrots, dearie. They're good for your eyes."

Candy was bad for my teeth. Carrots were good for my eyes. I hadn't counted on Miss Louise caring so much about my health. I stabbed one of the orange coins, poked it in my mouth, and wondered if the orphans at the Children's Home had to eat carrots. An awful taste spread across my tongue, but the thought of spitting the carrot into one of Miss Louise's pretty white napkins horrified me. Neither could I swallow because I was certain I would gag. I propped my chin on my palm, half listening to Miss Louise and Miss Redding discuss when the Germans might surrender.

I blinked and felt for the carrot with my tongue. It was still there.

"Tired?" Miss Louise asked. She turned to Miss Redding. "Kate, could you hand me another roll?"

Miss Redding passed her the plate, then patted my arm. "I think someone's getting sleepy."

I awoke to the moon shining through a window. At first, I didn't know where I was, but after I shook off my sleepiness and saw I was in bed, I probed for the carrot. Gone. If I swallowed it, it hadn't killed me. The old store and house was alive with creaks and moans, which grew louder and more ominous the longer I listened. To make things worse, I had to go to the bathroom.

Miss Louise was muttering to someone when I stepped into the dark hall. I had to use the light creeping from under her bedroom door to guide me toward the bathroom.

"You're the sheriff. You got to do something," she said in a high tremolo.

I froze. She was having one of those spells Grandpa had talked about.

"They have no shame, peeking in my windows like this," she said.

There was a pause.

"I want you to come over and get them off my porch roof, that's what I want you to do."

The door opened, and my jaw went slack. Apparently, I lacked the talent for snooping. Miss Louise waved me into the room and put her hand over the telephone's mouthpiece.

"What's the matter, dearie?" she whispered.

"I gotta go to the bathroom."

"You remember where it is?"

I nodded. Before she removed her hand from the mouthpiece, she stifled a giggle. She motioned for me to leave, but I was too curious.

"What good is a sheriff if he don't protect an old lady?" she asked into the phone. She smiled at me through another long pause. "It's them Parker twins. I'm lookin' at their little beady eyes right now, at this very minute."

She wasn't looking out the window. She was sitting on her bed, facing the opposite way. I edged past her toward the lace curtains, yellow with age. If she was crazy as some people thought, the sheriff was sure to take me away. I peeked out onto the moonlit roof of the front porch. Nothing. To be sure, I double checked. No Parker twins, no stray cats. I turned and looked blankly at Miss Louise. I was doomed unless John Caleb and I ran away to find Sam.

Miss Louise winked at me. "Well, if that's all you're going to do." She slammed the receiver down on the phone and winked again as if I were part of something.

"You'll keep my little secret, won't you?"

I nodded out of habit.

"I call the sheriff just to aggravate him. He's the poorest excuse of a lawman I've ever seen."

"You're not having a spell?"

She laughed. "Goodness, no."

Maybe she wasn't having one like everybody said, but neither was she ordinary. I'd have to keep her little secret or go to the Children's Home.

In a daze, I wandered back into the hall and past Miss Redding's bedroom. No light crept from under her door, but sobs choked and hushed trickled out. I'd heard my mother cry like that, and it brought back unhappy memories. Miss Louise walked up behind me and rested her bony hands on my shoulders.

"She's crying," I said.

"I hear. You go on to the bathroom."

"How come she's crying? Does she have a broken heart like my mama?"

Miss Louise sighed. "Oh, sweetheart, to have seen the sadness you've seen. Don't worry. I'll take care of Miss Redding. You go on."

She gave me an affectionate pat on my rear and waited until I was at the bathroom before she knocked on Miss Redding's door. "Kate, may I come in?"

On my way back to my room, I paused to listen at Miss Redding's door. I heard her talking to Miss Louise, too softly for me to understand. I returned to my bed. By then the shadows of the oak tree outside my window had turned into the Parker twins and the creaks in the floor were Miss Louise's high pitched voice lecturing the sheriff. But worst of all, every moan of the old two-story building had become Miss Redding's sobs. I pulled the covers over my head to close out the specters and sounds of my new home.

Word spread we had the smartest and prettiest teacher in the county. Monday morning, every kid was there early and, except for the Parkers, were combed and scrubbed as if it were the first day of school. John Caleb and I wandered onto the playground, taking care to avoid his brother Ernie. On the scale of meanness, Ernie was nicer than the twins but crueler than Luke, a brother rumored to have ended up at reform school. We headed toward the outhouses where yet another Parker huddled in the shadows.

"Hey, Wilma Rose," John Caleb said. "Teacher's here. Come inside and meet her."

The girl raised her head. She was four years older than John Caleb, and if her hair wasn't so tangled and greasy, she might have been pretty.

We heard laughter behind us.

"Wilma Rose, Wilma Rose, got a booger up her nose," Ernie and his gang chanted. They circled us.

John Caleb balled his fists in frustration. "You ought'n do that," he muttered under his breath. "She can't help it if she ain't right."

The boys were all bigger than we were. We stared at our feet, helpless.

The bell interrupted our dilemma. John Caleb grabbed our hands and dragged Wilma Rose and me across the yard to safety.

Ernie tromped last into the building and plopped down in the desk closest to the door. All the Parkers looked older than the students in their level, except for Wilma Rose, who didn't appear to belong in any grade. None of them ever had pencils or tablets. They never did homework. After reading class, Miss Redding reassigned them desks next to the smarter students, and I wondered if she hoped they would pick up the subject like oily rags gathered dust.

The weather was warm for a March day, and Miss Redding suggested we eat lunch outside. The girls chose the front steps while the boys ate by the ball field. Miss Redding surprised us when she joined the girls and brought a brush. She sat behind Wilma Rose. As we ate, she untangled the girl's hair with her fingers, then gently drew the brush through the greasy curls. Wilma Rose's mouth paused in midchew.

"Here, Maggie," Miss Redding said. She handed Wilma Rose's sister the brush and produced a tiny bottle of perfume. While Maggie brushed, Miss Redding dabbed a small amount behind both girls' ears.

The bottle was a magnet. Girls lined up to brush Wilma Rose's hair. Arguments broke out over whose turn came next. We hadn't finished eating when Wilma Rose's vacant expression cracked and a smile seeped out.

"My turn," Sally Becker said.

We shuffled out of her way, discreetly grumbling as we went. She was the oldest and the tallest girl in school, traits she used to boss the younger children when the teacher wasn't around.

She flung her long shiny hair over her shoulder and brushed. "Maybe we could put her hair up in a bun."

Miss Redding rested her hand on Wilma Rose's shoulder. "Would you like that?"

"Eewee. Look." Sally pointed to the sickly yellow dandruff accumulating on Wilma Rose's shoulders. We crowded in to look.

"She have cooties?" someone asked.

"Get away from her," Sally said, throwing the brush down.

We backed away, rubbing our hands on our dresses, gagging and laughing. Wilma Rose's chin trembled. A half moan, half bawl came out of her mouth. She darted through us like a scared lamb through greenbriers.

"Wilma Rose!" Miss Redding yelled. "Wilma Rose!"

On the kickball field, John Caleb took a called strike and ran to catch his sister. He followed her to the door of the girls' outhouse and shouted, "She locked herself in."

I didn't think teachers could run, but Miss Redding sprinted across the yard with us close behind.

She knocked on the door. "Wilma Rose, come out, honey. Sally didn't mean it."

"She won't come out until she's ready," Maggie said.

John Caleb nodded in agreement.

"But what if I have to go?" Sally's little sister asked.

Miss Redding whirled to face us. "Then you'll just have to use the boys' outhouse."

We gaped at her as if she'd asked us to rob a bank. She ignored our shock and pointed toward the school house. We fled. In the classroom, the girls told the boys what happened. A lookout was posted. The rest of us clustered around our desks and quietly discussed who was to blame. The clock's pendulum swung back and forth—fifteen minutes, then thirty before the lookout whistled a warning and hurried to his seat. Miss Redding marched into the room, dragging Wilma Rose by the arm. They wilted behind their desks. No one asked questions or even whispered the remainder of the afternoon. Twenty minutes before school was over, Miss Redding called Maggie Parker to her desk. A few seconds later, Maggie took Wilma Rose's hand and left.

At three-thirty, Miss Redding stood. "I hope you remember this day the rest of your lives."

She sat down, leaving us to ponder what she meant. We glanced at one another.

She reached into a drawer and gently set the hairbrush on her desktop. "You were cruel."

We ducked our heads in shame. Ernie Parker crept away first, followed by the others. John Caleb and I stayed, debating in whispers whether we should approach Miss Redding or not. Our kindness won out over our fears of a new teacher.

"Miss Redding," I said. "Want John Caleb and me to clean the erasers?"

Our offer seemed to brighten her. We gathered the erasers and slipped out the back door. Once we walked far enough to keep the chalk dust from drifting back into the building, we clapped the erasers together.

"I think she's gonna cry," John Caleb said.

I would have. She'd tried to help and made Wilma Rose smile. When we finished pounding the erasers until we succeeded in transferring most of the chalk dust to our hands, I followed John Caleb up the back steps.

He shoved me into the cloak room and whispered, "It's Pa."

"I'm not saying I blame you," Mr. Parker said.

Despite John Caleb's hold on my leg, I edged forward to peek around the corner.

George Parker was a spare man with a shapeless felt hat that hid his eyes. His expression was hardened and weary. He wore no special favors. His clothes were as patched and dirty, if not worse, than the rest of the Parker clan.

Miss Redding's face shimmered with tears. "If I had any idea it would have turned out like this—"

"Her mother can't get Wilma Rose to take a bath. The girl sits on the edge of the tub and refuses to get her feet wet." He slapped his hat against her desk for emphasis and raised his voice. "We've got nothing. Nothing but an old shack and a cistern."

"I meant—"

"I work from sunup to sundown and—" Something made him stop shouting.

John Caleb looked over my shoulder as Mr. Parker laid his grimy hand on Miss Redding's pretty sleeve.

"Maybe you could come by and teach my girls how to take care of themselves, proper and all."

"I want to help, but here at school." She stared at his hairy fingers crawling up her arm like a tarantula.

Miss Redding backed away from him, only to have him grab her wrist to hold her close. "You know you're every bit as beautiful as my Maggie said you are."

She yanked her arm free. "Don't you ever touch me again."

"Think you're too good, huh? Well, I don't want a woman like you teaching my children, anyways."

I swallowed a sob. Miss Redding and Mr. Parker snapped their heads in my direction.

"Gracie!" Miss Redding said. "Where are the erasers?"

Like Wilma Rose, I was struck mute. Saliva dribbled down my chin. John Caleb scrambled to his feet and marched into the room with the erasers stacked neatly in his arms.

"Here they are, teacher," he said. "All done."

Mr. Parker grabbed John Caleb by the shoulders. Erasers flew across the floor. "What are you doin' here. You causin' your teacher trouble?" Mr. Parker asked.

"No, Pa."

"Then why'd she keep you after school."

"He was helping me," Miss Redding said.

I shrank into the closet, the place Mama always promised I would be safe, away from Mr. Parker's hands, his voice.

Later, Miss Redding found me in the back corner hiding beneath my coat. No matter how much she assured me Mr. Parker had left, I couldn't stop sobbing. She sank onto the floor to pull me onto her lap. We sat there a long time, her trembling arms encircled around my chest. Over and over she sang a silly little tune about a spider and a rainspout, a poor choice of song considering Mr. Parker's tarantula fingers. Yet, I would rather she throw a jar full of daddy-long-legs on me than to have her stop.

Miss Redding called Mr. Becker when we got home. He came over that evening and talked with Miss Redding for a long time in the parlor. Miss Louise kept me busy peeling potatoes in the kitchen, two closed doors away.

"There are some things little girls shouldn't see or hear, and this is one of them," she said.

"Miss Redding's not in trouble, is she?" I asked.

Before she answered, I heard Miss Redding and Mr. Becker in the hallway. That was all I needed to drop the potato peeler and hurry out of the kitchen before Miss Louise's scolding could stop me.

"I only wanted to help," Miss Redding said.

"I know, dear," Miss Louise said from behind me. "Go on and rest a bit. Supper will be ready in a few minutes."

Miss Redding went to her room, but Mr. Becker lingered. He did his regular hem haw before he finally managed to get out what he wanted to say.

"Him pulling those kids out of school had nothing to do with her. It was spite. Their landlord told them to pack up the day before yesterday," he said. "There's not a one of them Parkers that are worth a plug nickel. Not a one. But I told George there'd be no trouble from us if he'd get out of our district."

"You should have used Old Bluster on him," Miss Louise said.

"Probably a good thing I didn't have it when I went over there." He stared straight at me as if to make a point. "I'd like to keep this quiet for Miss Redding's sake. You know how rumors spread."

"I do," Miss Louise said.

She waited until Mr. Becker went downstairs before she turned me around to look into my eyes. "John Caleb will be moving. He won't be going to school with you anymore."

Somehow, I knew that deep down, even before Mr. Becker came to the house.

Chapter 5

Other than the time the high school basketball team made it to the county finals, nothing significant ever happened in Iron Mound. Most folks liked it that way. A sign posted on Miss Louise's counter—*No spitting, No swearing*—summed up the usual public offenses.

In the weeks after Grandpa died, there was some interest in how I turned up at Miss Louise's, but with the death of President Roosevelt and the end of the war in Europe, my small bump in Iron Mound's road of tranquility was forgotten. No one knew about George Parker and Miss Redding.

As it turned out, George Parker moved his family a meager three miles southeast to the tarpapered shack across the river from the Cottonwood Flats, no more than a mile from town and just over the line from Iron Mound's school district. It was easy walking distance for John Caleb.

I was happy. Thoughts of my father drifted away. Sam remained my hero. Every day that summer, John Caleb was as dependable as the sun. Both appeared on the horizon at the same time. In exchange for buying wood and nails for a tree house in the backyard, Miss Redding insisted we read to her. She bought John Caleb a stack of comic books six inches high. And most importantly, I turned seven in June.

With August came the end of the war in the Pacific. For days, we anticipated it. Still, I wasn't prepared for Miss Redding's reaction. She took my hands, and we danced around the room until I grew dizzy. Every church bell in Iron Mound rang. I laughed, mimicking the joy around me. Since I had never known a world without war, I didn't understand peace.

By midafternoon, the streets filled with townspeople, farmers, orphans and dogs. Someone suggested a parade, and within thirty minutes as much of the high school band that could be found stood rank and file. Miss Redding and I joined

Miss Louise on the front porch of the store to watch the impromptu celebration. The drum major blew his whistle, the drummers beat their cadence and my insides vibrated with the rhythm. John Caleb waved to me as he darted in front of the ancient fire truck leading the procession. He hopped up beside me.

The route was short, due to Main Street's length of a single block. To compensate, the procession looped behind the bank, the funeral home and the lumber yard, returning to Main Street and the cheering crowd before starting the process again.

The third time the band emerged from behind the lumber yard, they were followed by the sheriff's big black car, Young Doc MacKay's Chrysler and the funeral home's hearse. I cheered the new participants. Everyone wanted to be part of the parade.

"What in the world?" Miss Louise muttered.

She watched the procession with eyes narrowed by age. They were little more than two slits, behind which secrets and wisdom could easily be hidden. The boisterous celebration dwindled to a few children's squeals, and while the unwitting band marched back to the high school, the three cars made a left turn into the funeral home's drive and stopped. Sheriff Lundy crawled out of his car to shake mud from his boots and wrinkled trousers.

"Anybody know of anybody missing?" he shouted as he hitched up his gun belt. "Found a body floating in the river this morning. Just down from the Cottonwood Flats. You're welcome to take a look and see if you can identify him."

The band became a distant echo. Two men came forward and nodded for the undertaker to pull back a blanket. They walked away, heads shaking, lips pressed together. They unlocked the crowd's curiosity. John Caleb grabbed my hand and pulled me into the flow.

"Ain't seen a dead man before," he said.

I shook my head. "I don't want to."

"Come on."

We lurched toward the front of the crowd in time to see Sheriff Lundy hold up his hands and grin. "No need to rush, folks. He ain't goin' anywhere."

Several people laughed. The sheriff grabbed a corner of the blanket and the collection of folks swayed like Johnson grass in a gust of wind. Despite John Caleb's persistent elbowing, I hid my eyes and refused to peek until I heard him sigh. We were on the wrong side of the blanket.

"Here, go on now," an old man said, flailing his arm at us.

We ducked. John Caleb dragged me to the other side as the second shift of rubber-neckers clambered in to gawk. A rumor rustled above us that the man was knifed.

"You mean murdered?" someone from the rear shouted.

Sheriff Lundy sneered at him. "I don't imagine he stuck himself."

The bodies around me jiggled with laughter. Their odors of hard labor ripened in the August heat. They pressed tighter. When a gap opened between Tom Lundy and the man next to him, I darted between them and came face to face with the dead man lying on a gurney. His mouth gaped open as if in midscream. Matted brown hair. . . a ghostly white face. This had not been a quiet death like my grandfather's. I couldn't move, couldn't stop staring at the body. Heads and shoulders and clear sky spun above me. Miss Redding had my arm in a pincer grip, and by the clacking of her heels as she dragged John Caleb and me across the brick street, I knew she was angry.

"I can't believe he'd do that. Just invite people to gawk," she said, depositing us beside Miss Louise. She pointed her finger at us. "Don't you dare step off of this porch."

She needn't have bothered. The look in Miss Louise's eyes had already glued my shoes to the floor.

"Satisfied?" Miss Louise asked as she watched the spectacle.

John Caleb frowned. "Didn't see nothing."

"You'll see plenty enough in your life. No need rushing it."

"He got stuck in the back. A Gypsy did it."

"Where'd you hear that?"

"Somebody said so."

"Who?"

John Caleb shrugged. "Dunno."

"Then don't go repeating it."

"John Caleb, that's how rumors get started and lynch mobs are formed," Miss Redding said. "Do you want that to happen?"

John Caleb looked uncertain. "No?"

Whatever a lynch mob was, John Caleb's answer seemed correct, if for no other reason than I wouldn't want anyone to blame Sam. Miss Redding ordered us inside, but we clung to a porch column a few minutes longer.

"You see anything?" John Caleb asked.

The dead man's image was drawn vivid in my memory, yet I shook my head. "Huh uh."

"Me neither. Shoot."

People walked away from the body with a shrug or a blank expression. I'd grown ashamed for dawdling when Rag emerged from the crowd. I tugged on John Caleb's arm to get his attention because my uncle was as ghostly white as the dead man. Rag gave us a cold glare as he hurried by, then he ducked his head and slipped into an alley. It was enough to send us scurrying inside.

After supper, I sat on the front porch to watch the last few cars sputter past me on their way out of town. A scrawny dog trotted along the deserted sidewalk. I rested my elbows on my knees and waited for Miss Redding. In the warm evenings, she liked to sit on the front porch until either the mosquitoes or my relentless chatter drove her inside. She joined me at sunset to watch the town dissolve into darkness. The smell of an approaching rain filled the night, and when a breeze stirred, flowers released their faint scent. Moonlight sifted through the clouds. The stars flitted like the last lightning bugs of summer. Miss Redding brushed my hair in an attempt to undo a day's worth of tangles, a torture I endured to feel her touch. All too quickly she finished.

"Let's go in before it rains," she said.

To stop her, I laid my head on her lap. I'd mulled over a question all afternoon without the courage to ask. I rolled my head to one side to watch her reaction.

"Does my daddy look like the dead man?"

Her lips parted. The answer wasn't there. It was too hard a question, even for her. Unlike John Caleb, the dark didn't frighten me, but every deepening shadow looked like the dead man.

"Let's go upstairs," Miss Redding said.

I agreed. It was not a night to linger outside alone.

Iron Mound had three churches, and by an act of God, all three preachers decided the dead man deserved a decent funeral and agreed to share the responsibility. Only the undertaker, Sheriff Lundy and the old men who played dominoes in the back of Miss Louise's store attended. The body was buried, quickly and quietly, late the next afternoon. For everyone else, work had to be done, shops tended and cows milked.

Like most problems though, the dead man didn't stay buried. Everyday he climbed from the grave to stir people's imaginations. Miss Louise posted another rule to her *No spitting, No swearing* sign on the counter: *No Gossiping*, a blow to the main activity of the store. At night, the dead man visited me in dreams. He lurked in the shadows of my room. In spite of Miss Louise's complaint I was using up her electricity, I left my bedroom light on while I slept.

A week later, while I waited on the back porch for John Caleb, a car rolled to a stop behind the store, and a man got out. It was early. The sun rose as high as the porch's eave, and for a second, it hung there like an escaped balloon before it slipped upward, out of reach. From the frumpy suit the man wore, I guessed he was a salesman. I yawned and followed his progress toward me with indifference. I'd grown used to salesmen's comings and goings. This one gave me a pat on the head as if I were a hound dog looking for affection.

"Store's around there," I said, pointing toward the front of the building. "It's not open yet. Miss Louise don't like to be bothered before breakfast."

He seemed determined to ignore my instructions. He climbed the steps to the back porch so I scooted out of his way and left him to Miss Louise. He rapped on the back door and went inside. I cocked my head to one side. He'd walked into the stock room without permission. I wasn't too worried. Miss Louise would soon have him cowering in a corner until she was ready to deal with him, something I wouldn't want to miss.

To give the pending ruckus a chance to heat up, I let the salesman have a few minutes head start before I followed. I looked for him in the deserted stockroom and peeked into the store. I almost believed the dead man got him when a deep male voice drifted down. He'd gone upstairs where we lived. Miss Louise was going to kill him.

I scrambled up the steps. When I heard him in the kitchen with Miss Louise and Miss Redding, I settled on the floor outside the door to eavesdrop. Miss Louise introduced him as Mr. Brown from the State Crime Bureau.

"They have a man missing," she explained, "and it appears we may have buried him last week."

The dead man. I should have known. That was all anybody talked about. I picked a sand burr from my socks and set it beside me. From what Miss Louise said, I gathered we weren't supposed to have buried him. Miss Louise had phoned the state, but the state being the state. . .

The man interrupted her to defend himself. "We called your sheriff."

"You might as well have called the town dog," Miss Louise said, "and I told you that."

I almost giggled. Nobody could out-argue Miss Louise, but the poor man wouldn't give up.

"We'd sent an agent out last week to see if he could turn up something on the bootlegging."

"And did he?" Miss Redding asked.

"As of last Saturday, he hadn't. That was the last we heard from him. Before I meet with the sheriff, I was wondering if you could give us any other information. You seem to know more than anyone."

"I've called you folks twice now and told you everything I know. Something's going on around here," Miss Louise said. "You're the ones who are supposed to investigate."

"I see," the man said slowly. "There's the child."

"She doesn't know a thing. Leave her out of this."

I shivered with fear. I had accidently looked at the murdered man for only a second, and now I was in trouble.

"I'd like you to leave the same way you come in," Miss Louise said. "People around here think I'm a little eccentric, and I'd like to keep it that way."

"Yes, ma'am. You will call again if you hear anything? Ask for me."

Chair legs scraped across the linoleum. When the man staggered from the kitchen, he braced one hand against the wall to avoid tripping over me.

"You're right," he said. "She doesn't like to be bothered before breakfast."

Other than pulling my legs out of his way, I ignored him.

"Gracie?" Miss Louise called.

"Yes, ma'am." I checked to make sure the man left.

"Are you out there in the hall?"

"Yes, ma'am."

There was a long pause. "Then come here."

I trudged into the kitchen. Sometimes, I got into trouble for just being.

That afternoon, Sheriff Lundy strutted into the crowded store to announce he had identified the victim as an agent with the State Crime Bureau. When he noticed the worried expressions and nervous murmurings, he assured everyone that more than likely the murder had been committed by a criminal from the city. I watched Miss Louise to see if she would correct him. She squeezed my hand. An hour later, the undertaker recalled the grave diggers. To the town's relief, the only man murdered in the history of Iron Mound was taken away, but his death was a bite that burned and itched long after the wasp flew away.

Chapter 6

After the war ended, I waited two months for my father to come home before I gave up asking if he would. Above Sullivan's store and away from the other children, I was Miss Redding's little girl. Toward the end of October, we were given an Indian summer day as warm and beautiful as the red and yellow foliage fluttering above me. Miss Redding spotted the oak guarding the entrance to the river road and sent me up the tree to gather its leaves for decorations.

"Climb up here, it's fun," I said.

Miss Redding brushed a leaf from her hair. "I'm tempted, but it's been a long time."

"You climbed trees?"

"Of course, silly. I had two brothers to keep up with. You don't believe me, do you?"

To egg her on, I drew out my "No."

"Look, Gypsies," she said.

At first, I supposed she was trying to weasel out of climbing up the trunk, then I saw the two cars and trailers turn onto the river road and head for the Cottonwood Flats.

"Is it Sam?" I asked. I had daydreams of him marrying Miss Redding and my becoming their little girl.

"I wouldn't know."

"Can we go see?" I asked though I knew her answer. The river road was one road she never took. Not only was it too rough for her sporty green Buick—George Parker lived across the bridge from the Cottonwood Flats. That was enough to make anyone's stomach toss.

The warmth of the day lingered into evening. Miss Redding suggested we put on our sweaters and sit on the front porch. I scattered my jacks across the uneven planks and bounced the rubber ball. It took an erratic jump. I caught it and thumped it against the floor several times before I started again.

"Onesey, twosey."

Miss Redding rocked her heel up and down to coax the swing into a lazy motion. "As soon as Miss Louise finishes her bath, it's your turn. No fussing."

An aimless whistle mercifully ended my game. Rag stepped into the pale light of the front porch. Miss Redding and my uncle acknowledged each other with a nod. He dug his hands deep into his pockets and grinned at her. His awkwardness caught my interest.

"I've been down at the café and thought I'd walk off my supper," he said.

"It's a beautiful evening," Miss Redding said. "I doubt we have many more."

"Probably not. Understand there's a cold snap coming down."

Sometimes I didn't understand adults. A skunk died under our neighbor's house, the Leer's son came home from the war with two medals, but Miss Redding and Rag talked about the weather.

"I'm going to the park and back," Rag said. "You're welcome to come along."

I caught my ball and stared up at him. He *loved* Miss Redding.

"Thank you for asking, but I need to help Gracie with her bath."

I sighed with relief.

Rag scowled at me. "You're not old enough to take a bath by yourself?"

"I get rat's nests in my hair," I said to defend my reputation.

"In that case." He touched the bill of his hat and sauntered down the sidewalk.

I watched him disappear into the shadows.

"He loves you," I said.

"Don't say that." She was quite peeved at me. "People will take it the wrong way."

I shrugged off her anger. How could I blame her? I wouldn't want Rag giving me goo goo eyes, either.

When I returned to my game, the ball hit my thumb and hopped down the sidewalk. Unable to anticipate its next skip, I grasped empty handed as it ricocheted toward the alley. I caught my breath. The tree branches hovering over the lane turned into skeleton fingers clutching the full moon.

"Gracie, come back," Miss Redding called.

"I lost my ball."

"We'll get it in the morning."

"Found it."

It lay on the fringe of a shadow. I edged into the alley. As I bent over, cool fingers touched mine. A hand clamped my mouth shut. I gagged. Chicken manure. It had to be one of the Parker twins. I didn't know which, because sometimes I had difficulty distinguishing them in daylight, let alone in a dimly lit alley.

"Stop squirming." The syllables slurred into one word. "I just wanna play with you. That's why you came isn't it? To find your ball and play with me?"

"Gracie," Miss Redding called with her teacher's voice. "Come. Back. Right. Now."

The twin dragged me toward Miss Louise's garage. I frantically looked for his brother among the shrubs. He would be close by. They were inseparable.

The one who held me bent over and whispered, "You'll see. It'll be fun."

His breath stank as bad as his hands.

Miss Redding ran toward us. "Let her go!"

She grabbed a handful of his hair and yanked his head back. I squirmed free, only to trip among the scuffling feet.

"Run, Gracie," Miss Redding said.

I scrambled to my feet—glanced both ways—the ends of the alley looked the same.

The twin knocked Miss Redding's hand away. "Hey, you're pretty."

"And you're drunk. Get out of here before I call the sheriff."

"Don't be in such a rush. I'm a lot more gentle with women than him."

He shoved Miss Redding against the garage and smashed his face and body into hers.

"Leave me alone," she said.

She pivoted her head side to side to avoid his mouth. It did little good when he pressed his forearm into her throat. She struggled to breathe under his mouth. I kicked his shin, twice, hard enough my toes wanted to crumble. Saliva and laughter spewed from his lips and rained on me. With his free hand, he tore at her blouse until the material ripped. Miss Redding gasped as he cuddled her exposed breast.

"Riley Parker," I shrieked. One name was as good as the other.

While Miss Redding clawed the arm pinning her to the garage, a hand grabbed my shoulder and spun me around. I found the other twin and was rewarded with a boney knee thrust into my stomach. My breath stolen, I collapsed, convinced I would suffocate.

"Please. . . don't," Miss Redding murmured.

The twins laughed.

An uncertain voice came from far away. "What's going on?"

Seconds passed. Then a closer and more forceful shout echoed down the alley. One of the twins screamed in pain and fell on top of me. All I could do was think about small dark places, places safe, places with no sounds of fear.

"Is she all right? Gracie, are you all right?" Miss Redding asked.

The words I mumbled became lost in the stumbling footsteps and strained breathing of the man who carried me up the stairs.

"Is she all right?" Miss Redding asked again.

I struggled for a breath.

"I can't tell," the man answered.

I lay in his arms and focused on his Gypsy dark eyes and the black hair tumbling over his sweaty forehead. Water dripped on my face from Miss Louise's wet hair. I gasped. My lungs filled. I squirmed from the arms holding me and raced down the hall to my bedroom.

"Want me to catch her?" the man asked.

"She doesn't know you," Miss Redding said.

I dove into my closet and wedged myself among the years of Miss Louise's accumulated clutter and dust where the semidarkness and isolation soothed me.

"Gracie?" Miss Redding called.

I hiccupped a sob. Her hair unraveled about her ears and neck when she peeked into the closet. She had an ugly red streak on her cheek. I pulled my legs in tighter to make myself smaller.

She knelt. "Did they hurt you?"

I nodded.

"Where?"

I pointed to my stomach.

"You had the wind knocked out of you. Does it still hurt?"

I shook my head.

"Are you sure?"

"It was Riley and Roland," I said. "They called me pipsqueak."

Miss Louise's head bobbed in and out of the closet opening. She handed Miss Redding a wet washrag to press against her cheek.

"I've called the sheriff. After you coax her out, bring her to the parlor," Miss Louise said, placing a robe around Miss Redding's shoulders.

I braced my leg against the wall. "I don't want to go to the parlor." Not with Sheriff Lundy waiting for me.

"I'll go with you," Miss Redding said.

She bribed me with a promise of a new set of jacks. I reluctantly followed her down the hall. At the same time, I planned to pose as a mute. The anticipation of talking to Sheriff Lundy's overhanging belly terrified me. At the parlor door, I refused to go another step.

"It's all right," Miss Redding whispered.

One glance into the room told me differently. The Gypsy was there. I darted behind Miss Redding to inspect him from the folds of her robe. He wore a crumpled soldier's uniform with stripes on his sleeves. His straggly whiskers and tousled hair made him look tired and worn, someone Miss Louise wouldn't allow upstairs. Yet he sat in her best chair, the one she reserved for company, and she'd served him coffee.

"Here we are," Miss Redding said.

The cup and saucer chattered in his hand. He clenched them, placed the set on the table beside him and cocked his head to one side.

"Gracie," Miss Louise asked, "do you know who this is?"

Her question and his uniform were my clues. If he was my father, he looked nothing like the wedding photograph. I'd studied that snapshot until I had his features memorized, until I no longer remembered the mother I'd known, only the young bride dancing in his arms.

"It's your father," Miss Louise said.

I was unable to respond. Somehow, I had gotten into a staring contest with him. He finally blinked first by shoving his glasses over his forehead to rub his face.

"Gracie, why don't you sit over here," Miss Louise said, pointing to a chair close to him.

Instead, I squeezed in next to Miss Redding on the sofa and waited.

He took a deep breath and lowered his hands. "Hello, Grace."

Miss Redding nudged me. "Say hello."

His hands shook like the neighbor's who had palsy. She nudged me again. I buried my face in her lap.

"Is she all right?" he asked Miss Redding. "Are *you* all right?"

Miss Redding shuddered despite answering yes. "Why didn't you warn us you were coming, that you were alive? We could have prepared her."

I raised my head to see his reaction. He pulled at the back of his neck and looked as if he was about to throw up in front of us.

"When I heard Annie and my parents were dead, I needed some time. I was telling Miss Louise that I got a transfer to Camp Chaffee over in Fort Smith. I hadn't planned on just showing up, but I hitched a ride with this Marine who fought across the Pacific, and when he heard where I had been, he—" He bowed his head. "He brought me straight here."

"Kate," Miss Louise murmured.

"I'm sorry, Mr. Timmons, I apologize," Miss Redding said. "If you hadn't come along."

"Ma'am, I've been whacked enough the last few years to know it addles your brain for awhile. You're going to have one ugly bruise on that cheek."

"I'm fine, really." She fingered the robe at her neck.

"We'll make the best of this, won't we?" Miss Louise said. "Kate, why don't you help Gracie get ready for bed. Aaron and I need to talk."

I bolted from the room, though I had no intention of closing my eyes with the Parker twins outside waiting to climb the tree and crawl through my window. My anxiety couldn't budge Miss Redding. She ordered me to bed.

"Do you think he liked me?" I asked.

"Your father? Of course he did."

"His eyes looked like brown beads."

"That's because of his glasses."

"They looked funny."

She patted my bed. I crawled on top of the bedspread.

"My toes hurt." I showed her my foot and made her wiggle each toe.

"Under the covers and close your eyes," she said.

"But Riley and Roland."

She picked up a book and lulled me into a compromise. I loved to hear her read. Her voice changed ordinary words into tone and meter. She read page after page until my eyelids grew heavy and gaps formed in a story I knew by heart.

I woke to someone crying. "Mama?" I whispered.

I struggled to separate the sounds and the shadows of my memory from what I saw and heard in my room. Miss Redding's eyes and tears reflected the moonlight streaming through the window. I touched her shoulder.

"Miss Redding?"

She jerked and clutched the robe to her throat.

"I must have fallen asleep," she said. "Sorry I woke you." The book she'd been reading fell to the floor. "Go back to sleep."

When she leaned over to retrieve the book, her muscles trembled. She sagged across the bed, coarse sobs alternated with her gasping for air. I crawled next to her and stroked her wet cheeks, but I couldn't dam the tears. Her fear and sadness shook the bed. I put my arms around her to stop the tremors in her body. I didn't know why, nor did I know what else to do. Grownups were too big to hide in closets.

Chapter 7

During the night, the temperature plunged as Rag predicted. I woke alone and tucked under two heavy quilts. While I dressed, I hopped from one foot to the other, wobbling like a drunken trapeze artist. I pulled a sweater over my head. Instead of taking the time to put on my shoes, I worked my toes into them while I clomped down the hall to Miss Redding's door. I was afraid to knock on her door. I wasn't supposed to. As a alternative, I thumped my back against the wall, hoping the sound would alert her that I waited outside her room.

Miss Louise came out of the kitchen. "What are you doing?"

"Waiting for Miss Redding?"

"Gracious, girl, leave her alone. After last night. How's your stomach? Does it still hurt?"

"A little." Enough to get me sympathy, but not enough to send for Young Doc MacKay.

"Your father spent the night on a cot downstairs. I heard him up awhile ago. Why don't you tell him breakfast is about ready."

An attack of bashfulness struck me. "Do I have to?"

"He won't bite."

I tiptoed down the top flight of stairs to peek over the railing. The room was as cold as an icehouse with the wind funneling through the open windows and the door. The cotton curtains flapped like flags. My father sat on a cot.

"Let the dead bury the dead," he read from a pocket-sized khaki Bible. The freezing air turned his breaths into tiny puffs of fog. "Let the dead bury the dead."

He rocked on the cot as he read. At least his disheveled look was gone. He'd shaved and combed his hair.

He stopped reading. His eyes flicked right, left. He cocked his head, as if to listen. Curious what he was doing, I leaned as far forward as I could. He jumped to his feet, twisting around in search of someone or something that might be hiding among the boxes stacked in the far corner. He spun around to look out the windows and the door. He froze, turned one more time and raised his gaze slowly up the stairs where his frantic hunt ended with me. I stepped away from the railing.

He exhaled a long breath. "Good morning, Grace."

He faced me where I could see the full front of his uniform. My curiosity grew bigger than my fear of his strangeness.

"You got any medals?" I asked.

"No."

"Oh." I'd thought every soldier came home with medals. "Jimmy Leer has two. He's a hero. How come you got the windows and door open? It's cold outside."

He hurried over and closed them. "Breakfast smells good."

"It's ready. Miss Louise said so. Did you sleep with them open?"

"It's stuffy in here."

When it was freezing outside? I fled up the stairway.

"You know what?" I announced walking into the kitchen. "He slept with all the windows open. He didn't know it was cold."

Miss Louise caught my arm. "Shhh! The war was hard on your daddy. What he needs is peace and quiet, not you making fun of him."

"The war?" I hadn't meant to make fun of him. If anything, he scared me, the way he frantically searched for something.

"Yes, he's been a prisoner of war for years. Go show him where the dining room is and be nice."

That part I understood. I found my father and led him to the dining room where he caressed the tablecloth. A faint smile creased his face. I rubbed my fingers across the white damask to see why. It felt the same as always. Puzzled, I looked up at him. He lowered his hands into his lap.

I plopped one elbow on the table to prop my chin on my palm. "John Caleb and I built a tree house in the backyard. Wanna see?"

"Maybe later." He rubbed his face and eyes. "I'm having a little trouble remembering how old you are."

"Seven. And a half."

His lack of knowledge didn't bother me. After all, I didn't know his age. I knew Miss Redding's. She was twenty-three. Miss Louise said she was sixteen, given that she had started over again. But I wondered if "nice" meant I should ask his. I decided it probably did.

He looked up at the ceiling the same way I did when struggling with an arithmetic problem. The way he drew out the "thirty" a long time before he tacked on the "three" made me wonder if he had forgotten how old he was.

I looked back at the kitchen and wished Miss Louise would hurry. "I have a calf. Her name is Peaches."

"Cute name."

"Grandpa gave her to me."

I rummaged around in my mind for something else to say, but my head turned into an upside-down pop bottle and my words ran out. All I could do was stare at him until Miss Louise brought a bowl of gravy into the room and sat at her usual place.

"We won't wait on Kate. She might want to sleep in," she said. "Let's give thanks for this day."

In case God was watching, I squeezed my eyes shut to keep from staring at my father.

"Dear Lord, thank you for keeping Kate and Gracie safe, for bringing Aaron home, and in a time when he was needed. We pray for the families who lost their loved ones. Thank you for this food, this home and for—"

I peeked. It didn't count if Miss Louise stopped praying. My father had stood and was gawking at Miss Redding standing inside the door. The red mark on her cheek had grown dark overnight. Her lips had puffed to twice their size.

"Sorry, I'm late," she said, sitting beside me.

"Oh, Lawd," Miss Louise said. "If I could catch those two, I'd pinch their heads off."

My father continued to gape mutely at Miss Redding.

She touched her cheek. "I guess I need a gunny sack."

"No, ma'am," my father said. "Don't do that. You're too. . . too. . . I wasn't looking at the bruise. I was looking at. . ." His bottom jaw sagged and a slow fiery red crept up his neck. "I was. . ." He gestured helplessly. "Ah, hell."

He had uttered a bad word in front of Miss Louise, not to mention God, and in the middle of a prayer as if he didn't know any better. He plopped in his chair. Despite Miss Louise's sign downstairs that forbid swearing, she smiled and winked at me. Neither Miss Redding nor my father noticed her. They had their heads bowed, no doubt waiting for her amen. At that age, grownups puzzled me to no end, and I was glad when Miss Louise passed the biscuits to my father.

She made the best biscuits and gravy in the county, but none of us seemed hungry except my father. He stuffed biscuits and sausage into his mouth with both hands as if he hadn't eaten in days. When he eyed the last remaining biscuit, Miss Louise handed him the plate. He reached for it, then retracted his hand when he caught me eyeing him. Miss Louise squeezed my knee until it hurt.

"But what's John Caleb gonna eat?" I whispered to her.

My father's neck turned red again.

Miss Louise beamed. "I made extra. I figured your father would love a good home-cooked breakfast. Eat up, Aaron. Eat to your heart's content." A knock interrupted her. "That's probably the sheriff. I told him when he telephoned to come on up."

I had two escape routes—into the hall or through the kitchen.

"Gracie, finish your breakfast," Miss Redding said.

I plopped onto my chair and banged my feet together. My habit had grown worse since seeing the dead man, and for me, the sheriff was as terrifying as any corpse.

Lundy stopped at the dining room door to look my father over. "We all thought you was dead."

"I heard," my father said.

"Good thing you got here when you did." The sheriff turned to Miss Louise. "I called out to Hampsons. They said they paid the twins yesterday afternoon and were told they were quitting. And I stopped off at their father's place. George hasn't seen them either, but he's been working over near Sapulpa trying to make ends meet."

"Working?" Miss Louise asked. "At what? Chewing tobacco? Ought to be thrown in jail for the way he neglects those children."

"I can't arrest a man just cause he's lazy."

"Of course, you can't. You'd have to arrest yourself."

"Ought to throw you in the booby hatch."

"The Parker twins?" Miss Redding said.

The sheriff pulled up his gun belt. "All right, ma'am, describe them. How tall were they? What color was their eyes? Their hair?"

"The alley was dark."

"So you couldn't identify them if you saw them again."

"I don't know," Miss Redding said. She looked over at Miss Louise.

Lundy raised his bushy eyebrows at my father. "And you?"

My father shrugged. "I didn't get a good look. I was busy pulling them off of her."

"So that leaves it all up to a six-year-old girl."

Lundy sauntered over to my chair. I looked up mostly to get my face out of his belly and corrected him on my age.

"Excuse me," he said. "So, what makes you so sure it was the Parker twins?"

"They stunk like chicken manure and called me pipsqueak."

Lundy snorted.

"You want me to chase them down and charge them with assault because they smelled like chicken manure? I'd be laughed out of the courthouse." The sheriff wandered toward the door and turned. "Ma'am, I'll warn you what George told me. He said right after you moved here you made a pass at him."

"He's lying!" Miss Redding said.

"You're pretty, used to men making over you—"

"That's not what happened." Miss Redding gave the sheriff a look that would have withered any of her students. "You're a bigger fool than I thought, if you think I'd consider—"

"Kate," Miss Louise said. She put her wrinkled hand over Miss Redding's arm. "Why don't you go relax in the parlor, and I'll bring you some ice for that bruise." She waited until Miss Redding stalked out of the room before she lit into Lundy. "I swear you're enough to curdle the cream on my table. Get out of my house." With that, she huffed into the kitchen.

The sheriff grinned. "Seems to me I struck a nerve."

"Seems to me you're a jerk." My father shoved back his chair. "She was protecting my daughter. Those two thugs did a number on her and you want to blame *her*? What kind of sheriff are you?"

"Somebody to keep in mind," Lundy said. "Ask your brother."

"I believe Miss Louise told you to get out of her house."

My father remembered me about then. His gaze flicked in my direction and with a jerk of his head, he indicated I was to leave the room. As I hopped out of my chair, Lundy held up his hands in surrender. For a moment, I thought my father might not need any medals to be brave. Then I bumped the table and Miss Louise's neat stack of plates and cups wobbled. To my horror, half of the dishes crashed to the floor along with any illusions my father was a hero. His expression splintered like the china. He collapsed, his arms over the top of his head and whimpering like Grandpa's hound dog when the coyotes howled. The sheriff jiggled with laughter. Why shouldn't he? He won the fight without raising a hand.

I scrambled across the floor to gather the dishes. "I didn't mean to." Not that either man paid any attention to me.

My father rolled over with a groan. A dark wet spot stained the front of his trousers. The sheriff smirked. My cheeks burned with heat. My father's gaze followed mine to his lap. His eyes filled with shame. He cursed. Dazed, I sat on my heels among the jagged pieces of cups and saucers as he struggled to his feet and fled in the direction of the stairs.

The sheriff, still laughing, followed him.

I cut myself on a fragment of china and jammed the bleeding finger into my mouth as Miss Louise skittered into the room.

"What happened?" she asked. "Where'd your father go? Where's the sheriff."

I pointed toward the stairs. Once she hurried from the room, I returned to picking up the fragments. If I gathered the pieces, maybe no one would be angry with me.

Arms, warm and secure, encircled me. Yet, I squirmed from their grasp. "I didn't mean to."

Miss Redding knelt beside me. "Your finger's bleeding. Let me see."

While she examined my finger, Miss Louise returned with my father's small khaki book.

"He's gone, but he left his New Testament," she said. A tiny smile came to her lips. "We must have stayed up past two o'clock this morning, talking. He'll be back. May take awhile, but he'll be back."

She hadn't seen his expression when he realized he wet his pants. I couldn't tell them what happened. To do so seemed cruel, like making fun of Wilma Rose and her hair.

Miss Louise carried the remaining dishes into the kitchen while Miss Redding went to find a bandage for my finger. I inched closer to the table. Broken hearts, broken cups. I'd had never stolen anything before, but I wanted my father's Bible. He may have abandoned me, yet I yearned for something of his.

I grabbed the book and sprinted to my closet where I squirmed into the corner. The Bible fell open to two grimy pages with a sentence underlined in pencil. *Let the dead bury the dead.* I shuddered at the word *dead*. I thumbed through the other pages, some missing, some torn, all stained and dirty. In the front leaf, someone had written, *To Daniel Lowell, From Mother and Father*. I reread the inscription.

The Bible wasn't my father's. He'd stolen it.

Chapter 8

John Caleb didn't come for breakfast that morning nor the next. My Saturdays and Sundays were turned upside down without him. If the weather was warm, I waited for him on the porch, doing a one-handed reel around a column until the yard and the trees tilted. If it was cold, I watched for him from the kitchen window. Two weeks went by without my seeing him. When I complained to Miss Louise, she told me his mother left Mr. Parker and took the baby and the three smaller children with her. Maybe, John Caleb shouldn't come around so much.

"How come?" I asked.

"It's probably for the best."

Adults used "for the best" when they didn't want to answer anymore questions. But I missed John Caleb and told her so.

She handed me a jar of silver polish, a rag and a fork. "There's plenty to do around here to keep you busy."

I wrinkled my nose. She'd made plans for a big Thanksgiving dinner. Not only the traditional turkey, but all the sweet things made with sugar we couldn't enjoy during the war. She invited the widows, widowers, and couples without children or whose children lived too far away. Fifteen people accepted the invitation.

Miss Louise picked up another spoon and polished it. "I got a letter from your father today. He wants to see you."

I watched the fork in my hand change from dull to bright, but my mood went the other way.

Miss Louise patted my hand. "He's made arrangements with Rag to stay at your grandfather's house. He wants to pick you up after Thanksgiving dinner and bring you back Sunday afternoon. He apologized for having to leave like he did. He told me to tell you he was sorry and hoped he didn't scare you."

Every night since my father left, I slipped into my closet and pulled his army Bible from its hiding place. The New Testament always fell open to the same page. *Let the dead bury the dead.* Words as cryptic as my father. After four weeks, I'd come to believe he had gone away forever like my mother and grandfather.

"I'm going with him?" If he came back, I assumed he'd stay at Miss Louise's like before.

"You two need to get to know each other, and it'll only be for a few days. I wrote him back and invited him to Thanksgiving dinner, so we'll all have a little time together beforehand."

My fingers trembled in panic. "But I don't know what to call him."

"I suppose you'll have to ask him."

Thanksgiving day, Miss Louise made me wear my best Sunday School dress and black patent leather shoes. I stuffed my pajamas into my cardboard suitcase that held my treasures. When Miss Redding examined the contents, she suggested I add more clothes. She loaned me another suitcase and packed my overalls and boots to wear to the barn, underwear, a sweater and socks.

The turkey baked in the oven. Miss Louise crumbled the cornbread for the dressing. Miss Redding peeled the sweet potatoes while I drew pictures on the frosty kitchen window. Later, women brought in their best casseroles and pies. Miss Louise fluttered, told them they needn't have, then shooed them out of the room. I pressed my face against the glass pane to make sure I hadn't missed my father's arrival. I wanted him to come, but at the same time, I worried he might wet his pants. The guests gathered in the dining room. Miss Redding came to get me.

"He's not here yet," I said.

"Something may have held him up." She pulled me away from the window.

He arrived after dinner in a light green pickup. The men who had eaten their fill went downstairs to huddle around the open hood of the truck. Miss Redding said they would stay there until the sun set or I went out with my suitcase.

"It will only be a few days," she said.

A few days felt like ten. What if he left me again? I would be alone at the farm with Rag.

"Come on." She took my elbow to usher me from my bedroom.

I looked up at her with eyes burning in tears. "Can I live with you forever and ever?"

A shadow swept across her face. "It's going to be all right." She smoothed my hair. Her eyes seemed to search for something in mine. When she looked away, I threw myself into her arms and begged to stay.

"But I don't know what I'm supposed to call him," I said, using the only excuse that came to mind. "What if he wants me to call him Pa?" George Parker had soured that name forever.

"You're making a mountain out of a mole hill. All you have to do is ask."

I trudged down the stairs behind her. Reverend Ponder stood on the back porch, his smile my final blessing before my world turned topsy-turvy, again. My father took the suitcases and placed them in back. With his white shirt and brown trousers, he no longer looked like a soldier.

"Gracie's been a little anxious," Miss Redding said. "We'd hoped you could have come for dinner so she'd feel a little more at ease."

My father's eyes shifted to the men still gathered around his truck's hood. "I'm sorry I couldn't make it. We better go."

I crawled in opposite of him. He was not going away, at least not forever.

He drove through the brown and gray landscape, asking how school was, asking about Miss Redding and if the twins had been found. I mumbled okays, yeses and noes while I mulled over my own question. Despite what Miss Redding said, figuring out what to call my father worried me. We crested the last hill before my grandfather's house. I had run out of time.

I took a deep breath. "What am I supposed to call you?"

"What do you mean?"

I counted off on my fingers. "Becky Becker calls hers Father, John Caleb calls his Pa, and Billy Pogue—"

"Let me say right off that I don't like Father. It makes me feel old. Don't most little girls call their fathers Daddy?" he asked.

All at once, it seemed so simple, and I giggled.

"Now, what am I supposed to call you, Miss Timmons?"

"Gracie."

"Glad we got that settled. Been worrying me." He turned onto the driveway, blared the horn and grinned. "Let's tell that brother of mine we're here."

Rag's car was gone. Only Grandpa's skinny hound was there to enjoy our arrival. Daddy parked under the elm tree, got out and slowly turned in a circle as if he had never seen the house and barns before. I mimicked him.

"Have you come out here much since your grandpa died?" he asked.

"We come to see Peaches and Beau." We usually came on summer evenings. Sometimes Rag was there. He liked to talk to Miss Redding while I brushed my calf. "I think Rag loves Miss Redding." The idea gagged me every time I thought about it.

"That so?" He rested one foot on the running board. "Does she love him?"

"I don't think so." I wanted her to marry Sam.

"You really like her, don't you?"

"Uh huh."

He smiled, then his lips hardened. I turned around to see what clouded his face. Rag was back. My uncle got out of his car, looked in our direction and slammed the door. He tramped to the house without saying anything. Daddy inhaled a deep breath.

"I guess we have to go to the mountain." He grabbed my suitcases from the back of his pickup.

I wondered if his mountain had anything to do with Miss Redding's mountain and what either one had to do with my uncle. I caught up with my father. I was curious what Grandpa's house looked like. Since he died, I hadn't been allowed inside except to pick up my things. Rag lived there, and Miss Redding thought it wasn't proper.

Daddy grabbed the handle to the screen door. His hand froze to the knob. I waited beside him, watching the dozens of little muscles in his face rearrange themselves.

"Do you miss your grandpa?"

I sat on the step. My eyes stung, but a cold hand shook my shoulder and didn't let me grieve.

"Buck up. Let's get this over with," Daddy said.

I wasn't sure if he was talking to me or himself. He had looked up at the bare orchard on the hill.

"Grandpa said just cause they look dead don't mean they are," I said to cheer up both of us. "You gotta keep believing so spring'll come, and they'll bloom."

He snorted as if I'd made the whole thing up. "Come on."

I followed him inside and let the door slam.

Rag had his feet propped on the kitchen table. "Hope you didn't expect a hero's welcome."

"A 'glad you survived' would've done," Daddy said.

"Coffee's on the stove." Rag nodded at the greasy range. "But I imagine you'll want something stronger. Right side of the sink."

Daddy pulled a chair from the table and nodded I was to sit there. He opened the cupboard doors. Dozens of gleaming quart jars filled the four shelves from side to side.

He grinned. "You've been busy. Hey, thanks for letting me. . . us stay here."

"You didn't give me much choice, did you? Actually, I'm surprised you showed up."

Daddy poured a clear liquid into a cup and took a sip. His eyes widened. "Forgot how potent this stuff is." He took another drink and leaned against the cabinet. "I want to get to know my daughter and I thought—"

"Since when did she become your daughter? When she was born or when you found out Dad left her everything? I bet you don't even know how old she is."

Daddy looked at me. "Seven?" He forgot the half.

"Good guess. When's her birthday?"

Daddy's mouth sagged. He didn't know.

"Doesn't matter anyhow," Rag said. "The farm's all tied up with some lawyer in Guthrie, and Miss Louise has control over the kid. All I got was Dad's old car and a lousy job."

"I came home to make things right."

Rag raised his eyebrows. "You get religion over there?"

"I saw hell."

"Don't expect any sympathy from me. Annie rotted away with TB. According to Dad, when they found her, Gracie was trying to feed her. She was too weak to open her mouth."

I couldn't remember if this was true or not. Daddy must have thought so. His shoulders drooped, and Rag watched with his one good eye and grinned.

"Let me tell you about your daddy," Rag said. "There was this girl who thought she loved him, but her father didn't want any of your daddy's Indian blood infecting his family."

I wasn't sure what infecting meant, but I popped off what Grandpa told me. "Daddy's mama was a Shawnee. That's why he's so handsome."

"Hah!"

Daddy raised his head as Rag lit into him.

"Old man Jenkins didn't think so. He sent Jessie away as far as he could get her. Until then, your grandpa thought Aaron the good son. I was the bad one. But after your daddy realized he was nothin' more than a half-breed to most folks, he raised a crop of hell that could've filled the barn."

He explained how my father fought as dirty as anybody, drank more than most but was lousy at cards and ended up owing a man a lot of money.

"Your daddy came hat in hand to me. I might have felt sorry for him, but he had his eye on another girl." He punched his chest with his thumb. "My girl, your mother."

"My mama?" I asked.

"The same. Anyhow, he broke into Miss Louise's store and made off with her money."

To my amazement, Miss Louise didn't turn my father into a tea strainer. Instead, she went to Grandpa and asked for her money back. Rag sputtered on how my father had already given it to the man he owed.

"So your grandpa hauls your daddy to the county seat and signs him up with the army. Said it'd teach him to be a man. Too bad it didn't work."

I'd heard enough. I tried to slip away. Rag grabbed my arm to plop me back in the chair.

"Not until I'm finished," he said.

Daddy seemed to have withdrawn to a painful place and couldn't defend me. That left plugging my ears with my fingers. Rag only talked louder.

"I tried to warn your mother. On one of your daddy's leaves back here, they got married. When his enlistment ended, he comes home, builds a house and everything seems hunky-dory until *Jessie* comes back. Your daddy didn't even have the guts to tell your mama he was walking out. Didn't care how much he hurt her, or if he disgraced the family. Didn't care if he was leaving your mama to raise you all by herself. He just took off, and we never heard from him again. Only way we knew your daddy reenlisted was a buddy of mine ended up in his platoon. By the way what happened to Luke."

Daddy finally raised his head. "Dead."

"That's a shame. He was a better man than you."

"I know."

"You do?" Rag grinned. "Did you know I got Annie back? We loved each other. Of course, we had to keep it all a secret."

"Not in front of the girl. I don't care what you say about me, but don't drag Annie down in front of Gracie."

"I got her pregnant."

Another word I was unsure of. Daddy grabbed my uncle's shoulders and yelled for him to shut up. Rag slammed his fist into my father's stomach. Daddy gasped. He fell against a chair, sending it screeching across the floor. I dove under the table. He grabbed its edge to right himself. I crept closer to my grandfather's bedroom where the darkness of the closet once comforted me. My uncle delivered a second blow that knocked Daddy across the door, blocking my way.

As my father struggled to stand, Rag brought his fists down between his shoulders. To stay upright, Daddy clawed at the wall. My uncle spun him around and punched him again in the belly. I crawled from under the table and eased toward the back door. Neither man noticed me as I slipped through the gap. For once, I didn't let the screen door slam.

Chapter 9

I darted across our road and crouched in the waist-high grass of Garfield's meadow to see if anyone followed me. Rag stalked outside, got into his car and fishtailed onto the road. A few minutes later, Daddy stumbled from the house, clutching his stomach.

"Gracie, where are you? I'm sorry."

No matter how much he begged, I wouldn't go back. Even if I had to walk the five miles to town on my own. When my father staggered to the barn, I sprinted for a grove of blackjack trees deeper in the pasture.

With my mind set on getting home, I followed cow trails that wound through stands of cedars until the direction I came from and the direction I wanted to go became as entangled as the greenbriers grabbing my bare legs. Blisters formed on my heels due to Miss Louise's insistence I wear my Sunday School shoes. Barbed wire fences snagged my coat. Ahead, dogs bayed in the distance.

When the sun slipped further in the sky, the trees overshadowed the steepness of the cow path. I descended into a gully. Grabbing an exposed root for support, I skidded down the bank, feet first. My handhold broke, and I landed in a heap of misery and buck brush at the bottom. A hawk screeched at me for disturbing him. Somewhere nearby, there was the rustling of leaves. Footsteps. I wondered through a list of possibilities. Daddy's? Rag's? Or the dead man's? Maybe his killer? I rolled over on my stomach to bury my face in my arms.

"Sneaked up on you like I was a real Indian, didn't I?" John Caleb said.

I raised my head. He sank to his knees to show me his homemade bow and arrow. He was dirtier and skinnier since I'd seen him last. His hair hung past his eyes and ears.

"Heard you coming from a long ways off," he said. "You was making enough noise to wake up the dead. Where's Miss Redding? How come she ain't with you?"

I rolled over and sat up. "She made me go with Daddy to Grandpa's house, and he and Uncle Rag got into a fight."

"A real fight? With punching and hitting?" He scrambled to his feet to shadowbox. "Who won?"

"Rag."

"How many licks did your pa get in?"

"None."

"He let Rag beat him up? Sheesh. What for?"

It did seem odd if Daddy was supposed to know how to fight and fight dirty as Rag said. Then nothing about my father made sense—from leaving the windows open in winter to peeing his pants in front of the sheriff.

John Caleb pulled me up and steered me down the creek bed until it ended at a small spring. We crawled up the bank there where a path led to an impenetrable mound of brush.

"Crawl in," he whispered, parting the briers to reveal a tunnel.

I balked. I had enough scratches on my legs to use up a box of bandages. He jabbed his finger at the passageway. I dropped to all fours and crawled in. It ended in a domed-shaped area half as big as my bed. A moth-eaten blanket was spread across the ground. John Caleb snaked in behind me and crossed his legs Indian style.

"What do you think?" he asked.

My hair snagged a thorn behind me when I tried to nod my approval. The darkness and closeness reminded me of Grandpa's closet. The memory let the day's weariness return. I curled into a ball beside John Caleb.

"Want a drink?" he whispered. He thumped a rusted canteen on my shoulder.

I sat up to take the water.

"Guess what? I'm gonna run away with Gypsies," he said.

"Can you take me home first?" I asked between gulps.

"Nope. They're leaving tonight, and I ain't goin' home again, ever." He pulled a chicken feed sack over in front of me. "Got all my stuff right here. Pa got us a new ma a couple weeks ago. She took one look at Wilma Rose and said she wasn't taking on an idiot. I told her Wilma Rose didn't belong to her. Anyhow I took care of Wilma Rose. So my new ma slapped me for sassing her."

"What'd your Pa do?"

John Caleb's eyes reddened. He turned his face to study a dried up berry the birds hadn't found.

"Yesterday he hauled Wilma Rose off to some place where he said they'd teach her how to brush her teeth and tie her shoelaces."

"Sheesh."

"Maggie already ran away." He leaned close to my ear. "With a boy. So you can run away with me."

"Sheesh." I'd heard nothing about any of this.

"Yeah."

"But Miss Redding'll get mad."

"You ain't running away from her. You're running away from your pa. Everybody says he ain't right. You send her a letter and tell her Sam's taking care of you."

I bolted upright. "You've seen Sam?"

"Shhh. Keep it down. Don't you got any idea where you are?"

"No."

"The Cottonwood Flats are right over there. So are the Gypsies."

And John Caleb's house was on the other side of the river. From there it was another mile to town. Which meant I had walked at least four miles. The dilemmas piled one on top of the other until I had a mountain peak taller than Miss Redding's and Daddy's molehills. Finally, John Caleb convinced me I couldn't sit in the middle of a greenbrier patch all night. And if I did change my mind about running away, Sam would take me home.

John Caleb gathered his blanket, stuffed it into his sack and handed it to me. I followed his exaggerated tiptoe. At every sound, he froze and raised his bow and arrow. My feet hurt. Two slobbering dogs crashed through the brush to block the path. John Caleb raised his bow, but his hands shook too much to keep his arrow balanced on the string. Not that it mattered. His bow was made from a green willow branch and the arrow from a sunflower stalk. I stooped and groped for something more substantial.

We edged around the dogs. They shadowed our moves like two game pieces pursuing us across a checkerboard. When the Gypsy camp came into view, we raced toward its center with the animals snapping at our feet. A boy jumped from behind a tree to throw rocks at the mongrels until they retreated. At the same time, a mob of younger children crowded around us. Their fingers stroked our faces and hands and worked their way into our pockets. John Caleb jammed his fist into his overalls to keep his arrowhead and quarter safe.

As quickly as they appeared, the children scurried behind the trailers. John Caleb nudged me with his elbow and nodded at a group of men sauntering toward us, their eyes narrowed with suspicion and anger. With a sinking heart, I searched for Sam. He wasn't among the men.

"If you want your fortune told," one of the Gypsies said, "come back tonight." A gold watch chain looped from a button hole to his vest pocket.

"He must be their chief," John Caleb whispered. He squared his shoulders and faced the Gypsy. "Where's Sam? Our business is with him."

I turned to gawk at John Caleb. Since when had he grown so brave?

The chief held out his hands and shrugged. "Sam? Is that a name for a woman? No one here."

A little of John Caleb's courage spilled over on me. "But John Caleb saw him."

"I think I did," John Caleb said shrugging at my alarm. "You told me he was a Gypsy."

The chief waved his arms at us. "Go home before we decide to keep you as slaves."

I jumped back into a cluster of guffaws. Hands pushed me forward again.

"They're joshing," John Caleb whispered.

"You sure?" I asked. If he wasn't, I wanted to take my waning courage and run.

"Yeah." But his voice turned squeaky. "We don't wanna be slaves. We wanna be Gypsies."

"Ah well, that changes things," the chief said, grinning at the others. "You must give us something in exchange. Horses, chickens. . . *money?*"

John Caleb reached into his pocket to pull out his quarter.

"Two bits for you," the chief said. He grabbed the quarter to flip it in the air. "But we need two bits for the girl, or she'll be our slave."

I groped in my coat pocket, praying I'd forgotten to give my dime to the Sunday School collection. All I came up with was lint. I had been good last week.

"I haven't got any," I whispered to John Caleb. "What am I gonna do?"

While John Caleb went back to his pocket, one of the other men winked at me. Either he liked me or thought he had a new slave. Both ideas terrified me. John Caleb came up with his arrowhead.

"A rock?" the chief asked, holding John Caleb's arrowhead high for everyone to see.

"It's a honest to goodness Indian arrowhead."

The chief shrugged. "To me, it is a rock. The girl, she is our slave."

John Caleb looked at me helplessly. We had to get his arrowhead back and escape. I kicked the chief on the shin. He dropped the arrowhead in surprise. I made a grab for it and missed. Somebody had me by my coat collar and wasn't letting go no matter how hard I squirmed.

A question sliced through the camp. "Is this what Roma do? Frighten little ones and take their small possessions?"

Little ones. Sam's nickname for me.

The men shuffled out of his way as he appeared through the campfire smoke.

The not-so-chief man said, "It'll teach them to stay away. They belong to the *Gadžè*."

"They mean no harm," Sam said.

The man picked up the arrowhead and slapped it onto Sam's outstretched hand. His eyes flared at me. He spat. "Harm? That one kicks like a *Gadjè* foal."

Sam gave the arrowhead back to John Caleb. "You cannot stay here."

"He took my quarter, too," John Caleb said.

The man flipped the coin to him.

"Why are you here?" Sam asked us.

"We're running away," John Caleb said.

"I will take you home."

There was nothing to do but drag behind him when he stalked to a car and unhooked a trailer. An older man with steel gray hair stared over his shoulder at us as he poked a stick at a nearby fire.

"If the *Gadžè* see you with the young ones, you will find yourself in the *Gadjè* jail," he said in a quiet voice, unlike the others in the camp.

Sam kicked the tongue of the trailer. *"Bàjo! Bàjo!"* He turned to glare at us. "You bring trouble on us. What am I to do with you?"

"Send them away," the older man said.

"Ah! Emile. But as you say, they are children."

My chin quivered in pity. Sam didn't want us. Nobody did. With the sun resting among the cottonwood trees and John Caleb afraid of the dark, I was sure to get lost. No one would care.

"Little one, do not cry. I would take you home, but I cannot, not yet. You must stay here a while longer, until it is night," Sam said. He pointed his finger at John Caleb. "You live across the river. You go now."

"Ain't leaving Gracie here by herself, and you can't make me."

I squeezed John Caleb's hand so hard he winced.

"Ah! *Bàjo*," Sam said. "Then you will sit on those stumps by the door of my trailer and not move, not an inch. I will tell my wife you are here."

"And what will you do if the *Gadžè* come looking for them?" Emile asked.

"Do I look like God in the heaven?"

Emile shrugged and returned to tending his fire.

Strange but delicious smells came from the trailer. My stomach growled. It had been a long time since Thanksgiving dinner. A woman stepped outside to pour steaming water into a basin. She nodded at us and smiled.

"This is Berta, my wife," Sam said.

"Such a brave one and so sick," she said, shaking her head.

She must have been the lady in my dream.

While Sam scrubbed his hands and face, two girls and a boy gawked at us through the trailer windows. They slipped past the doorway to join Sam as he sat at the table outside. Berta ladled a thick stew onto his plate. Everyone, even the children, gestured with their hands, and their voices rose above the din of the camp. A baby's cry from the trailer interrupted them. The oldest girl went inside and returned with the infant on one hip.

When Sam caught us staring at the stew, he frowned, forked a chunk and held it up. "Chicken. Is very good. Even better when one wanders into my pot."

I didn't dare glance at John Caleb. We were eating stolen goods. Sam laughed so loud the other Gypsies stopped eating to stare at us.

He nodded at his daughter. "Nikola, give our guests some stew."

Sam was right. Pilfered chicken tasted better. I ate everything on my plate, except the carrots, which John Caleb volunteered to eat.

The sun set. Sam lit two lanterns. With the coming of darkness, the children quieted, but across the camp, men sang and clapped their hands to a hypnotic rhythm. Others talked, their voices only slightly softer than before supper. Sam nodded his head to the time of the music while the aroma of his pipe mixed with the strong smell of the campfires. Everyone seemed to move slowly as if the night would linger for weeks. I shivered in the cold.

Berta brought a blanket to spread over me. "We must wait, little one."

I closed my eyes and asked Jesus if Sam could be my father. As an afterthought, I promised I would never run away, again.

"Wake up, Sweetheart," Miss Redding said. She shook my shoulder. "It's time to go home."

My eyelids felt pasted shut. The warmth of my blanket made it hard to crawl into the damp cold. Before I wobbled to my feet, Miss Redding smothered me with a hug that made me forget the frost-filled air.

"I was terrified when we couldn't find you. Are you all right?"

I focused my half-opened eyes on John Caleb huddled next to Sam's trailer.

"Let's get you to the car."

She directed my faltering feet past a dying campfire. I stumbled. She hadn't come by herself. Daddy stood in the glow of the headbeams, his face half in light, half in shadow. The remaining illumination in the campground came from Sam's fire. All the others were out. The Gypsies had broken camp while I slept.

Berta flailed her hand at Daddy. "We do not steal children. We know how to make our own."

"Enough!" Sam said. He motioned she was to close the door. "The children came to our camp."

"You were taking your sweet time in bringing them back," Daddy said.

I let go of Miss Redding's hand to throw my arms around Sam's waist. "I want to stay with you."

Daddy pulled me away. I broke from his grasp, only to have Sam hold me at arm's length. His eyes pleaded with me to stay back.

"Are you the one who found Gracie after her grandfather died?" Miss Redding asked.

Sam nodded.

"Mr. Timmons," Miss Redding said. "This man wouldn't harm Gracie. He saved her."

My father's shoulders drooped. He dug his hands into his coat pockets and continued to stare into Sam's black eyes. A contest he couldn't win.

His voice crackled like the dying embers. "Sorry, I hope you can catch up with your family."

Except for the slight nod Sam gave my daddy, his expression never changed. "Roma travel in many directions, but they will let me know which road to take." He smiled at me. "You must go."

I ran sobbing to the car. John Caleb was already there and scooted across the back seat to make room for me.

"Ain't fair," he said. "Just ain't fair." His eyes shined with the injustice of belonging to someone who didn't care.

Daddy opened the door for Miss Redding. She didn't thank him for the gesture, nor wait for him to get into the passenger seat before she started the engine and gunned it. If he hadn't run, I believed she would have left him, which would have been fine with me.

"The boy tells me water's washed out a ditch in front of the bridge," Daddy said. "Car like yours can't get through. Not only that, he doesn't have a phone, and no one's home. He can stay with me, and I'll take him home in the morning."

Miss Redding glanced at the rearview mirror. "Is that true?"

"Yessum," John Caleb said. "Pa usually don't come in until after sunup."

We sped down the road. Miss Redding swerved to miss a rock. We were bucked from one side of the car to the other. The motor roared in the tense stillness. Daddy braced an arm against the dashboard as the front tires skidded into a rut.

"We should've taken my truck," he said. "Saved you all the wear on your car."

She whipped the steering wheel around. The car bounced free. "I prefer to drive myself and I had an idea where to find her. You didn't."

John Caleb and I stared at each other in the dark. First, the sheriff, then Rag, now Miss Redding. How many fights was my father going to pick before he gave up?

At Grandpa's house, we parked under the yard light. John Caleb crawled from the car.

"Get out," Miss Redding said, opening my door.

"Aren't we going home?" I asked.

"I am. You're not. Listen to me, young lady, don't you ever run away again."

"I was looking for you."

"Don't you remember I said you were never to go off by yourself?"

"John Caleb was with me."

"That included him, if I recall. I was scared to death something happened to you. Did you forget about the moonshiners and the murder? Why did you think I went with you two every time you went fishing or wanted to go on a picnic last summer?"

I steeled myself for more of Miss Redding's anger, but instead, she kissed me on the cheek and hugged me.

"Now, go with your father. I'll see you Sunday afternoon."

She gave the order as if nothing horrible happened, as if the fight hadn't terrified me. My pride wouldn't let me throw myself to the ground, not with John Caleb watching, which left arguing, something I'd never tried with Miss Redding. I stamped my foot.

"He got into a fight with Uncle Rag, and they hit each other, and it scared me."

"Your father told me what happened and promised it won't occur again. He's told Rag to stay away until Monday. Give him another chance. Please."

"I don't want to. I hate him."

"You don't know him."

"I hate him."

"Stop that."

"I won't. I hate him."

She pointed her index finger at me. "Go to the house."

I went a few yards before I dared to turn around. John Caleb still lurked beside the car. He looked even skinnier under the yard light. When Miss Redding and my father noticed him, he fast walked to catch up with me.

Daddy opened the car door for Miss Redding. "I'm sorry. I really am."

"At least you had the sense to call me first thing. You and your brother'd better not pull something idiotic like this again. She's gone through enough."

"I understand."

"Do you?"

"What do you want me to do? Grovel? I've done enough of that to last a lifetime."

"I want you to start acting like a father."

Not wanting to be seen dawdling, I ran to the back steps. Miss Redding's door slammed. John Caleb nudged me as her car fishtailed onto the road in a way that would have made Rag proud.

The light from the yard streamed through the kitchen window to pool at my feet. John Caleb huddled beside me in the cold room. A chickenfeed sack with his belongings brushed back and forth against his leg, marking the seconds that passed. With each minute, I regretted telling Miss Redding that I hated my father, or at least so many times in front of him. The door opened. Daddy switched on the ceiling light, blinding me in the sudden brightness.

He sank into a chair. "I don't know what to say, other than I'm sorry it ever happened." He leaned his head back and released a breath, mumbling something about Rag getting to him and the argument having nothing to do with anything. I shouldn't worry about something. I didn't listen very closely. He asked me if I understood. I stared at him blankly until he raised his hands into the air and sighed. He went to the kitchen cabinet where he shuffled through the cupboard and found the jar Rag offered him earlier in the day.

"It's late. I guess. . ." He lost his way in the middle of the sentence.

I helped him out by pointing in the direction of my bedroom. "I sleep in there."

He turned to see which way I aimed my finger.

"John Caleb," he said. "I guess that means you and me bunk in the bedroom across the hall. Either one of you hungry?"

I shook my head.

"What about you, son?"

"Mr. Henry used to say I'd eat about anything anytime."

I gave John Caleb a fiery glare that should have given him a stomach ache. He ignored me.

"If you don't want anything, I guess you might as well go to bed," Daddy said to me. "Don't forget to brush your teeth."

I grabbed my cardboard suitcase and bolted from the kitchen. Once settled on my bed, I opened the suitcase to pull out my A-B-C book. Mama had cut out the pictures and pasted them onto the first page, making it as sacred as Miss Louise's Bible. I'd worked on the second letter of the alphabet, whacking every which way with the scissors. My mother never scolded me for my messiness. I wished I could give Sam my book so he could learn to read. I loved him that much.

"Must be pretty important," Daddy said from the doorway.

He put down my other suitcase and sat on the bed. Convinced any page he touched would crumble like a dried flower, I squirmed to the other side,

"What have you got there?"

I wrapped my arms around the memory of my mother and whispered, "A book Mama and me made."

"That is special then."

I bobbed my head. "I wanna give it to Sam."

"The Gypsy? Whatever for? If it's that special, then—"

"'Cause he wants to learn to read, and Grandpa wouldn't teach him."

"You'd give it to a stranger because—"

"Sam knew Mama. He liked her. He said so."

Daddy tilted his head to one side and narrowed his eyes. "He *liked* her?"

He was suspicious of *liked*, but after Miss Redding's reaction to my saying Rag loved her, I was becoming wise of the word. It either made people happy or angry, and I hadn't figured out which.

"Lots of people don't like Gypsies," I said. "She was nice to him and gave him a chicken."

"I see." He rubbed his chin. "Do you remember much about your mama?"

"She was really, really pretty. She had pretty blue eyes and... and brown hair and she liked to put it up with pretty combs."

Daddy squinted and shook his head. "I guess for someone your age, it's a long time to remember, but your mama had red hair and green eyes."

"No." I crawled across the bed to look through my suitcase for the photograph I kept of her. "See?"

He took the snapshot from me. "You can't tell from this. It's black and white. Your mama always said her parents must have been Irish because she had bright red hair."

"No, her hair was brown. I remember." A wave of sleep washed over me.

He gave me back the photograph. "Maybe you have her mixed up with Miss Redding. Her hair's brown and she wears it up."

I shook my head no, but a tiny bit of memory escaped from where all forgotten things go to hide. Mama had twirled a red curl around her index finger whenever she fretted over something. He was right, but I wanted to scream at him, to hit him with my fists. It didn't matter if Miss Redding had brown hair or Mama's hair was red or black—I wanted him to be wrong.

"Mama said she had a broken heart," I yelled. "She did and she died."

The red spider webs floated in his eyes. My words had come without thinking, but once spoken, I saw their effect and understood their meaning. Rag had tried to tell me this afternoon. I'd heard it in the whispers of others and found it in the sadness of my grandpa's eyes. My father broke my mother's heart. When the lady from the county took me away from her, it was only the last bit of Mama's heart left to crumble.

"Want me to tuck you in?" Daddy asked, turning to look out a window the night had painted black.

"No."

He jiggled the change in his pocket. "Want me to stick around while you say your prayers?"

"Miss Redding listens to my prayers." At the top of my list was Sam being my father, not the man in my room. I returned my book to my suitcase.

"All right. I'll come back and turn the light out after you get in your pajamas."

But I had already dimmed the light in his eyes.

Chapter 10

The next morning, Daddy knocked on my door and told me to get up in a voice that creaked like cold wooden floors in winter. His footsteps faded when I answered. Bright sunshine lit my room. I pulled on the heavy sweater and overalls Miss Redding had packed for me and shuffled down the hall, looking for John Caleb to console me. In the kitchen, I found my father rubbing the temples of his bowed head. He looked at me through half-closed eyelids.

"Where's John Caleb?" I asked.

Daddy went to the stove and scraped a spoon of cold oatmeal from a pan. "Home. He said he'd walk. My deal with Rag is I do the chores. The milking's done and I've got the milk can loaded. Eat this, and let's go. We're late." He handed me the bowl of oatmeal, and as if to hurry me along, he put on his coat. "I want you to stay away from that Parker boy."

I put the spoon down. The oatmeal was gummy.

"I like him," I said.

"From everything I've heard, the family's trouble."

"Not John Caleb."

"Not yet." He nodded at my bowl. "Hurry up and don't waste any."

The morning turned as sour as my stomach.

My daddy had a long jerky gait like a man on stilts, making it difficult for me to keep up as we hurried from the house to the pickup. Thick frost covered the windshield. I watched him send a shower of diamonds into the air as he scratched and chipped at the ice. The sun caught the crystals and turned them into the colors of a rainbow before they fell away to lose their sparkle, much like my dreams of a father.

"Get inside the pickup where it's warmer."

The cab was as icy as outside. I tucked my feet underneath myself. His eyes watered from the cold when he got inside. He wound the engine to a sputter and rested his forehead against the steering wheel until the motor ran smooth.

"All right, let's give it a try," he said. The pickup lurched forward. We rode in silence until we came to the highway. "Seems to me we aren't getting off to a very good start here."

If he thought the pickup was about to die in the middle of the road, he could be right, or if he thought I still hated him, now even more this morning, then he was right about that as well. He lit a cigarette. The cab filled with smoke. I gulped a breath and held it until, like a balloon let loose, air burst from my lungs. My head felt so light, I gripped the seat for support.

"What are you doing?" Daddy asked.

"Reverend Ponder says smoking is a sin."

"If that's all he's worried about."

"Miss Louise says it don't say so anywhere in the Bible, but she figures for all the money and trouble that it is, you might as well stick your head down a chimney."

"Everybody has an opinion."

Only a stub remained of his cigarette. He stuck it in the ashtray and wiped the fog from the windshield.

"Like I said, we aren't getting off to a good start. We need to get to know each other better. I mean, Rag was right. I don't even know when your birthday is. You don't know me. We need to spend some time together."

A shiver ran down my back.

"I've decided to put in for a pass every weekend," he said. "I'm going to talk to the chaplain."

"Miss Redding's promised to take me to Tulsa to see the Christmas lights and Santa Claus and get me a brand new dress for the Christmas program. We're going to stay all night," I mumbled.

"I'm sorry. What'd you say?"

I repeated Miss Redding's promise.

Daddy tightened his fingers around the steering wheel. "Okay, there's lots of weekends."

"We're gonna chop down our very own Christmas tree. Miss Redding's already found an axe in Miss Louise's garage."

"I see."

The heater blew cold air, adding more misery than warmth. He didn't mention coming back again, easing the fear that made me tremble deep inside.

On my window's foggy canvas, I carved pictures with my fingernail—Miss Redding, Sam, John Caleb and me.

The morning's flames in the cast iron stove had dwindled to red embers by the time we returned to Grandpa's house. Daddy took off his coat and hat, laid them over a chair and added more logs to the fire. As he revived the fire, the bells on the telephone clanged, one long followed by two shorts. Four neighboring families shared the same telephone line, but each home had a different ring.

Daddy closed the door to the stove. "Is that ours?"

I shrugged. It was when I lived with Grandpa, but to answer someone else's ring brought a gruff rebuke from the other parties. Grandpa told me proper manners required giving the person called time to answer before gently picking up and eavesdropping.

Daddy dusted bark and wood slivers off his sleeves. "Is it or not?" He reached for the earpiece.

I shrugged again and took off my coat. If I told him wrong, he'd get mad. The phone rang again.

He picked up the earpiece. "I wasn't sure if it was our ring or not. What do you want?"

Angry breaths whistled through his nose. When he turned to stare at me, I slumped into the easy chair by the fire and wished I could ooze between the cushions. His glare never left me until he hung up and stalked outside. He let the door slam. His hat and gloves slipped off the chair back and fell on top of me. Despite the cold, he forgot them. A few minutes passed before I gathered enough courage to creep to the window and pull the curtain aside.

He hadn't gone far. With his hands jammed in his pockets, he marched in a square underneath the elm—four steps each side. Gusts of wind whipped his black hair. The wintry day bent his back and shoulders like the weathered limbs above him. He kept marching—four steps, turn, four steps, turn. I shivered and let the curtain fall back into place before he caught me.

While he was outside, I found one of my old school tablets in the desk and labored over a drawing of Miss Redding, Sam, John Caleb and me with a heart above Miss Redding and Sam. The door opened, and the wind blew my father inside. Without stopping to warm his hands, he tramped straight to the telephone to pick up the earpiece.

"Long distance," he said. He looked over at me. "Go to your room."

The sharp order sent me running for the hall. Somebody had died, the only reason I knew to call long distance. I hoped it was Rag. Outside my window, redbirds hopped from twig to twig on a bare lilac bush. Their fluttering wings brushed strokes of red against the grays of winter. Like my father, they didn't seem to notice the cold. I hadn't been there long when Daddy marched straight to my window.

"Those are cardinals. Did you know that?" he said over his shoulder. His presence made the birds nervous. He touched the glass near one of the cardinals. "I never thought I'd see one again." A smile lingered for a second after he turned to face me.

I shrugged. The redbirds were outside my window every day.

His smile disappeared. "That was Rag. He's not coming back."

My uncle hadn't died, after all. Still, never seeing him again was almost as good. "How come?"

"Could be a dozen reasons. Most likely because of me or he just got tired of working."

"Who's gonna take care of Peaches and Beau? They'll get hungry."

"I guess I will from now on."

I mulled over his unpleasant news. If Miss Louise would let me keep Beau and Peaches in her garage, I could take care of them and avoid my father at the same time.

He sat on the bed and fumbled with a piece of paper in his shirt pocket. It was the drawing I'd worked on while waiting for him to come inside. He held it in front of my face and pointed to the heart I colored above Sam and Miss Redding.

"I wouldn't do this again if I were you. At least don't put their names on it. I don't imagine your Miss Redding would appreciate a drawing of her holding hands with a Gypsy. Even if a child drew it, believe me, some folks around here'd get riled."

I waited for him to say something about John Caleb and me in the drawing. I had all four of my wishful family holding hands. Instead, he wadded up the paper and crumpled my dream.

"We'll go by Miss Louise's this evening and pick up the rest of your clothes and things," he said. "I'm going to take care of you. It's what your mother would have wanted."

I stared at the crushed drawing in his hand. "Grandpa wanted me to live with Miss Redding and Miss Louise."

"Miss Redding is your teacher. Miss Louise is a shriveled up old maid that's due to die anytime. They're not your family. I am."

I glared at him through burning eyes. "I wanna live with Miss Redding."

"She's not your mother."

"I don't care. I love her. I hate you."

With a sigh that sounded more like a moan, he knelt in front of me. "Look, she grew up in a big city, and one day she'll get married and will go back there. She has to be lonely here."

"She has me."

"It's not the same. Besides, she'll want children of her own."

I looked down at my hands and counted fingers. One for Sam, one for Miss Redding, one for John Caleb, one for me. And if Miss Redding had a baby, a girl, I hoped, one for my little sister.

"Gracie, look at me." He raised my chin. "When that happens, no matter how much you want to go with Miss Redding, you'll have to stay here. This is where you belong. With me. I'm your father." He handed me his handkerchief. "Here, blow your nose. You're too big to cry."

I refused to take his hankie. "I wanna go home."

He struggled to his feet, a tired angry giant. "I can see that you and Miss Redding are very attached to each other, maybe too much. So I don't want to hear anymore about it."

When he tried to put his hand on my head, I ducked. His lips grew thin, their corners tucked into his cheeks. With one last glance at me, he raised his arms in the air and retreated from my room.

I rummaged through my suitcase for the picture of my mother, checked the hall, then raced into the bathroom and kicked the door shut. Grandpa had kept a footstool under the sink for me. I used it to look in the mirror. With the snapshot held next to my cheek, I squeezed my eyes halfway shut. Miss Louise told me she squinted to make fuzzy words in her books and newspapers clearer. The method didn't work with my blurry photo. I put the picture in my pocket. Mama was dead. I couldn't belong to her anymore. I moved my face closer to the mirror and opened my eyes as wide as I could. Mine were brown like Daddy's. My hair as black as his. I turned sideways to get a better view of my nose.

Daddy knocked on the door. "Gracie, are you in there?"

"Yes." I jumped down and opened the door a crack.

Brown eyes, black hair.

"Dinner's ready," he said.

"My tummy hurts."

Brown eyes, black hair.

"Does it hurt too much to eat dinner? It'll be a long time until supper."

I shook my head.

"Then wash your hands and come on."

I climbed up on the footstool and ran enough water on my hands to get them wet. As I hopped off, I caught one last glimpse of myself in the mirror. Miss Redding didn't look like me. Someday she would go away. I belonged to my father the same as John Caleb belonged to his.

After we delivered the evening milk to the Children's Home, Daddy parked his pickup in front of Sullivan's store a few minutes before closing time. He took my hand and gave it a squeeze, which did nothing to make me feel better about him or what he was about to do.

Miss Louise stood at her meat case with one last customer. Once the lady moved aside, Daddy whispered something to Miss Louise. She winked at me and pointed at the jar of candy corn. I took a handful, though I didn't have my usual craving. Most I stuck in my coat pocket for later, but I ate a few and waited next to the stove until the woman left. Miss Louise pulled the shades down over the windows and locked the door.

"Is everything all right?"

I ran to her and wrapped my arms around her tiny waist. With my fingers locked together, no one, not even my father could pry me away from her.

"Rag's quitting," Daddy said.

"I was afraid something like this would happen after yesterday. I wished you two could have put your disputes aside for awhile. I guess I shouldn't be surprised." She placed her hand on the back of my head. "This makes for a problem."

"I called the chaplain. He thinks he can get me an extended furlough, maybe even push up my discharge. Doesn't make any difference. I'm not going back."

"Won't that get you in trouble?"

"What are they going to do? Throw me in the stockade and call it punishment?"

"What's a stockade?" I asked.

"Jail."

He was a criminal like my uncle. It shouldn't have surprised me. He'd stolen somebody's Bible. I wouldn't care if he went to jail. God might, so I didn't ask him, but I double and triple wished with my fingers crossed.

"I assume you know what you're doing, but if you could stay on, it would make things easier," Miss Louise said.

"There's one other thing we need to talk about."

"I understand. When your father left the farm to Gracie and not you and Rag, he wanted to make sure she had a secure future. Still, no one expects you to work like an ordinary hired hand."

"We can talk about that later. What I'm here for today is Gracie. I appreciate what you and Miss Redding have done, but she needs to be with me."

Miss Louise stroked my face with her spidery fingers. "We'd best go upstairs. I'm sure Gracie would like a cookie."

I shook my head.

"Of course you do," she said.

If Daddy hadn't held my shoulders between his hands, I would have collapsed into a pile of bones on the floor. I'd counted on Miss Louise to stop him. My knees wobbled as I climbed her stairs. The steps had grown twice as steep and twice as long during the last two days. Once inside Miss Louise's hallway, she pointed me toward the kitchen.

"I want you to stay in there until your daddy and I finish talking."

I glared at my father. "I don't wanna go with him. I hate him. I wanna stay with you and Miss Redding."

"Gracie, that's enough," Daddy said.

Miss Louise's weary lines followed a hundred wandering paths across her face. "Now, now. Your daddy and I will have a nice talk about what's best for you. If you finish that cookie, you can have another."

A door opening down the hallway wrenched my attention away from her. Miss Redding stepped out of her room and waved to me. My father put his hand on my shoulder as a tether.

"Hello, sweetheart," she said. "Anything wrong?"

Daddy nudged me. "You do like Miss Louise told you."

I kicked him right below the knee. He grabbed his shin while Miss Redding and Miss Louise shouted at me. I glared at him, hoping I'd whacked him hard enough his leg would fall off. He made a grab for my shoulder, but I ducked into the kitchen and under the table.

"What in the world's going on?" Miss Redding asked in the hallway.

"You might as well be a part of this," Daddy said.

They left me alone. While I waited, I took a cookie and hopscotched it back and forth across Miss Louise's checkered tablecloth. The voices in the parlor grew angrier. When Miss Redding's rose above the others, I sneaked across the hall to huddle by the door.

"She's gone through enough," she said. "She doesn't need to be uprooted so soon, especially by a stranger."

"The Japs didn't hand out weekend passes," Daddy said.

"What about the years before the war? What was your excuse then?"

"The way you act, you'd think she was your daughter, not mine."

"Keep your voices down," Miss Louise said. Her rocking chair creaked her irritation.

"I know I've hurt a lot of people," Daddy said. "Haven't you ever made any mistakes?"

Miss Redding didn't answer. Miss Louise's chair slowed to a crippled pace. For adults, mistakes didn't mean they'd missed an arithmetic problem or they couldn't remember the year the pilgrims landed on Plymouth Rock. They meant big mistakes—shooting at Gypsies or burying a dead man in the wrong grave or my father's breaking my mama's heart. Things that hurt people and made them angry. Miss Redding wouldn't make those kind of mistakes. Unlike Daddy, everybody loved her.

"Aaron, that first night you came back and we sat up talking half the night, I told you the past can't be undone. It can only be forgiven," Miss Louise said. "It's Gracie we have to consider." She resumed her steady rocking. "Kate, maybe he's right."

"He doesn't love her," Miss Redding said. "How could he?"

"It may seem that way, but I've been told by a man who's been there, that there's places in this old rocky world you wouldn't think a seed of love could sprout and grow, but it can."

"At least give her a few weeks to adjust to the idea," Miss Redding said. "Please."

"Listen to me. The sooner you make the break, the better. You have to let her go. She won't accept Aaron as her father until you do."

"No," Miss Redding murmured.

"Aaron, I have one piece of advice. Love, like a flower, needs watering. If you can't give your little flower love, then give her up before you ruin her life like you did Annie's."

I stuffed the rest of the cookie in my mouth and covered my ears with my hands. They had planned all along for me to live with my father. I wasn't any different from John Caleb. Miss Redding rushed out of the parlor. By then, the sweet bribe in my mouth had turned into a soggy glob dribbling down my chin. She pulled me to my feet and handed me her hankie.

"Spit it out and come with me."

I handed the soggy embroidered cloth back to her. "I hate you."

"Come with me." She caught my arm to drag me to her room. Despite my shouting and attempts to wrench free, she said nothing until she had closed the door behind us and sat me into the easy chair that crowded one corner. She took two hankies from her dresser, handed one to me and wiped her eyes and nose with the other.

"We'll still see each other at school," she said.

A few hours at school wouldn't be the same as having her to myself every night, to laugh and sing on the way to school, to hold me when the dead man chased me through my dreams.

"You can't hug me," I said.

"Of course, I can still hug you."

"Teacher hugs, not the kind I like."

She knelt in front of me. A cry escaped her throat as she pulled me onto her lap to rock me. Then without reason, she pushed me away.

"You better go. I have papers to grade. And close the door, please."

She lied. She graded papers at the dining room table, not in her room.

"Please," she said.

She turned away and busied herself with smoothing the cushion on her chair and fluffing the pillows on her bed. First, she needed to grade papers. Now, she straighten her room, still, I couldn't hate her. I'd lied when I told her that in the hallway. Despite what she said, her heart was as broken as mine.

Miss Louise had my things packed in a box when I went into my bedroom. My anger had mysteriously faded, replaced with a numbness that couldn't fight back or beg to stay.

"I'll miss you," Miss Louise said, "but your father will take good care of you. He wants to love you. Give him a chance."

I waited until she left the room before squeezing into my closet one last time. It was still there between two boxes. When I pulled it out, it fell open to the familiar page. *Let the dead bury the dead.* I slipped the New Testament into my pocket and went with my father. Winter had come again.

Daddy, carrying the cardboard carton of my things, limped to the pickup. Though his leg hadn't fallen off, I held to the hope he'd have to drag it the rest of his life. He dropped the box into the truck bed and slid behind the steering wheel.

"Don't ever kick me again. For that matter, don't ever kick anybody again, you hear me?"

I nodded, but he kept going.

"It's not ladylike."

"I don't wanna be a lady."

"That's not the point. Now promise me."

His face smoldered as red as the sunset all the way home. I had another worry, his New Testament to hide before he found it and took it away from me. The obvious places, under the mattress or in my suitcase under the bed, wouldn't do. While he washed the milk can, I lay flat on the floor and slid the book under the dresser. My hand came out covered with lint. Perfect. I rolled over to see my father's legs, his boots still wet from his cleaning.

"When I was a kid," he said. "I used to hide all sorts of stuff under my dresser. Worst place there is. My mother would come along and clean under it at least once a week. Let me have it." He held out his palm. "What is it?"

"Nothing." I retrieved the Bible, but slipped it behind my back.

"Let me see," Daddy said.

When I showed him, he grabbed the New Testament from my hands.

"Where did you get this?" he asked.

"Miss Louise found it."

His hands swallowed the little book.

"I didn't hurt it," I said.

He nodded and thumbed through the Bible with the same care I held my A-B-C book.

When he came to the missing pages, I said, "Somebody else tore them out."

"I know. I did. For cigarette papers."

While I pondered why he would have done such a thing, let alone admit it, he sat on the bed and stared across the room at things I couldn't see or hear. I only caught glimpses of their shadows in his eyes and in the quivering muscles of his face. The clock chimed in the living room, bringing him back to the present. He shuddered.

"Did Miss Louise give this to you?" he asked.

"No."

"Don't take things that don't belong to you."

"How come your name isn't in it?"

I prepared myself for a harsh answer, but his rough fingers touched my cheek as tenderly as they had stroked the cover of the New Testament.

"It was a gift. From a friend."

Daddy sent me to bed early when he caught me yawning during supper. I left him at the table, reading his New Testament and mumbling to himself about the dead burying the dead. In my room, I pleaded with God to let me go home to Miss Redding. I vowed never to kick anyone again. I'd eat Miss Louise's carrots if that's what it took, though I was certain they'd kill me. When I ran out of promises to make, I buried my head in my pillow and fantasized Sam would come before morning to kidnap me.

A scream snatched me from a dream. Down the hallway, Daddy choked and shrieked. The dead man came to mind. I searched for him in the shadows of my room. A light came on at the far end of the hallway. I scooted under the blankets where I hoped my father couldn't find me, even as his heavy footsteps clomped toward my room.

"Gracie," he whispered. "Gracie, are you awake?"

I felt his hand on my head and cringed. He withdrew his palm. When the floor boards creaked and I was sure he left, I peeked from under my blankets to find him staring at me. He'd knelt beside my bed, close enough his breath tickled my nose. His nightmare clung to him like his sweaty pajamas.

"I scared you. Sorry. I didn't mean to. Sometimes, I have nightmares and scream like bloody murder. But I'm just having a bad dream." Without his glasses, his eyes looked twice as big. "Everybody has bad dreams," he said. "Don't you?"

"A dead man chases me."

His back stiffened. "Dead men chase me too."

"Miss Redding says he's not real, but I saw him. They dug him up and took him away, but he still tries to catch me. Can you make him go away?"

He walked as far as the door. "I wish I could. Go back to sleep."

How could I go back to sleep with the dead man lurking under my eyelids and Daddy having nightmares down the hall? They made my night into a tangled ball of yarn with no beginning and no end. I glanced about the room before I dove under the covers. Saturday and Sunday had to come and go before I saw Miss Redding. What if there weren't enough tears in me to last that long?

Chapter 11

Monday morning, I watched the wind blow cottony clouds across the sky while the rest of my classmates bent their heads over their math books. Miss Redding tapped my desk. She had assigned pages and pages of arithmetic problems.

"You're awfully quiet today," she said, feeling my forehead.

Before I left home, my father made me promise never to tell her or anyone about the dead men. In my desk was a drawing of Miss Redding, Sam, John Caleb and me. I couldn't show her that either. That only left daydreams and a question. Did clouds ever float to where they wanted to go?

"I have a surprise for you," she whispered. She walked to the front of the room. "Finish your work, class. Mrs. Becker is coming to help us with our Christmas program."

After school, I sprinted most of the way home, stopping only to adjust a sock that had slipped down my heel. I flew over the stone threshold of the barn and danced my way through hungry cats. My father had the top of his head pressed against a cow's flank to balance himself and to discourage her from kicking. Streams of milk drummed against the bottom of his tin bucket. Other than a momentary stutter in the rhythm of his hands, he took no notice of me.

"Daddy?"

He shuddered. Milk lapped over the top of the bucket and onto his knee. He closed his eyes and swallowed. "I told you don't sneak up on me. Wait until I see you."

I had waited, but I nodded anyway.

"I thought I told you to come straight home from school."

"I'm going to sing. . . Miss Redding said—"

"I've got Bess left, then I'm through. Go change your clothes and gather the eggs. Miss Louise said she'd buy our extras."

I lingered in silence, hoping he would ask about my school day the way Miss Louise always did. Besides, I hated Spurs. Though the rooster had grown old and lost most of its tail feathers, he still came at me with wings and toes when I gathered the eggs. A yellow cat snaked around my shins until my skin prickled. I gave in to the itch as Daddy picked up his t-shaped stool and straightened his back.

"Get going. I had a cow come down with milk fever, and now I'm running late."

"Spurs'll get me."

"Just keep the egg basket between you and him." He hung the bucket on a high hook to keep the cats out of the milk while he released the cow from its stanchion. "Hurry now."

On the way to town, my father didn't take the time to light his usual cigarette. Occasionally, he looked into the rearview mirror to make sure the milk can remained upright. We jiggled through a section of washboard road jarring enough to churn cream into butter. I shoved myself back into the cushion and braced my feet against the dash to keep from bouncing onto the floor.

"Miss Redding gave us our parts for the Christmas program. She said I could sing a song all by myself. It's called *I Saw Three Ships*."

"Never heard of it."

"Me neither. She kept me after school to teach it to me. I remember some of it." I wanted to sing for him but wanted him to ask.

He turned onto the driveway that meandered up the hill to the Children's Home. The superintendent of the orphanage rushed out of the building as Daddy backed toward the kitchen.

My father left me in the pickup. I spun around to watch through the rear window. Mr. Archer's pussy willow eyebrows fascinated me. They wiggled when he shouted, which he did even when he wasn't trying to be heard over his orphans' clamor.

"You're late," he said.

I strained to hear Daddy's explanation of the sick cow.

"Half the time Rag didn't get our milk here until after breakfast," Mr. Archer said. "If it hadn't been my respect for your father, I'd have told Rag to peddle his milk elsewhere. I'd hoped you'd do better." His glasses bobbed along with his eyebrows. "I've a couple of big dairies after me to buy their milk. They've got milking machines and the men to run them."

Daddy looked over the top of his glasses at the smoke belching from the incinerator as if neither the smell nor the superintendent bothered him. Once Mr. Archer sputtered to an end, Daddy wrestled the milk can from the pickup and carried it through the back door. The superintendent caught me staring at him. I turned around and sank deep into the seat. Neither Rag nor Gypsies scared me nearly as much as being left at Mr. Archer's orphanage.

When Daddy returned, he lit a cigarette. I sat up and looked out the rear window. The superintendent was gone.

"Mr. Archer's mad at us," I said. My attempt at wiggling my eyebrows produced a wrinkled nose. "Isn't he?"

"Not nearly as much as I am at Rag. The lazy son of a—" He glanced at me. The rest of his sentence morphed into a reminder to get gloves at Miss Louise's. He rolled down the window a crack to flick the cigarette's ashes into the air.

The familiar odors of Miss Louise's store welcomed me—meat and new overalls, leather boots and cabbages, coffee and yard goods. A warm feeling spread through my chest. I was home. Daddy stopped a half dozen steps inside the door. I scooted past him and the waiting customers to set the eggs on the counter. Usually by five o'clock, everyone had gone home for supper and Miss Louise had pulled down the blinds, but the room was full of people shopping for groceries, hardware and rumors. Miss Louise gave me a quick smile. I headed for the jar filled with candy corn, where I hoped if I stood long enough, she would give me a handful, a hug and maybe whisper she wanted me back.

"Candy's a nickel a bag, ma'am."

No one had ever called me ma'am before. I was too young. John Caleb grinned at me from beside the counter. He leaned on a broom, the one Miss Louise let me use. His apron hung to the floor.

"How come you got that on? Miss Louise don't like for other folks to wear her apron."

"It's mine," he said. "I'm taking care of her store." He pulled the apron back to show me his new jeans and white shirt. "She told me if I'm gonna be a businessman, I gotta dress like a businessman. She's gonna pay me." He took a lazy sweep with the broom.

"I'm gonna sing in the Christmas program all by myself, in front of everybody."

"Miss Louise hollered at me on the way home from school and said she needed some good help."

"No, she didn't. I'm her helper."

"She did so." He shrank into his apron and lowered his voice. "If this hadn't come along, I'd be thinking about heading out to find Sam, but as long as she needs me. . ." He stared over my shoulder. "What's wrong with your pa?"

The chatter in the store died to whispers. I turned around. Everyone was staring at my father. He stood at attention. Sweat poured down his face despite the chill in the room.

He mumbled, "Let the dead bury the dead," as he walked backwards toward the door. It opened and old Mr. Tanner, who came by every evening at five o'clock to buy a Dr. Pepper, stepped inside.

"Excuse me, son," he said.

Daddy spun around. His elbow caught Mr. Tanner in the chest, knocking him to the floor. Daddy hesitated only a second before he stumbled from the building. The warmth of Miss Louise's store fled with him. Cold air rushed through the open door. What was I supposed to do if he didn't come back?

Sheriff Lundy walked over to the counter and tossed down a pair of leather gloves and a dollar. "They tell me the Japs broke him."

Two farmers standing by the pop machine helped Mr. Tanner to his feet and dusted him off. Everyone else listened to the sheriff. The back of my eyes throbbed with anger. The sheriff didn't know what he was talking about. My father wasn't broken. He didn't have any bandages or crutches. The blister on his hand was from digging the new posthole for the barnyard gate.

Lundy raised his gun belt over his belly. "Heard they had to tie some of those boys down just to get 'em home."

"Hush!" Miss Louise snapped at him. "Gracie?" Her voice became gentle. She gave me a handful of candy corn. "You better go on, now."

"But Daddy forgot his gloves," I said. "He's got blisters."

She gave me the gloves the sheriff intended to buy. "You can take him these. Don't worry about paying for them. The sheriff's offered to."

He huffed at this. Although everyone stepped aside to make room for me, I had to walk through their silence to get to the door. Only Mr. Tanner smiled as he gripped the pop machine to steady himself.

"I'm sorry," I said to him.

"Don't you fret about it. It'll be all right in time. You'll see, it will."

With so many people staring at me, I bolted from the store the same way Daddy had. The truck door swung open. The engine was running. As soon as I climbed in, he shoved the gearshift into reverse and wheeled back into the street.

"Miss Louise said to give you these." I scooted the gloves over next to his leg. "The sheriff's paying for them."

Without taking his gaze from the road, he rolled down the window and threw those brand new gloves out of the cab. He might not be broken, but he was as mysterious and unsolvable as long division. I sucked on my candy, one piece at a time, in an attempt to make the nineteen yellow and orange kernels last.

Daddy rolled a cigarette and lit it. "Tomorrow, you tell your teacher that you're not going to be in her Christmas program."

"But I get to sing by myself."

"I'm sorry, but it just can't be helped."

"How come?" I banged my shoes together, making scuff marks across the toes.

"Stop that!"

I pulled my feet beneath me. Inside my mind I kept pounding them louder than I ever had before. Still, he must have heard them. His hand shook as he raised the cigarette to his mouth.

In the night, the dead men chased my father. As long as they couldn't find me, I didn't care if they caught him. I squeezed my eyes shut. My song settled around me during the silence between Daddy's screams. After I had gathered the words and notes, I poked my fingers into my ears and sang softly so the dead men wouldn't hear me.

"*I saw three ships. . . come sailing in. . . on Christmas day. . . on Christmas day.*"

When my daddy's screaming wiggled past my fingers, I buried my face in my pillow and raised my voice.

"I saw three ships come sailing in,
on Christmas day, on Christmas day,
I saw three ships come sailing in,
on Christmas day in the morning."

"Don't forget to tell Miss Redding that you can't be in the program," Daddy said the next morning. He pulled a can of Prince Albert tobacco from his pocket as soft rain pelted the windshield of the pickup. "Grandpa and Rag let things go around here. A lot of things need fixing. The stock tank—"

"Sam was gonna fix the tank," I said.

"I don't care what Sam was *gonna* do." He peppered a layer of tobacco on the cigarette paper. "A good half mile of fence needs to be replaced. You know how many postholes that is?"

I shook my head.

"A lot." He rolled the paper and licked the edge. "I'd like to take you to that Christmas program, but by supper time, I'm worn out."

The other fathers I knew, except John Caleb's, worked hard, and went to Christmas programs and church and Co-op meetings.

"I'm sorry," he said. "Go on. Be sure to thank her for asking you."

I jumped from his truck and trudged through the puddles to the side door of the school, which had an old rug to wipe my feet. Miss Redding didn't like us to leave cookie crumbs of mud on the classroom floor. She was writing the day's lessons on the blackboard when I slipped inside. Feeling as small and shy as the first time I met her, I ducked into the cloak room. It wasn't as dark as Grandpa's closet, but was a place to hide from Miss Redding's eyes. One look at me and she'd know I wasn't supposed to sing in the Christmas program.

I hung my coat and hat on a peg. A pool of muddy water formed on the floor under my boots. My heart argued with my stomach. One wanted to jump into Miss Redding's arms and cry. The other wanted to stay hidden in the cloak room forever.

Miss Redding peered into the closet. "What are you doing in here?"

"I can't get my boots off."

"You should have said something. Let me have your foot."

"They're muddy."

"Foot."

She tugged on my boot until it slipped off. While she worked on my other foot, three boys came inside, punching each other on their arms.

She sighed. "John, Billy, stop that. Pete."

She gave my boot one last pull, then hurried back to the classroom after the boys. I would have to tell her later.

A lie meant telling something not true. What was it when never told?

A day passed, then another. Every afternoon I practiced. Miss Redding thought I was going to sing. Daddy assumed I wasn't. A week and a half slipped away, too late to even lie. The morning of the program, I hid behind the girl's outhouse, a lonely place where no one bothered me. Maybe that was why Wilma Rose stayed there so much. I wiggled my numb toes inside my boots and wondered if she had learned to tie her shoelaces.

Miss Redding rang the bell. Once my classmates' laughter faded, I ran to the door to march last in line into the building. During the morning, the older boys stacked the desks on one side of the room and hung a clothesline and bed sheets to make a curtain. One of the fathers brought a huge evergreen to set in one corner for us to decorate with colored paper chains and strings of popcorn. After lunch, we had our last practice. Until then, I believed something would happen to untangle the problem. I sat in the chair and tapped my toes together.

Miss Redding put her hand on my shoulder. "Shhh."

I scooted forward to put one foot on top the other to hold them in place. The moment I forgot them, they tapped again.

Miss Redding squeezed my shoulder. "Don't be nervous. It'll be all right."

Miss Redding and old Mr. Tanner were wrong. It wouldn't be all right.

My chin quivered. I barely said the words. "I can't sing."

"Of course you can."

"Daddy won't let me."

"Why?"

I shrugged. "He's tired."

"That's all he said?"

I nodded.

Mrs. Becker, the accompanist, waved to Miss Redding. "Could you come here? Hurry."

"Stay after school," Miss Redding said. She handed me her hankie. "I'll take you home and have a talk with him."

She rushed to the front. Joey Wriggins forgot his lines. His face turned white. Miss Redding pulled him to a chair and fanned him. She was too busy to notice when I pulled on my coat and boots and walked outside, past the outhouse and past the schoolyard gate. It snowed the night before. Cars had cut ugly gashes in the road. I bent my shoulders into the bitter cold that numbed my feet and hands. After I stepped over the stone threshold of the barn, I waited for my father to notice me. He looked up as I wiped the sting from my eyes. I found a three-legged stool and piled as many cats as I could on my lap for warmth. When Daddy finished milking the cow, he opened the stanchion to shoo her out of the barn. The next two cows stood hip to hip. He shoved them apart and set his stool on the floor.

"What are you doing home so early?" he asked.

I crossed my fingers behind my back. "Miss Redding let us out because of the program. I'll change my clothes and go gather the eggs."

He returned to milking for a few minutes. "No hurry. I found a Christmas tree."

His hands moved up and down in rhythm as he talked of cutting down a cedar on our way home, even if it was so dark we had to use a flashlight to see. I could decorate it after supper. The promise gave me no joy. It would be as temporary as the steam rising from the warm milk when he heard what I did. He had two cows left to milk when a car door slammed. I jumped, spilling cats from my lap.

"Mr. Timmons," Miss Redding called. "Have you seen Gracie?"

Spurs seemed less threatening than the glare my daddy gave me. I sank onto the stool.

"She's in here," he said.

The words glued to my tongue for the last three weeks slid like cold gummy oatmeal into my stomach. I felt as sick as Joey Wriggins. Seconds, minutes, maybe an hour passed before Miss Redding finally stepped into the barn.

"Thank goodness you're all right," she said.

Daddy raised his eyebrows. "Having trouble keeping up with my daughter?"

"I was busy with the program and didn't notice her missing until it was her turn to sing."

He stopped milking. I wrapped my arms around myself to keep from throwing up.

"Mr. Timmons, Gracie said you won't allow her to come tonight. She's practiced so hard and looked forward to this."

Daddy unwound his legs from the stool and hung the full bucket from a hook on the wall. He returned to release the cow. It headed to the door, crowding Miss Redding against the wall, but she pressed past the animal as if it were nothing more than a child.

"If you can't bring her, I'll be happy to," she said.

"No."

"Mr. Timmons."

"No. She was supposed to have told you three weeks ago."

I had no closet, no place to hide. Tears for every note I sang for Miss Redding ran down my cheeks and dripped cold onto my hands and lap. She wrapped her arms around me. I tried to whisper I was sorry, but my voice couldn't squeeze between the sobs, not with my father staring at me with a face as blank and unseeing as my Raggedy Ann's.

That evening, we didn't cut the cedar. My father thought it too late, that all the color had faded from the day. I was too ashamed and too heartbroken to remind him of the flashlight. After he fixed my supper, he went to his room, closed the door and didn't come out to eat. The chink of my fork on my empty plate must have told him I finished. He shuffled into the kitchen with the duffle bag he used to carry his clothes.

"What time does that program of yours supposed to start?" he asked.

"Seven-thirty."

"Then you better hurry."

I ran to get my coat. He was taking me to the Christmas program. He shouldered his bag and I followed him outside. Was he going away? He tossed the duffle into the back of the truck. What was I to do? Miss Louise didn't need me anymore. She had John Caleb.

When we got to school, cars and trucks had filled the yard in front, forcing Daddy to park down the road. He reached across the seat to open my door. The sleeve of his denim coat smelled of evening damp, sweet feed and milk.

Disappointment welled into my eyes. "Aren't you gonna come?"

"No."

"Are you gonna be here when—"

"Go."

I tiptoed through the slush and darted between the men smoking on the front steps. Inside, Miss Redding had the first grade angels gathered for inspection. When she saw me, she waved me over.

"He let you come. Here, let me brush your hair."

I took off my coat. "I didn't have time to put on my church clothes like you said."

"You're so pretty—"

"Do grownups run away?"

The comb snagged one of my tangles and didn't budge. She turned me around.

"Do they?" I asked.

She hesitated a moment. "Sometimes."

"Daddy is."

"What makes you think that?"

"He isn't coming to hear me sing." I pulled Miss Redding's comb from my hair. "He put his clothes in his bag."

"He wouldn't leave you."

"What am I supposed to do if he does?"

Mrs. Becker scurried past us on her way to the piano. "We're ready to start. My husband said it's so full out there that some of the men have agreed that they'll stand outside until it's their children's turn."

"After the program, wait for me," Miss Redding said to me. "I'll go with you."

I nodded and shrank back into a corner. Two eighth grade boys pulled back the curtain. Miss Redding lined up the angels and shepherded them on stage. While snowflakes, wise men, and choirs jostled past me, I whispered my song over and over. If I stopped, tears burned my eyes. I hated him. At the same time, I wanted him to hear me sing.

Miss Redding shook my shoulder and helped me to my feet. "You're next. Remember, if you get nervous, pick out one person and sing to them."

"Who?"

"Miss Louise is here. She's sitting on the second or third row." She led me to the center of the stage and straightened my dress one last time. "Don't forget to wait until Mrs. Becker finishes the introduction."

I looked for Miss Louise. I'd sung to my classmates, the bathroom mirror at home and my doll, but not to a room full of adults. The music stopped. I stared at the audience. They stared at me.

Miss Redding whispered, "I saw three ships. Sing to Miss Louise."

I couldn't find Miss Louise. I glanced from one side of the room to the other until the faces blurred. She wasn't there. Mrs. Becker began the introduction again.

"Don't look at the audience," Miss Redding said above the music.

An orange light flared outside one of the windows, dimmed and settled into the night. It rose and fell, out of rhythm with Mrs. Becker's music. I wondered what it was. Miss Redding whispered the first word to my song. The glow was a sun, a tiny sun shining into the room. I watched it rise.

"I saw three ships come sailing in
On Christmas day, on Christmas day;
I saw three ships come sailing in
On Christmas day in the morning.

"And what was in those ship—"
I stumbled over the rest of the words. The light paused and flickered until I remembered the next line. As I began to sing, the orange sun rose again.

"On Christmas day, on Christmas day?
And what was in those ships all three,
On Christmas day in the morning?"

Traces of yesterday's snow reflected the half moon and made the night brighter than it should have been. I gripped my paper bag and pretended to skate across a patch of slush turned solid. Miss Redding let go of my hand to walk around my make-believe ice rink. Without her coat and hat to keep her warm, her breaths made little puffy clouds.

My father's pickup was parked where I left it. He hadn't run away after all, leaving me to figure out if I should be happy or sad. Miss Redding opened the door for me. Daddy huddled behind the steering wheel, his arms wrapped across his chest. I felt his shivers through the seat.

Miss Redding rubbed her arms to keep warm. "Thank you for bringing Gracie. You should have come in and listened to her. She sang beautifully."

"Figured she'd do better without me."

"But it was too cold to stay out here."

"You should know." He turned his head slightly when she laughed.

In the moonlight, her dress and hair shimmered like that of the angel's on the Christmas tree. Daddy didn't start the engine. Miss Redding didn't go back inside. My toes ached from the cold that neither adult seemed to feel.

"Gracie thought you were going to run away," she said. "You'd packed your bag."

"Oh." He rapped his thumbs on the steering wheel and glanced at his duffle bag in back. "The clothes. I don't know how to wash them. At least I'm not very good at it."

Every Saturday he scrubbed his overalls and my school dress on a washboard, but before I could tell Miss Redding that he lied, his tapping stopped. He looked at me out of the corner of his eye. I understood his signal and slid down in the seat.

"I was going to find someone to do it for me. But," he said, "I changed my mind."

"I see," Miss Redding said. She put her hand on the back of my head and combed a tangle with her fingers. "You don't have to do it all by yourself."

"Yes, ma'am."

"I need to get back. The other parents..."

"Yes, ma'am."

"Miss Louise is having Christmas dinner."

My heart rose and fell as quickly as it took him to shake his head.

"I should get Gracie home," he said.

"Of course."

She kissed me goodbye. Daddy turned on the headlights to watch her walk up the road.

"What you got?" he asked.

I held up my sack. "An apple and some candy."

He cleared the window with the back of his hand. The engine sputtered and shimmied as if protesting the cold. We drove in silence for a few minutes before he hummed a couple of notes.

"Your mama sang. In church, she'd get the whole congregation in tears."

He listened to Mama sing, but not me.

He lit a cigarette. Its end smoldered in the pale dash lights. I watched the orange glow rise to his mouth. It burned brighter for an instant, then he lowered it and gripped the steering wheel. The little sun outside the school window was orange. But it couldn't have been my father's cigarette. He'd stayed in the pickup. He told Miss Redding so.

"Something the matter?" he asked. "You hate it when I smoke. I guess it is a lot like sticking your head down a chimney." He opened the window and tossed the unfinished cigarette.

He whistled a few notes of the tune written in my head. I looked out the back window to see if the cigarette still glowed and if it did, would it melt a hole in the snow? It couldn't have been him. It couldn't have, but I sang, as soft as a whisper, the song I wanted him to hear.

"And all the angels in Heav'n shall sing,
On Christmas day, on Christmas day;
And all the angels in Heav'n shall sing,
On Christmas day in the morning."

Chapter 12

All through Christmas, my song frightened away the dead men who chased my father in the night. But then the tree was tossed outside and the decorations put in the attic as if the season never happened. At school, I asked if we could sing *Away in the Manger*, but Miss Redding told me the holiday was over. With my song packed in a box along with the tinsel and the angel for the top of the tree, I couldn't keep the dead men from returning. The coldest and grayest months of winter settled over our house. Dreary days and frostbite nights dragged endlessly into February. Though it was much too early, I searched the yard for the first cowboy rose, a secret gift I hoped to give Miss Redding. At least twice a week, I begged Daddy to take the river road, each time, praying he wouldn't realize I wanted to see if Sam returned.

One evening in March when gusts of wind rattled our windows and doors to get inside, Daddy sat at Grandpa's desk and studied pictures of milking machines in *Hoard's Dairyman*. He added and subtracted numbers in his ledger, and scratched out his answers until he squinted and blinked at the paper. Finally, his chest heaved, and he dropped his pencil.

"Go to bed, please," he said.

The clock hadn't chimed eight. To delay my bedtime, I circled the outside ring of the braided rug. He wasn't watching me. He was lost among his worry lines.

"Miss Redding said tomorrow's the first day of spring. That means the peaches are gonna bloom," I said.

He bent over the problems in his black book. "It's still winter. They're predicting snow tomorrow."

"Bet you I can find a flower."

"You can look, but you won't find any."

"I'll find one and take it to Miss Redding."

Even those words couldn't get a rise out of him. I gave up and hopscotched to my room, spun around and fell backwards onto my bed. He didn't believe I could find a flower. Unlike Miss Redding, he'd stopped believing in spring, if he ever had.

Under the dusting of snow, I discovered Spurs lying by the chicken yard gate when I came home from school the next day. His remaining feathers fluttered in the afternoon wind like the last fall leaves hanging on long after winter began. I nudged him with my shoe. He was stiff. His toes had curled under, turning them into useless weapons. He was no longer scary, but he brought back the sadness of being left alone. I sank to my knees.

"I'll get the shovel," Daddy said.

I didn't know how long he had been there. The cold ground had numbed my knees. He left as silently as he came. A few minutes later, he returned with a garden spade balanced on his shoulder and handed me his handkerchief.

"What are you crying for?" he asked, picking up the rooster. "You hated him."

"He was Grandpa's."

"Your grandpa had a dozen different roosters named Spurs, and every one was meaner than the last."

"He did not, and Spurs wasn't mean."

He stared at me until I wanted to shrink inside my coat.

"Archer's probably watching his clock, just hoping I'll be late. Let's get this done."

He carried the rooster and the shovel behind the chicken yard. With four sharp jabs, he made a hole big enough to push Spurs into. Another four scrapes of the blade, and the rooster was covered with dirt. The muscles in Daddy's jaw twitched. He pressed his hand against his mouth the way people do when they're about to laugh or cry and don't want anybody to know which. Except my father never laughed. He raised the shovel above his head, took a deep breath and slammed the back of the blade hard against the little mound. Clods of dirt exploded. The fierceness of the second blow shook the ground under my feet.

"You'll stay buried," Daddy mumbled each time he swung the tool like a sledge hammer.

I grabbed the handle. "You're hurting him!"

"Let go."

Every way Daddy yanked the shovel, I went with it. He peeled my fingers off the handle one by one, and one by one, I wrapped them back on.

"He's dead. He can't feel anything," he said between his clenched jaws. "Let go."

I heard a familiar laugh that made Daddy's head snap up.

Rag grinned at us from the chicken yard fence. "How do you know he can't feel anything? You ever been dead? Just who did we bury, anyhow?"

"What are you here for?" Daddy asked.

"Figured it'd been a while since I saw ya'll."

Daddy twisted the shovel out of my hands to hurl at Rag's feet.

My uncle hopped over the handle, laughing as if he were playing jump rope in the schoolyard. "Hey, that's not much of a welcome."

"You're lucky I didn't throw it at your head. Gracie, gather the eggs."

"Tell you the truth," Rag said. "I was wondering if I could borrow your couch for a few nights."

Daddy shoved the egg basket into my hands as he trudged by me. "Hurry up. I'll wait in the truck." He left me alone with Rag.

My uncle was too quick, the tiny gap between him and the fence was too narrow. He caught me around the waist. "Whoa there."

His usual sneer disappeared. "He act like this all the time?"

I closed one of my eyes and used the other to look into his good eye. That earned me a shaking and another question as to what I thought I was doing. Everything in front of me was still wiggling when he turned me loose and I managed a lopsided shrug.

"Suppose the war made him that way," Rag said.

I didn't tell him that was Miss Louise's idea of why my father did the things he did.

My uncle made a face at me. "You've got snot running out your nose."

Before I could duck, he pulled his handkerchief from his pocket and wiped my nose. Whether the cloth was clean or dirty, it belonged to my uncle. I gagged and made complaining noises as I scrubbed my face with my coat sleeve.

"That's not very ladylike," he said. "What would your pretty Miss Redding think?"

Rather than answer, I bolted for the chicken house where I gathered the eggs and my courage. When I peeked out the door, Rag was gone. I hoped forever. His absence didn't keep me from sprinting to my father's pickup. Two eggs cracked on the way, but Daddy was too busy steering the truck down the driveway to notice.

I made up my mind to mope and never talk to him or Rag ever again. Daddy because of Spurs. And Rag, because he was Rag. To get away with my plan, I pretended the fence posts zooming past fascinated me, but I could only hold on two miles before a worry evoked a question from me.

"Are you going to let Rag borrow Grandpa's couch?"

Daddy scowled at the road in front of him. "No, and I don't plan on letting him sleep on it either."

I let out a long breath of relief. If Rag had taken Grandpa's couch, he might have kept it. With that problem taken care of, I returned to pouting.

"Spurs. I wasn't being mean to him," Daddy said. "And I wasn't hitting him. After I buried him, I packed the dirt over him, so an animal wouldn't find him. Understand?"

I shook my head.

He tucked the corners of his mouth into his cheeks, which he did when he didn't seem to know what else to do. "If I hadn't, in a few days Spurs would start to... to smell."

"Like the possums and skunks that get run over?"

"Yes. And then some other animal would dig him up. You wouldn't want Beau or a coyote to dig up Spurs and eat him, would you?"

I wrinkled my nose. "Miss Louise said they buried Grandpa in the ground. Was it because he was gonna stink?" I sniffed and almost smelled the sweet tobacco of Grandpa's pipe. No, Grandpa was too nice.

The muscles in Daddy's jaw twitched as he stomped on the brake and stumbled from the cab. By the time I crawled across the seat, he was bent over, hands on knees, his body shaking like a scared dog in a thunderstorm, reminding me of Mama before the county took her away.

If he died, I would have to sit alone in the pickup until someone found me. The thought made me tremble as much as my father.

He wrapped his arms around his stomach and vomited. "It was just a chicken," he mumbled between heaves. "It was just a chicken.

Several minutes passed before Daddy could stand up straight and pull himself into the pickup. While he rested his forehead against the steering wheel, I banged one foot against the door and studied his chest going up and down.

"Are you going to die?" I asked.

Daddy shook his head a tiny bit, which didn't help my worrying.

"Are you sure?" I asked.

"Archer'll kill me first."

Before I could untangle my arms and legs, dust and gravel churned beneath the pickup's wheels. He muttered to himself while he drove with one hand

and fumbled to unwrap a stick of chewing gum with the other. I braced myself for a bumpy ride. If he planned on dying, he'd decided to wait until after he delivered the milk.

When he hadn't passed away by the time we got home, I returned to worrying about Rag. We found him inside the house, snoring on Grandpa's couch. From halfway across the room, Daddy tossed a book at my uncle. When it hit Rag on the shoulder, he rolled onto the floor and came to his knees with a gun pointed at us.

Daddy shoved me aside. "What do you think you're doing?"

I hoped my uncle was playing cops and robbers. His good eye rolled back and forth. Once it finally focused on Daddy, he muttered something under his breath and lowered his gun.

"You in trouble, again?" Daddy asked, wiping a dribble of saliva from the corner of his mouth.

Rag put his gun back into his coat pocket. "Not nearly as much as you could've been. Ever think of giving me a gentle shake?"

"I learned not to be within an arm's length when it comes to rousting a man out of his sleep."

"Yeah, well." Rag picked up the book, read the title and tossed it to Daddy. "My, my, the stuff you read."

Daddy caught the book and tramped to the kitchen. Not wanting to be left alone with Rag, I followed. I found no comfort watching my father's hand shake as he poured himself a drink from one of the last jars in the cupboard.

"Was Rag gonna shoot you?" I asked.

"No, he enjoys aggravating me too much to ever shoot me on purpose."

"What about me?"

"You don't have a thing to worry about."

"Unless you're a brat," my uncle said as he ambled into the room. He winked at me with his good eye.

Rag found a glass and held it out for Daddy to fill. "My supply here has been what you might say, depleted. Been hitting it a little hard, haven't you?"

"Guess you should've taken it with you," Daddy said.

"Guess I should've. Got ten bucks? That'll pay me back and get you all you want."

Daddy pulled his wallet out of his back pocket and handed Rag two dollars.

"That's it?" Rag asked.

"All I can spare. Archer's threatening to take our contract somewhere else."

"We've been selling milk there since before I was born."

"Says he can buy cheaper. I'm fixing to buy a milking machine and more cows. That way Archer gets his price, and I still come out all right by selling the cream off the extra milk."

"Big dreams for somebody who won't pay his debts. Not to mention this place ain't yours. Remember?"

"I've got back pay coming from the Army."

"Oh, I forgot. You're taking care of it for the kid." Rag took a long drink and pointed out the kitchen window. "You never did tell me whose grave you were beating on this afternoon."

"Dad's rooster."

"If I'd known that, I'd been out there stomping on it with you."

"Shut up, Rag."

"If there's a heaven for animals, I can guarantee you one thing. That old bird ain't gonna be there."

Daddy slammed his glass on the counter. "Shut. Up."

"Shut up, Rag, but you'll drink me dry. How much a day does he drink?" Rag raised his eyebrows at me. "If Miss Louise hears you're drinking in front of the kid, she'll have your hide."

"I don't drink in front of her, except on special occasions when you're here."

"I had several dozen in here when I left. Now I got three lousy jars."

"What do you care?"

"It's my whiskey."

They were drinking moonshine—something as sinful as walking around with money robbed from a bank.

"I didn't drink any," I said. "Will I have to go to jail?"

Daddy shook his head. "No."

"What'd I tell you," Rag said. "A year with Miss Louise and she's spouting nonsense." He raised his hands. "Yeah, I know. Shut up, Rag."

"While you're at it. Leave."

"No place to go."

I leaned against the counter and tapped my toes together. Rag was staying. Daddy couldn't make him go away, anymore than he could chase the dead men from our nightmares. He gulped down the last of his drink and went into the hall.

"Why are you always banging your feet like that?" Rag said.

I didn't answer. The more important question to me was why my father kept leaving me alone with my uncle.

"I don't like it, so stop," Rag said. "Come here."

He set his empty glass beside the sink and squatted on the floor like a big spider waiting for the little ladybug to crawl to the web. There was no use running. I shuffled across the kitchen to him, only to be surprised by his gently patting my head and smiling as if he were nice.

"Do you like living here with your daddy? I can't believe that old prune of a storekeeper let him take you, as strange as he's acting."

"Miss Redding didn't want me to go. She and Daddy got into a fight."

"And I bet you it was a knock down drag out. She'd fight tooth and nail for her little girl. She knows what's what. That's because she's got a good head on her shoulders, and a pretty one at that. Yes, siree."

His good eye narrowed until he looked at me through two slits. A bad sign. He grabbed my chin.

"You're a chatty little brat, so you better listen up. Don't you dare say a peep about my whiskey to nobody— nobody, you hear? I'll squash you like a bug if you do. Then I'll turn you over to the sheriff, and he'll throw you in jail. Now promise me, hope to die."

I didn't need to look under his droopy lid to see if that eye was thinking the same thing as his other.

"Well?" he asked.

My mouth went dry. With his hand squeezing my chin, I was unable to nod my agreement. I grunted an "uh huh" the best I could as Daddy came back into the kitchen and threw a blanket at Rag.

"Leave her alone."

Rag caught the blanket. "I'm not hurting her. Am I, darling?"

"He's gonna squash me like a bug," I whined.

"Oh, hush," Rag said. "Didn't you see me wink?"

"Winking means he's lying, which he does a lot even when he doesn't wink," Daddy said.

When Rag laughed, his stinky breath went up my nose. I made a face and dove under the table.

"There's that room in the milk barn that Dad let the fruit pickers have," Daddy said. "You can stay there, but not under my roof."

"Now that's true hospitality, but not so fast. I want to know what's going on here. I mean, first, you pick a fight with me and let me beat the crap out of you. Then I come back and find you beating the tar out of a rooster's grave and drinking like a fish."

"Get out of here."

Rag looked under the table and winked at me. "Don't you worry about him. I'm here now to keep an eye on him for you. Just remember to keep your mouth shut about my whiskey."

As usual, my uncle let the screen door slam on his way out.

I spent the evening staring at the light in the milk barn until Daddy slapped his book closed and told me to get away from the window and go to bed. On my way out of the living room, he reminded me that, for the most part, Rag was nothing but a bag of wind. His assurance didn't help me sleep. Whirlwinds were winds, and so were tornados.

To add to my worries, a pack of coyotes in the orchard woke me up in the middle of the night. The longer I listened to them, the closer they sounded until it seemed they were beneath my window. Dead men I could hide from, but coyotes had noses and could sniff me out. I crawled out of bed and peeked down the hall. The house was dark except for the light in the living room. Daddy had moved Grandpa's chair closer to the fire and was staring out an open window. As he raised Rag's jar for a drink, he saw me and lowered it out of sight behind the arm of his chair.

"Whatcha in here for?" His voice sounded like a windup record player that had run down.

"I heard coyotes."

"Oh." His head wobbled. "They won't hurt you."

"What if they jump in the window?"

He leaned his head against the back of the chair and laughed. Something was wrong with him. His ears and hair and glasses were the same, but the rest of his face and his voice belonged to someone else.

He wagged his finger at me as he grinned. "You're... you're... you're a worry wart, know that?"

Two of his upper teeth had the corners chipped out, making a little v-shaped notch that I'd never noticed before. He bent over the book he'd thrown at Rag and flipped through the pages, first one way, then the other.

"You like Whitman?" he asked.

I didn't know anyone named Whitman, nor did I care. All I wanted was to make sure the coyotes didn't dig up Spurs or eat me.

Daddy's smile disappeared. "Too bad. Maybe when you're older."

His head nodded a few times before his chin settled on his chest and little snorts and whiffles escaped with his breath. I'd headed back to my room when the coyotes howled again. Their cries made me shiver as much as the cold breeze fluttering past the living room curtains.

"Dogs," Daddy mumbled. "They're always diggin' up the bodies and stringin' bones all over. Next morning you gotta gather up what's left and bury 'em 'fore you dig the next pit and start over on another day's corpses."

I made a face. I didn't like my imagination painting a picture of dogs digging up dead chickens.

"Don't let them dig up Grandpa's rooster," I said.

"Won't let 'em. Cross my heart and. . .whatever."

He tried to stand, only to collapse half in the chair and half on the floor. He freed an arm from behind his back and pointed at the window.

"Moon's still almost full," he whispered. "See it?"

"Uh huh." The moon I had seen hundreds of times, but not my father like this. He was nothing more than eyes shining through crooked glasses and a heap of arms and legs.

"Look down, fair moon, and. . . and bathe this scene;
Pour softly down night's. . ."

He rubbed the back of his head. "Can't remember. Something floods. Oh, well."

His cheek bones glowed with tears.

"Got it," he said. He tried to straighten his glasses and ended up knocking them off his face.

"On faces ghastly, swollen, purple;
On the dead, on their backs, with their arms toss'd wide,
Pour down your unstinted. . . unstinted. . . nimbus, sacred moon."

He stretched out his arms. "Nimbus moon. That's it. Nimbus moon. What'd you think of Whitman's poetry?"

"It doesn't rhyme," I said. "I like poems that rhyme."

"Doesn't rhyme." He chuckled. "Nothing rhymes anymore. Poems, life. Nothing."

"And chickens don't have arms. They got wings. The poem said arms."

Daddy blinked his eyes and repeated what I had said. He shook his head. "Doesn't make any difference, sweetheart. Go to bed."

He'd never called me sweetheart before, a name Miss Redding used when she wanted me to know she loved me. Most of the time, he didn't bother with my name. It was simply do this or do that.

"Go on." He waved me off. *"Leave the dead to bury the dead."*

So I left him crumpled on the cold bare floor, alone with his coyotes howling and with his moon and his book and his tears.

Chapter 13

After school, I grabbed the egg basket and sprinted for the back of the chicken house to see if the coyotes dug up the rooster. There were no feathers lying about—only my father's huge footprints and a flat rock over the grave in which he'd scratched Spurs' name into the soft red sandstone. He'd kept his promise. I hoped he kept his smile. Using his boot marks as squares, I hopscotched back to the pen where the hens clucked contentedly as if they didn't miss Spurs. Neither did I.

Without Spurs threatening me, it didn't take long to finish my chores and trot to the pickup. Some time during the day, my father put the stock racks on the truck. Their wood slats were rungs of a ladder to the bluebird sky. Up that high, the sunshine felt warmer on my face, the breeze softer. Barn swallows flew within my reach. I'd never climbed that close to heaven without having to peer through leaves or a window. From my perch on the top board, I leaned back as far as I dared to let my hair dance free. The sky became a sea covering the top of the world. Wind sculpted the clouds into ships from Spain, waiting to sail across the Atlantic.

The door to the stock racks creaked opened. Daddy heaved the milk can onto the pickup bed. I hadn't seen him all day. He woke me that morning with a flip of the light switch, grumbling he'd overslept. Before I could unglue my eyelids, the kitchen door slammed and he left for town.

He leaned his head against the stock racks and looked up at me through his red spider webs. Since last night, he seemed to have put himself together again, though somewhere in the patching, he lost his smile.

"The coyotes didn't get Spurs," I said.

I hoped my good news would bring his smile back.

He turned his face away from me. "Climb down."

"I can't. The wind's about to blow the Niña, Pinta and Santa Maria across the ocean."

"I see."

"No, you don't. You aren't looking."

"Where?"

He shaded his eyes as I waved my finger at the three clouds separated from the others.

"They're up there by the Big Dipper," I said. "See?"

He looked in the wrong direction. "Yeah, now let's go."

"Was Mr. Archer mad this morning?"

"No, I made it on time. Rag helped."

"I thought he hated you."

"Apparently, he hates Archer worse. Get in the pickup."

Even if it meant a scolding, I wasn't ready to give up heaven for another long ride to town with my father. My ships had to sail past the Little Dipper first, wherever it was in the sky.

"Do you know stars don't go away during the day?" I asked. "Miss Redding says they're still up in the sky shining. It's just we can't see them 'cause of the sun."

"You learn that in school today?"

"No. Sometimes last summer we took a blanket outside at night to watch them. If you look at them long enough, you can see all kinds of animals. They got names, but most of them sound funny."

For all the hurry he was in, he took the time to roll a cigarette. I stuck out my tongue at it. When that didn't cause him to snuff it out, I gagged and asked him if he had run out of gum. His face turned to rusty iron, and in his sigh, I heard my last warning to get into the pickup. Yet he leaned his head back against the stock racks to watch my ships sail from one constellation to the next. When the boats were halfway across the Atlantic, his face softened, and he began to work his jaw back and forth, and I wondered if, maybe, his everyday frown hid the smile I saw last night the same way the daytime sun hid the stars.

On the way home from town, Daddy took the river road. We hadn't gone that way for weeks, despite my pestering. At the Parker's, their old truck remained in the front yard as immovable and deep-rooted as the tree it was parked beneath. Two of the windows John Caleb's father replaced last fall had panes missing. At one time, a flood left a brown stain a foot above the foundation and porch. Seeing the house again brought back bad memories.

"I don't like Mr. Parker," I said.

Daddy coasted to the bridge while he rolled a cigarette. "Never met the man. Don't care to."

"He's mean."

"There's worse than him, believe me." He lit a match.

"Miss Louise said people were mean to you."

"You've been pestering me for a month to come this way. You gonna look out the window or talk?" His hand with the match wobbled uselessly around the cigarette until the flame reached his fingertips and forced him to give up. "Which is it?"

"The window."

Miss Redding would have told him cranky people make no friends. Beneath our tires, the bridge crackled as if it were made of twigs instead of planks. Cold muddy water swirled between the banks. To make ourselves lighter, I raised my feet off the floor and silently urged Daddy to drive faster. We reached safety, only for one of the pickup wheels to drop into what Daddy called "a shortcut to China." While the truck crawled up the other side, I lowered my legs and peered out the window looking for Gypsies. No smoke rose from the fire rings. The flat plain was deserted except for the raggedy brown leaves blowing among the tree trunks.

"They're not here," I whispered. I'd hoped when the Gypsies returned to the Cottonwood Flats, winter would go away and the orchard would bloom.

My father grumbled the patches of chugholes in the road had multiplied due to the laziness of the county graderman. We bounced from one abyss to another until the springs in the seat croaked louder than frogs after a rain. As we approached the intersection, a car skidded around the corner from the south and like a bully, took the better part of the road.

"Durn fool," Daddy said, swerving to the opposite side. "He's driving like a bat out of hell."

I squinted through the dust shimmering in the late afternoon sun. "It's Miss Redding."

Her dark green Buick fishtailed past us, spewing pellets of clay at our pickup. I ducked until the hailstorm ended, then spun around to see the car plow into the soft bank beside the road. Daddy slammed his foot on the brake, knocking me to the floor. Before I could untangle my feet and legs, he barreled from the pickup, leaving his door to flap like a broken wing. He sprinted to Miss Redding's car.

"Ma'am are you all right?" He asked the question so politely I stumbled over a rut.

Miss Redding got out of her Buick and slammed the door. "No, I'm not all right. I just drove into a ditch." She tramped through the weeds to examine her car, tugging to straighten her dress as she went. "I must have been going a little fast."

"I'd say so," Daddy said. "Any faster and you would've flown over the ditch and right up that tree. What were you doing driving your nice car on this road, anyhow?"

"It's a public road."

"I know that, but not a very good one. What's going on?"

"Nothing."

"The last time I saw you this upset, you had my tail in the wringer."

"There's nothing wrong."

She swept a bit of hair from her forehead, got back into her car and gunned it, spewing dirt out the back. Daddy sent me to stand next to the fence. Miss Redding shifted into reverse. He crossed his arms and scowled at the tires digging deeper into the soft dirt. After her fourth or fifth try to free her Buick, he walked to her door, and they went after each other, again.

"Ma'am, if you'd get out of the car, please."

"It's stuck!"

"That it is."

"Would you please help me get it back on the road?"

"I'll see what I can do. If you'd just go stand up there by Gracie, out of the way."

He circled the car and stopped to peer under the front fender, then he slid behind the steering wheel.

Miss Redding stumbled back to her car. "What are you doing?"

"Putting on the emergency brake before I crawl underneath."

"Mr. Timmons, you don't have to."

The rest of her sentence dribbled into muddled syllables. Daddy bent over to study a sheet of tablet paper, turning it over twice before he shook it at her.

"Is this what it's about?" he asked.

Her face bloomed red.

From where I stood by the fence, all I could see was a line of writing underneath a sketch, enough to tease me into thrashing through the weeds for a better look. I jumped over the last few stalks of sunflowers, only to have my daddy wad up the paper the same way he'd crumpled my drawing of Miss Redding holding hands with Sam. That was it. I'd pieced together the puzzle and danced to the silent chant of *Miss Redding loves Sam, Miss Redding loves Sam.*

"Mr. Timmons, let me have that. I'll take care of it myself."

"Like you did your car?" He unwrinkled the note a little. "You know, except for their names, they can't spell worth a darn. Can't believe they'd be stupid enough to sign this."

They? I'd put together the wrong puzzle.

"Tell you what though," he said, "whichever one drew this is not too bad an artist."

"Can I see?" I asked.

They both snapped *no* at the same time. Miss Redding ripped the paper from his hand and jammed it into her pocket, too deep for it ever to fall out by accident. Grumbling, he squirmed underneath her car. A few minutes later he crawled out and stood to jiggle the dirt from his clothes. As he did, he glared in the direction of the bridge.

"You're not going to do something stupid, are you?" he asked.

"I'm not going to let the twins intimidate me," she said.

Twins? The word alone sent my stomach on a carnival ride. "I thought they ran away," I whispered, in case the boys lurked nearby in the blackjack trees.

"Don't worry," Miss Redding said. Adults often recited those words with the same attention they gave to tying their shoes every morning.

To be safe, I wormed myself under her arm.

Daddy's expression turned sour. "You going to talk to Parker is about the most idiotic thing I've ever heard."

"You can't stop me."

"Probably not, except a tie rod's broke and you're going nowhere. Get in my pickup. I'll take you home, and you can call Darrell at the garage to get your car."

"Would you please take me to see Mr. Parker, first?"

"No, I won't. I'm taking you home by the highway and into town. If you want to go by the Parker place, you'll have to walk."

"I can't let them get away with this."

"Make up your mind. I'd like to get home by suppertime."

"Then I'll just have to sit here." She opened the car door as if to do just that.

For once, I hoped my father won an argument. Despite what he told me about meaner people in the world, in Iron Mound, that title went to Mr. Parker and the twins. Daddy, though, didn't have much chance against someone like Miss Redding. She had inseparable parts of pretty and smart with a pinch of stubborn, which was why everyone respected her.

"We'll go by the sheriff's office on the way back," Daddy said. "Let him take care of it."

"Sheriff Lundy can't catch butterflies with a net," I said, repeating Miss Louise's philosophy.

Daddy lolled his head at me as if I were a bothersome gnat. "Get in the truck, Gracie."

In hopes of satisfying him, I shuffled a couple feet toward the pickup, then stopped.

Miss Redding returned to shaking the paper at him. "And show him this note? He very well might thumbtack it to his bulletin board. No, thank you."

"You've no business going up to that house in broad daylight, let alone this time of day. Why don't you let me talk to Parker tomorrow?"

"I take care of my own problems."

"You're an obstreperous woman."

"How dare you say something like that to me."

"Is it a bad word?" I asked.

"Yes," Daddy said, swatting his hat against his thigh. A cloud of dust rose from his overalls. He sighed and hooked his thumb at the pickup. "All right, ma'am. I'll take you wherever you want to go. Just get in the pickup, please?"

As usual, Miss Redding won.

We drove back to Parker's tarpapered shack. No one seemed to be around. No smoke rose from the chimney. Daddy stopped by an old gate and the last remains of a crumpled fence. On the front porch, two mongrels lounged on a rotting sofa. They raised their heads. Daddy drummed his fingers on the steering wheel and stared at them.

"I'll go knock," Miss Redding said.

"Wait," he said. "Somebody knows we're here. Curtain moved." He honked the horn. When no one came outside, he rolled down his window to lean out the truck. "Parker! George Parker!"

"Obviously, he's more obstreperous than I am," she said.

To keep from giggling, I clamped my hand over my mouth.

"Here's what we're going to do. We'll both get out and go as far as the front of the pickup," he said. "But if I tell you to get back in here, you'll do it."

Miss Redding huffed at him.

"You'll do it," Daddy said. "Now, if any of the Parkers have the nerve to come out, you say what's on your mind, then we leave."

"I plan to tell him to get his children under control."

"Whatever."

He frowned at me and told me to stay put. I waited a few seconds, then scooted over to the driver's side to listen through his open window.

"Parker," he called as he and Miss Redding walked around to the front.

The stubby-eared dog crawled off the sofa to stretch while a sad-faced hound arched his back like a coon's. Daddy told Miss Redding to get behind him. She'd barely moved when the mongrels sprang from the porch.

"Get in the truck," he yelled.

He faced the charging dogs until he heard her door creak open, then he turned and sprinted for his side of the pickup. He lunged at the stock racks. The sad-faced hound hurtled past my window and locked its jaws on my father's boot. Daddy grabbed a wood slat an arm's length above his head to pull himself higher. He groaned. The hound seemed determined to tear off my father's leg and carry it away. Daddy's ramblings last night about dogs and bones hadn't faded from my imagination.

With the weight of the dog straining his arms, Daddy's body sagged within reach of the second mongrel. He lashed at the stubby-eared mutt, using his free foot to keep it away. The cab thundered overhead.

"Get out of here," Miss Redding shouted.

She stood on the running board to pound her fists on the top of the pickup. Instead of obeying, the stubby-eared dog stormed around the corner of the pickup, scaring Miss Redding back inside.

"Does your father have a hammer or something I can use for a weapon?"

She needed her paddle. As far as I knew, my father didn't own one. But she'd lured one of the dogs away from him. With the stubby-eared dog slobbering on Miss Redding's window, he had one less mongrel to fight off. He was able to kick the sad-faced hound on the nose. It yelped. When it turned loose of his boot, Daddy jumped over the top of the racks.

"Gracie," he gasped. "Get back from the window."

I scrambled across the seat onto the safety of Miss Redding's lap. Now that the mongrels had treed Daddy in the back of the truck, they roamed back and forth until Mr. Parker stepped out of the house to whistle at them. Wagging their tails, they trotted back to their couch.

"What you want?" Mr. Parker called.

Daddy peered through the stock racks as if they were bars of a jail. "You ought not to have dogs like that around."

"You ought not to come on to a man's place without an invite. That's trespassing the last I heard."

Miss Redding shoved me off her lap and opened her door. "Mr. Parker." She marched halfway to the porch before Daddy could scramble over the stock racks and catch up with her. "I want you to tell your boys to stop harassing me or I'll have to do something about it."

"Harassing?" Mr. Parker asked.

"Pestering," Daddy said.

Miss Redding pulled the note from her pocket. "They left this on the seat of my car."

Mr. Parker asked the same question I had earlier. "Can I see it?"

"No," Miss Redding said, "it's obscene!"

"Dirty," Daddy said.

Mr. Parker grinned. "I see."

"No you don't," Daddy said. "Let me explain what Miss Redding's trying to tell you. If I catch up with your boys, I'll wear their butts out, and if they pester her again, I'll beat the crap out of them."

A bit of pride for my father ignited in my heart. If not brave, he was smart with words.

He nudged Miss Redding's elbow. "Get back in the truck."

Mr. Parker puffed up like a balloon. "Heard you was crazy. Holin' up in that house all the time."

"Yeah, I'm crazy, so you better tell your boys to leave Miss Redding alone."

With that, Daddy stalked back to the truck, not once glancing over his shoulder at the dogs as if to prove he was as crazy as everyone said. A little trickle of sweat dripped from his jaw. His hands shook. Not much had changed with him. The dogs and Mr. Parker scared him.

"Mr. Timmons?" Miss Redding's voice warbled. She got into the truck. "I'm sorry. How's your foot?"

Daddy examined the tear in his overall's leg. "All he got was a mouthful of boot. If you don't mind, can I take you home now?"

Miss Louise met us when Daddy parked the pickup beside the store. After Miss Redding explained what happened to her car, I told Miss Louise about Daddy and Miss Redding's fuss and the note. How the sad-faced hound almost bit off Daddy's foot and how Mr. Parker called Daddy crazy. And how all the way to town, I saw the dogs' eyes shining in the headlights. Daddy grumbled I had seen a raccoon or possum. Even so, Miss Louise gobbled up my story as if it were Sunday dinner.

"I think Sheriff Lundy needs to hear about this," Miss Louise said. "I'll give him a call tonight." To be sure I understood, she winked at me.

"What are you giggling about?" Daddy asked me.

I shrugged.

"We better be going. I've got chores to finish," he said.

Miss Redding opened the pickup door to get out. "I'm sorry about this afternoon."

A smile tugged at the corners of Daddy's mouth. "Apologizing fifteen times is enough. You don't have to keep at it."

"I feel embarrassed."

He looked up through the windshield. "Stars are bright tonight. Gracie told me they don't go away in the daytime."

"No, they don't. Thank you."

She ran up the steps to the porch, turned and waved. His mouth twitched when she wiggled her fingers at us one last time. Even after she went inside and he took off his boot to rub the ankle the hound grabbed, he continued to stare at the door. I leaned back against the seat and closed my heavy eyelids.

"Does Miss Redding have a friend?" he asked. "A man? You know, a man that she likes? A lot?"

I scowled. She did, but not Sam, the one I wanted her to marry. "Gene Kelly. She says she loves him."

"He from around here?"

It was one too many questions. Why did he care? I peered at him through a half-opened eye like Rag.

"Is he?" he asked.

Miss Redding had shown me a picture of Gene Kelly in a movie magazine, and we'd gone to see his movies, though I'd never seen him in the store. Everybody within fifteen miles shopped at Miss Louise's.

"I don't think so," I said.

"Probably some rich guy in Tulsa."

From the way his shoulders sagged, he didn't like Gene Kelly any more than I did.

Chapter 14

Daddy woke me earlier than usual the following morning. He had the milk can loaded and the engine running when I curled up half asleep on the seat. The hum of the tires lulled me into closing my eyes. The pickup stuttered across a patch of washboard. I raised my head. He had turned onto the river road, something he'd never done when taking the milk to town. For Grandpa's "shortcut" past the Cottonwood Flats, we went at least a mile out of the way. When I questioned him, he mumbled something about gathering his thoughts.

"What about the dogs?" I asked.

I'd had enough of them and George Parker from the night before. Since then, my father favored the foot the sad-faced hound grabbed. It seemed to me, he could better keep his thoughts together without having to worry about dogs chasing them all over the place.

"I want to check on Miss Redding's car. It's too nice to leave sitting beside the road."

I loved Miss Redding's green Buick more than anyone. No one in Iron Mound except the banker's wife had a prettier car, not even Young Doc MacKay. And no one had uglier and meaner dogs than George Parker.

"Looks like Darrell came out and towed it back to town," Daddy said.

As we lurched past the tracks Miss Redding's Buick plowed, I looked with dismay at the intersection behind us. We could have seen the car from the corner, then turned around and went back to the highway. The right front pickup wheel dropped into one of his holes to the other side of the world, and any thoughts I'd gathered bounced out of my head. The truck crawled back onto the road, and Daddy pressed the gas pedal to the floor. By the time we topped the last hill before the Cottonwood Flats, he was driving faster than Miss Redding's bat out of hell. He would have flown over the bridge if it weren't for a dozen children who appeared out of a cloud of gray campfire smoke and ran onto the road.

I sat up on my knees. "Gypsies!" Among the cottonwoods, a circle of old cars and trailers had popped up overnight as magically as a fairy ring of mushrooms.

"Beggars," Daddy said.

"No, they're not!"

The children ran beside us with their hands outstretched. One little girl couldn't keep up with the others. I spun around on the seat to wave my fingers at her. She smiled shyly at me. The men of the camp warmed their hands over a blazing fire. I searched each face, hoping to see Sam's smile among the scowls. Though he wasn't there, my dream was—Sam, Miss Redding, John Caleb and me.

"They'll steal you blind," Daddy said as our pickup rattled over the bridge. He stared at me out of the corner of his eye. I glared back until he gave up and fumbled for a cigarette.

When we returned home, Daddy loaded three steers into the back of the truck to take to the Coler Brother's Sale Barn at the county seat. The auction was held in a tall square barn surrounded by pens of cattle, sheep and hogs. We waited for a cowboy to paint a number on our calves' rumps and give Daddy a ticket before we could go inside.

Daddy hesitated as he peered into the dark building. "They're selling sheep." He leaned against the outside wall as if he planned to stay there for the rest of the day.

A man with a stick prodded four black-faced lambs toward us.

"Open her up," somebody yelled from a window high above me.

A boy chomping on a wad of bubble gum hopped off the top plank of the fence to grab a rope and haul down. A solid wood gate creaked against its iron tracks. It inched higher. Sweat dribbled off the boy's chin. Once the man herded his sheep through the dark opening, the boy let the door drop, then climbed back to his seat to pop a bubble.

"Can we go inside?" I asked. "I want to see the baby lambs."

Before Daddy could answer, I trotted into the barn. The air carried the fresh scent of sawdust covering the floor. Above the show ring, the auctioneer pounded a wooden gavel on a table. The lambs bleated. I couldn't see them for the buyers draping their arms over the top rail of the fence and resting one foot on the bottom rung.

I ran back outside. "Can we sit in the bleachers?"

Daddy shoved himself away from the wall to peer through the door. About the time I thought he would refuse, he straightened his shoulders and marched inside.

The auctioneer pounded his gavel again. "Sold!"

A semicircle of bleachers rose from the floor to the wood-planked ceiling. Partway up the steps, I watched the show ring's back door raise for a red-haired man to herd the lambs outside. I'd missed them. Daddy trudged past me to the top row, high above everyone else. While we settled into our seats, the man with the stick prodded another flock of big black-faced sheep into the ring.

"What kind are they?" I asked.

"Hamps. Ewes."

The auctioneer chanted a singsong jumble of syllables with a number thrown in every once in a while to let me know it wasn't complete gibberish.

"Do you know what he's saying?" I asked.

Daddy propped his elbows on his knee and closed his eyes. I thought he fell asleep, but he finally mumbled the auctioneer was calling out bids and asking for more.

I pointed to a farmer sitting below us. "Does he know what that man's saying?"

My father shrugged. The auction began. No one offered a bid that I could see, though the auctioneer pointed his gavel at one man, then another.

"Sold," he shouted in English and banged his gavel. "Hog's coming up next."

Daddy jerked his head, looked around, then sprinted down the steps two at a time. Farmers scrambled to get out of his way. Though I wasn't ready to leave, I followed him outside where I found him sitting on a bench, his head in his hands. I plopped next to him. I should have known better than to take him inside. Still, I wondered why the crowd and the clamor of voices never bothered other men. Some of them went through "the war."

A man with a string tie stopped in front of us. "You all right, son?"

Daddy nodded.

"Who's that?" I asked once the man went inside.

"Mr. Coler, the owner. Let's go."

Daddy unbolted a narrow gate between the pens and the yard. We plodded along the lane the cowboys used to move the livestock to the sale barn. I lagged behind, wandering between the first few pens, looking for an animal to pet. I found the four spring lambs in the third from the end.

"Didn't anybody buy them?" I asked.

Daddy glanced over his shoulder at the lambs. "Haven't picked them up yet."

I reached through the fence to touch the smallest one's nose. "I wish we'd bought them."

Daddy was no longer there. He had shuffled several pens away to watch a hog wallow in the sour mud of an overflowing water tank. We turned left along a row of calves, then another left before he settled down to study a Holstein cow.

"We gonna buy her?" I asked.

"No."

To pass the time, I played hopscotch around the cow piles until the game ended when one foot landed in the wrong place. I scraped off the bottom of my shoe by stubbing it into the dirt, then climbed the fence beside Daddy.

"When are we going home? I'm hungry," I said.

"On the back side of the sale barn, there's a kitchen. Go get us a couple of hamburgers and pops."

I backtracked twice before I found the lane with the lambs. The littlest one trotted to the fence as if it remembered me. While it slobbered on my sleeve, I worked my fingers into the dense wool on its back and asked if it wanted to come home with me. Someone snickered from the next pen. A red-haired man tossed a shovelful of manure into a wheelbarrow. He was an older, taller Riley or Roland. Not wanting to take any chances he might recognize me, I bolted past him to the sale barn and didn't stop until I was in the kitchen.

Behind the counter, a round woman wiped her hands on her apron. "My goodness, but you must be hungry to come running into my kitchen like that. What can I get for you?"

I walked backwards to the counter to keep an eye on the door. The cook put her hand on my head and twirled me to face her.

"My daddy wants me to get two hamburgers and pops," I said.

"And what kind of pop would you like?"

"Grape."

"And your daddy?"

"RC Cola."

While she cooked the hamburgers and I watched for the twins, I learned her name was Lilah. She had three great-grandchildren my age, and they lived in Meridian where they went to the Missionary Baptist Church. I handed her Daddy's two quarters, and she gave me the change with a kiss. The hamburgers and bottles of pop were a handful to carry. Still, when I saw the wheelbarrow gone, I stopped to talk to the lambs one last time. A hand reached over my shoulder and snatched a hamburger.

"Hey, Riley, you hungry?"

My hamburger flew through the air to the cross-eyed Riley. Roland grabbed the RC Cola. I swung my bottle of grape at him, missed and ended up penned against the fence while he drank half the RC Cola in one gulp and poured the rest on the ground.

"You tell your old man, we ain't scared of him," Riley said. "We'll be right here waiting on him if he thinks different. Go on. Tell him."

I took off with feet pumping. Somehow, I made all the right turns and found Daddy where I left him. His back was toward me. When I grabbed his hand, he jerked his arm and knocked me flat on the ground.

"The twins," I wailed and pointed down the lane. "They took our hamburgers."

He ordered me to stay there until he returned. That he could hobble down the lane so fast, not to mention his bravery, surprised me. I supposed he hated the twins as much as I did. He turned a corner, and I lost sight of him.

When he caught up with the twins, he'd kill them, a thought that made me smile. I cringed—the twin's message. I forgot to give it to him. While I mulled over whether I could find him in time, a cowboy with a belt buckle as big as a saucer trotted up on a horse.

"That your daddy that took out of here?" he asked. He shot a stream of tobacco juice at the fence.

"Yes."

"Where's he off to in such a rush?"

"He went after the twins."

"He shouldn't have left you here alone. We're about to start moving the bulls. You better come along with me."

"He told me to stay put."

"In that case, crawl up on that fence there and don't fall off."

A few minutes later, he herded a big black Angus past me, but not before he shot another stream of tobacco juice at the board beneath my shoes. He made a bull's eye, and I raised my feet another rung.

"Your daddy not back yet?"

I eased off the top of the fence. "Nope. Can I go look for him?"

"You stay right there on your perch. I got another two bulls to go."

Due to his accuracy with tobacco juice, I thought it best to listen to him. He rode by again. I wondered if Daddy lost me among the rows of pens or forgot me and left. The idea of spending the night on a fence by myself scared me. It was enough to suck in my bottom lip.

Another cowboy rode up to me. "Whoa there, you bawling? Your daddy's at the office with Mr. Coler." He pulled me onto the front of his saddle and flicked his whip over the top of a half a dozen wild-eyed heifers. "I need you to whistle at them to get them moving."

I always believed that whistling came naturally to boys, but not girls. As I blew an airy note through my lips, I felt him chuckle, which irked me. It had been my best ever attempt. I tried again and had congratulated myself when he let loose a fire engine siren of a whistle. I clamped my hands over my ears even while I formed my mouth for another effort. By the time we had herded the heifers to the barn, my cheeks ached and my head swam. Once the calves were inside, the cowboy let me have the reins the last few yards to the office.

"You ever need a job herding cattle, you let me know," he said, setting me on the ground.

I grew at least an inch because of his compliment.

In the office, my father sat humped over in a chair. Blood dribbled from an egg-sized bump on his forehead. No doubt, he lost another fight. This time with the twins. A lady taped a piece of gauze over his cut while Mr. Coler watched from his desk. Daddy winced.

"Sorry to say, those boys work for me," Mr. Coler said. "They're turning out to be worth less than what I hired them to scoop. Roberta, when they come in for their pay, you tell them we won't be needing them anymore." He smiled at me. "So those boys stole your hamburger?"

I nodded.

"You have your daddy go back to the kitchen and tell Lilah to get you another. Roberta, have the Timmons' calves sold yet?"

"I don't have the paper work, if they have," Roberta said.

"I'll send for you as soon as it comes in," Mr. Coler said to Daddy.

We went outside to sit on a bench near the door. I was eager to hear the details and if he caught the twins.

He shook his head. "No, somebody tripped me."

With his sore foot, I should have known. Maybe if he'd had his shovel, he could have thrown it and knocked one of them down, but more than likely they would have jumped over it and laughed at him the same way Rag had. Daddy leaned his head against the wall and closed his eyes.

"I'm hungry," I said, tapping my toes.

"You heard Mr. Coler. Go to the kitchen and tell Lilah you want another hamburger."

"What if the twins are there?"

"They won't be."

"But what if they are?"

Daddy half opened his eyes. The auction had ended and a dozen or so farmers gathered outside the office to wait for their checks.

"Stay put," he said.

As soon as he left, I banged my feet together. The idea occurred to me the twins might be lurking among the livestock pens instead of the kitchen. Someone laughed from the other side of the fence.

"If I want to find the little one, I say to myself, I must listen. She will tell me where she is."

I hopped off the bench and scrambled over the fence. For months, I tucked away all the things I wanted to tell Sam. Now that he stood in front of me, they scattered like startled birds.

He laughed. "Your tongue is wood?"

He held a frayed rope attached to a black and white gelding's halter. The scrawny horse's head hung low. I scratched its velvety chin and received a weary whicker for my kindness.

"What's wrong with him?" I whispered.

"His spirit is broken. He needs good grass and kind hands."

"Is he gonna die? Spurs did, Grandpa's rooster. Daddy buried him so the coyotes wouldn't eat him."

"Where is your papa?"

I pointed to the building.

"Is he feeling better?" Sam asked.

Like Miss Redding, he seemed to know what everyone was up to any time of the day. Miss Redding told me she'd taken a special class to learn how to read children's minds. I supposed with Sam, it must've had something to do with his being a Gypsy.

"He has a big goose egg," I said.

"Perhaps he was clumsy?"

"He was chasing the twins, and somebody tripped him. They stole my hamburger."

"He must be careful who he chases."

His smile disappeared. Daddy stood, scowling, arms crossed, on the other side of the fence.

"You seem to know a lot, so maybe you know who tripped me?" he asked.

Sam shrugged. "There were many, many farmers."

Daddy mumbled something about not getting a straight answer from a Gypsy. "Maybe you can tell me if you saw those two boys I was after and which way they went."

"You see two boys," Sam said. "I see four."

"No, two."

For once Daddy was right, and Sam gave up the squabble over how many boys it took to make a set of twins. Sam shrugged and smiled, but Daddy wasn't ready to quit. He picked another argument.

"You buy that horse here? I don't know what you paid for it. It was too much."

"You ask many questions, then answer them to yourself."

"Come on, Gracie."

Before I climbed the fence, I threw my arms around Sam. The way the Gypsy came and went, I might not have another chance.

"Perhaps, your papa wants a hug," Sam whispered as he unwound my arms.

Daddy's head drooped as wearily as the horse's. Hugging Sam, Miss Louise or Miss Redding came naturally. My hugs would probably frighten my father. I scrambled over the fence and ran a half dozen steps ahead. He caught up with me to give me a hamburger before he turned to Sam.

"Four boys?"

Sam nodded. He walked down the empty lane, humming a mysterious and faraway tune that mingled with the low whicker and soft clomps of the horse's hooves. We watched him until he disappeared behind the loading chutes.

Daddy shoved his hat back on his head. "He tripped me."

Chapter 15

On the way home, I pestered Daddy for the reason Sam tripped him. He refused to answer. It got to the point he threatened to put me in the back of the pickup if I didn't hush. Standing in calf manure the rest of the way home from Trades Day sounded pretty miserable, so I pouted. For the rest of the afternoon, he rattled around in a bad mood and filled the pickup cab with smoke on our way to deliver the milk. As he pulled into a parking space in front of the general store, he lit yet another cigarette.

"Don't say anything to Miss Louise about what happened today," he said. "I don't want her telling Miss Redding and getting her upset. And get me a pound of bacon, some cornmeal."

While he mumbled his shopping list, I daydreamed about Sam and his horse.

"Got that?" Daddy asked.

I thought a shrug safer than an outright *no*. He sighed and ran two fingers around the outside of his bump. Sometime during the milking, he'd stripped off the bandage, leaving a less noticeable goose egg and cut.

"Can I tell John Caleb about Sam?" I asked.

"No. That'll bring up the whole mess with the Parker twins."

"But John Caleb's not really a Parker. His pa stole him from the Gypsies."

"Not another word about Gypsies." He gave me the egg basket. "Tell me what you're supposed to get."

"Bacon?" There was something else. Maybe two or three things for all I knew. I'd lost his list sometime during my daydream.

He looked at the empty parking places on either side to judge how many people were in the store. It was almost closing time, and most customers had finished their shopping and gone home to supper.

"I'll go with you," he muttered. "I could use a headache powder."

In the store, I noticed something out of kilter as soon as I trotted through the doorway. The old men who played dominoes in back had given up their warm stove to stand by the cold glass of the meat case. They weren't interested in the bacon or the hams either. Miss Redding behind the cash register had caught their attention.

In Iron Mound, Reverend Ponder preached from behind his pulpit every Sunday. The other six days, Miss Louise stood behind her counter and rang up groceries, overalls and yarn. She never allowed anyone to touch her cash register, except me, and then only to press *Sale* and never the keys with numbers. From the way Daddy stared at Miss Redding, he must have wondered at the strangeness too.

Mrs. Lockwood, the banker's wife, lumbered up to the counter with her basket of groceries. She twisted her gray curls into tight knots while Miss Redding pecked at keys one finger at a time instead of the five Miss Louise used.

Daddy grabbed my shoulder. "Go get me a headache powder," he said without taking his eyes off of Miss Redding.

I had to walk by Rag and another man leaning against the pop machine to get to the cash register. For once, Rag didn't snarl at me. Mrs. Lockwood turned around to give him a heated glare that should have turned him into a puddle on the floor. He grinned back at her. She puffed. Miss Redding ignored them and tapped the keys. The front door banged open, and John Caleb raced into the store.

"I'm back!" He grinned at me but didn't slow down.

"Just in time," Miss Redding said. "Mrs. Lockwood needs help with her groceries."

"Yessum." He darted past Rag and around the corner of the counter. At the cash register, he banged the *Sale* key with his fist, jangling the bell into a fit. "Mrs. Fox gave me an extra dime."

He spread a handful of money across the counter and counted it against the paper he had in his hand.

"To the penny. Very good," Miss Redding said.

He dropped the coins and dollars into their bins, then like a whirlwind gathering dust, he grabbed Mrs. Lockwood's bag of groceries and flew out the door.

I set my egg basket on the counter. "You're not supposed to press the number keys on Miss Louise's cash register," I whispered. As upset as I was, I only wanted to warn her, not get her into trouble.

Miss Redding leaned across the counter until we were almost nose to nose. "It's all right. Miss Louise has a headache and asked me to watch the store."

"Did she bump her head?" I cringed. Secrets were mounding up in my head.

"No."

"How come John Caleb can use the cash register? All he's supposed to do is sweep."

"Miss Louise promoted him to delivery boy."

I dropped the whisper. "It's not fair. I'm her best helper."

"I believe there's a green-eyed monster in the room."

I looked around the store. Rag stood by the pop machine, but his one good eye was blue.

Miss Redding tapped my shoulder. "I meant don't be jealous. What happened to your father?"

He had too many bungles to keep up with. Finding the right words to explain them was harder than finding the fattest worm in a can full of night crawlers.

"I don't remember his bumping his head yesterday," she said.

"No, ma'am. He wants a headache powder."

"All right. Let's see."

She searched the shelves behind her where Miss Louise kept the castor oil, cough syrup and all the other things that tasted bad—except the cans of carrots, which were on the aisle with the peas and green beans. Once Miss Redding handed me a packet, I hurried back to Daddy before she could ask more questions. He shooed Rag and the other man away from the pop machine.

"Miss Louise doesn't feel good," I said.

I might as well have been a dead roly-poly on the floor for all the notice they paid to my explanation. They were concentrating on Miss Redding. Daddy dug two nickels out of his pocket for an RC Cola and a root beer. After he opened the bottles, he handed me the root beer.

"Hey, little brother," Rag said. "You remember Earl Schofield?"

Daddy poured the headache powder into his bottle. "No, but any friend of yours I try to avoid."

Earl whistled softly, which brought a scowl from Miss Redding. "You know, she's pretty, even when she's put out with us."

"You two might as well reel your eyeballs back into your heads. She's taken," Daddy said.

Rag snorted. "By you?"

"No, somebody away from here. Sounds pretty serious." Daddy looked to me for confirmation. "Is that right? Gene Kelly?"

"Who?" Rag clasped his hands over his head and moaned.

"Kelly? Gene?"

"Your sweet kid led you down the merry path, little brother. Gene Kelly's a movie star. That lady over there and half the women in the country are in love with him."

"Yeah," Earl said, "and the rest are screaming for Frank Sinatra. You know who he is, don't you? Frank Sinatra?"

Daddy's gaze shifted from me to Miss Redding to the floor. Earl's laughter bounced from the walls to the ceiling. The old men by the meat case stared at us. For once, I wanted my father to run away and not pick a fight.

Rag stopped laughing. "Aaron?"

"Bet you Miss Redding'd like to hear about her *boyfriend*," Earl said.

Rag grabbed Earl's arm. "Hey, let it go, man."

"Nah." Earl hurried to the counter. "Hey, ma'am. I hear you and Gene Kelly are gonna get married."

Daddy dragged me out of the store. A mile out of town, I finally gathered the courage to peek at him. All his little telltale habits he expressed before he went to that other place he sometimes inhabited were there—the fumbling for a cigarette, the working his jaw back and forth, the constant drumming and twitching of his fingers on the steering wheel.

"I didn't mean to," I said, hoping to bring him back.

As we drove past our windmill and over the cattle guard separating the yard from the pasture, my old urge to hide in my grandfather's closet returned. My father stopped and slipped the truck into neutral.

"Can we go to the house?" I asked.

He peered beneath the sun visor at the hill where the peach trees waited to bloom. Maybe he wanted to see if spring had finally come. But no, we hadn't sat there long when he shoved the gearshift into low and the pickup crawled up the orchard lane. We passed the first row of trees, the second, the fifth. I counted them on my fingers. He headed the truck down the other side of the hill to the old house where Grandpa said I once lived with my mother. It sat empty in a yard overcome with Johnson grass. Since I'd seen it last, lightning struck the cedar tree in the front yard, slashing its trunk to the roots. Daddy let the truck roll to a stop while he stared at the broken windows, the gaping holes in the roof.

He pounded his fists on the steering wheel. I shrank back into my corner of the cab as he slammed the pickup door and paced back and forth between the pickup and the tree. The cedar's dead limbs hung above him like hands of a skeleton reaching for his head. He moaned and pulled his hair.

"No!" His scream echoed across the pasture.

He charged the gate and kicked it off its hinges, sending part of it flying into the weeds. The rest he pried on until he pulled loose a cross-brace the size of a baseball bat. He staggered up the porch steps and swung his club at the front window. The glass shattered into diamond confetti. He battered the door into splinters.

I waited until he went inside before I sneaked from the pickup and up the front steps. Though every floorboard underneath my feet shrieked at me to go back to the truck, I peeked in the front window.

In his anger, my father couldn't see me. He pounded the wall with his bat, oblivious to me and the white plaster dust fogging the room. He hammered until he made a hole large enough he could rip the lath ribs from the house with his bloodied hands. A pile of wood grew at his feet. Tears plowed furrows in his dusty face. When he dropped his club, I hoped his rage had worked its way and was ready to leave. Instead, he tore strips of wallpaper free to stuff beneath the broken slats. Sinking to his knees, he fumbled with his box of matches, lit one, and held it to the paper. It caught fire and blazed. As if to pray, he bowed his head and sighed. Spellbound, I backed away from what I witnessed. Miss Louise had told me about certain things little girls weren't meant to see. I'd seen my share with Daddy.

He tilted his head a notch, the only warning I had.

"Get back to the truck and stay there," he whispered in a way that terrified me.

I bounded off the porch without bothering to take the steps. In my mind, I leaped halfway to the pickup, but I left my feet behind and ended up sprawled on the ground, stunned and gasping for a breath. Inside the house, a spasm of coughing overcame Daddy. All the air in the world was sucked from the sky, leaving none for us. Once I relearned to breathe, I smiled at the prettiest cowboy rose I'd ever seen growing in front of my nose. On Monday, Miss Redding could put the blossom in a glass on her desk for everyone to see.

Not far from the flower lay a headless doll cradled in tickleweed the winter winds had gathered for her bed. I slipped the blossom into my pocket and reached for the doll. Part of her cotton stuffing hung like a shawl about her shoulders. I poked the wadding through the hole where her head had been and tried to brush the dirt from her, but my fingers couldn't rub away the stain of being left behind. Had she belonged to me or Wilma Rose? According to Grandpa, the Parkers lived here once.

Daddy lurched onto the porch. He slumped on the steps not far from me and rested his head in his bleeding hands. Fat drops of sweat dripping from his face made pockmarks in the dust at his feet. I tucked the doll under my jacket and edged toward the pickup.

He looked at me over his fogged glasses. "What's that?"

"A doll," I stammered.

"Let me see."

I showed him.

"Throw it away," he said. "I've seen enough headless bodies."

"I'm gonna bury it."

Another spasm of coughing hit him. I used that moment to sprint for the dead tree where I dug a shallow grave with the toe and heel of my shoe and gently lay the doll in the soft earth. A car clattered and squeaked its way down the rutted lane toward us. I didn't recognize the ramshackle automobile as belonging to our neighbors. I hurried to scrape dirt, leaves and twigs over the doll. By the time I'd stamped the little mound flat to keep the coyotes away, the car creaked to a stop next to our pickup.

"Sam," I whispered with wonder. He came to help me.

I ran to his door before he scooted from behind the steering wheel.

"Daddy made a fire in the house," I said. "Make him put it out."

Sam watched the smoke curling from the windows. "I will talk to your papa."

Despite the heat pouring from the fire, Daddy hadn't budged from the front porch. He sat with his torn hands cupped in his lap, his shirt clinging wet to his chest. Sam pulled a handkerchief out of his pocket, gripped one edge between his teeth and ripped the cloth in two. He offered the pieces to my father to wrap his palms. Daddy refused to look at Sam. Blood dripped from his fingers. Fire licked at his back.

Why? It was the same mystery as when Miss Louise gave him the sheriff's gloves, and he threw them away. Why did he refuse help? I had no answer. Sam patted my shoulder as if he understood my bewilderment.

Daddy mumbled to his feet. "Can't seem to get rid of you. You can't find anybody else to trip?"

"I saw smoke," Sam said.

"What happened to your fiery steed? Die on the way back?"

"It is true he is weary, but also skittish. He does not recognize the smell of the river or the paths. I tell my little brother to be patient, take two days and be no more than a snowflake on the horse's back. The boy will do well. He is anxious to show he is a man. You sit on a porch as the house burns?"

Daddy rubbed the back of his neck, his fingers clutching and pulling the straggly black hairs that grew there. "It's not worth anything."

"Wood can be sold. Or maybe you burn not the house so much as the memories."

Daddy gave the flames roaring in the living room a long look before turning back and accepting the torn handkerchief to wrap his bleeding palms. Neither he nor Sam seemed to feel the fire's breath. Nor did they give Rag's car tearing down the lane a second look. As usual, a whirlwind of dust and trouble followed my uncle. He parked on the other side of Sam's car and stalked toward us.

"What's he doing here?" he asked before he turned his attention to me. "Why do you always bang your feet together like that? Drives me up a wall."

I grabbed my toes. I hadn't noticed them doing anything.

"He saw the smoke," Daddy said.

"Saw the chance to steal something." Rag grinned at Sam. "Hey, on your way out, be sure and leave our windmill."

"Alas," Sam said, "my wife is not with me, and I have no skirt to hide it under."

I clamped my hands over my mouth to stifle a giggle.

Rag scowled at me. "What's the matter with you? Your daddy feeding you maggots?"

"Maybe the question ought to be what are *you* doing here," Daddy said to Rag.

"Me? Miss Redding threatened to peel my hide if I didn't come and check on you. Though, it'd be worth the pain just to feel her fingers running over me."

"Everybody thinks I'm crazy," Daddy said to Sam. "I don't know. Am I?"

"What are you asking him for?" my uncle asked.

"Shut up, Rag."

"He's a stinking Gypsy."

"Shut up, Rag."

"Is that all you can say to me?"

"Dammit, Rag, shut up." He asked Sam again, "Am I crazy?"

Sam smiled. "All *Gadžè* are crazy."

"What's that supposed to mean?"

"My people are *Romani*." Sam dismissed us with a wave of his hand. "All others are *Gadžè*."

Rag snorted at this.

"The sun sets. I must go," Sam said. He turned to my uncle. "Your windmill, it is good?"

"Yeah."

"Then I must stop to admire it." He smiled at Daddy. "Aaron Timmons, when my horse is strong, you come see."

Daddy's eyelids flickered. His gaze followed Sam back to the car, waiting until the Gypsy pulled away before he said, "I will."

I gasped. "I'll tell him." I turned to run after Sam.

Rag grabbed the back of my jacket. "You'll tell him nothing." He whirled me around and dragged me to the other end of the porch. "Forget that Gypsy."

"I wanna go home to Miss Redding."

"Don't blame you. I'd love to go with you." He scowled at the burning house. "Your daddy have any particular reason to set fire to this place?"

At my shrug, he gave up on me and tramped back to Daddy.

"What's eating you? Earl and me were just joking around," he asked.

Daddy raised his head. "All these years in my mind, the front door was green, the living room had those white lace curtains Annie made. Seems every night I'd dream about this place, the way you could look out the kitchen window at the sunrise."

"What kind of answer is that?"

A good one, I thought, as I imagined the green door and the lace curtains fluttering in the morning breeze.

"Crazy thing," Daddy said, "since I got back, I haven't been able to make myself come over here. Break out in a sweat every time I think about it." He shoved his glasses up on top of his head to rub his eyes. "She wanted me to paint the dining room blue. I never got around to it."

"After Annie left, the Parkers moved in. They weren't much into decorating, either."

"The Parkers?" Daddy spat on the ground.

"Agreed," Rag said. Something changed in his voice. The harshness disappeared along with the smirk on his face. "Come on, let's get out of here and go home."

Daddy squinted at my uncle. "Where's home? Annie, Mother and Dad's gone. I don't recognize any of the boys playing for the Cardinals. The president's some man I've never heard of."

"Most of us never heard of Truman until Roosevelt died."

"Everybody's running around wanting bigger farms and tractors. How can I keep up?"

"All I know is that you can't sit here much longer."

"When did Johnny Mize get traded?"

Rag shrugged. "Forty-one, forty-two."

"With his batting average?"

"The Giants had to fork over at least three players and some change."

They kept their voices low, relaxed. Their resonance calmed my fear. The fire crackled quietly inside the house. My eyes grew heavy. As much as I hated Rag, I found myself leaning against him. His arm slipped around my shoulders to steady me.

"You plan on burning up with this house?" Rag asked as if it were just another question.

It almost slipped past me. I fought through my sleepiness and uncurled myself from my uncle's grasp.

"What do you care?" Daddy asked.

"Don't, but Annie wouldn't want Gracie watching her daddy roast himself. If you can't get a handle on things, maybe you ought to let her go. It might be for the best."

"No," Daddy said as he stood. He walked a few feet away, then looked over his shoulder. "You're scaring Gracie."

"I'm scaring Gracie?" Rag asked in his usual snarl. "What do you think you're doing?"

"I'm okay, but I'm not ready to leave yet. Not until the fire's out."

"Oh man, I've got business to tend to. I can't hang around here watching you mope."

"I said I was okay. Go back to your moonshine. I'll put Gracie in the pickup where she'll be safe."

Rag touched the brim of his hat. "I'm gone."

He left in a boiling cloud of dust. The surprising thing was he took with him a feeling of safety, an emotion I never experienced around him before. I was alone.

"It'll be awhile," Daddy said without looking at me. "I'll have to make sure the fire doesn't get into the pasture, but I won't be far. Stay in the pickup. If you get cold, roll up the window."

He chased down sparks with an old gunny sack. The fire ate the walls and roof and slithered down the porch posts. When nothing was left but glowing ashes, he sat under the tree, his head down, his arms hugging his knees. I no longer worried about him burning up in the house. I pulled my flower from my pocket and floated away with dreams of Sam and cowboys.

"Wake up," Daddy said. "Can't get the truck started. We'll have to walk."

I opened my eyes halfway. My flower was gone. I raised up on one elbow to look beneath me.

"Come on," he said.

I touched something soft above my head as he grabbed my ankles to scoot me across the seat.

"Moon's not up yet. Better let me carry you," he said.

My fingers wrapped around my flower as Daddy lifted me to the sky. If the night hadn't the stars, and the pebbles hadn't crunched beneath his feet, the world could have been turned upside down in the blackness, and I never would have known. We'd left the pickup long behind when Daddy stopped to shift me to his other shoulder.

"Your stars," he whispered.

The angels had pasted thousands and thousands of twinkling jewels on the black velvet of the sky. More than I could ever hope to count. While we watched the moon rise into the cold air and light the dew clinging to the grass, Daddy's chest shuddered.

"Oh, God," he prayed. He seemed to inhale all the night, yet his voice became as soft as an April breeze.

"As I marched alone with death across the desert of my soul
Where neither thistle nor the thorn endured the sun's embrace
I came upon a flow'r with petals pale and dewy leaf
And wondered how this fragile bloom flourished in such a place."

"Is this a poem? It rhymes," I asked. I supposed it was one from his book.

"Yes, it's a poem."

"Miss Redding taught me how to rhyme. Place…lace. See? Was it a cowboy rose? I found one. I told you I would, but you didn't believe me." I twirled the flower between my fingers, letting its petals brush against Daddy's neck. "Was the flower purple like mine and pretty?"

I laid my head on his shoulder. Beneath the stars, he felt strong.

"I believe so. Shhh."

"Is there more?"

His gait settled into a steady rhythm.

"Whether of forgotten God or demented mind, it quivered in the wind
And a dying man asks no questions but devours both dew and blossom.
With petal's sweet scent upon my hands, I cried out in despair
For wilted stalk and fallow ground, for the man that I'd become.

"In dreams, I wept for headless flowers and legions of headless men
That tramped through night—"

"The doll I found didn't have a head."

"No, it didn't.

"In dreams, I wept for headless dolls and legions of headless men
That tramped through night in rank and file beneath the naked moon.
Bound to orders of gentle mercy, they chanted a timeless dirge
And searched for those who would to die and heed their hypnotic tune.

"Though I wished to follow them, to leave this hell behind
I woke to find the stalk revived; its leaf tipped with dew
And while I watched in wonder, a fragile bud burst forth
To beckon me to carry it with life and faith anew.

"So I march along with death across the desert of my soul
Where neither thistle nor the thorn endure the sun's embrace
I pray the blossom will guide me home, but should this soldier fall
I smelled the fragrant flower of hope, the flower God christened Grace."

"That's my real name."
"Yes," Daddy said in a voice that crackled like the fire. "Yes, I know."

Chapter 16

Overnight, most of the poem my father had recited faded away, leaving me but a few rhymes and my name. I woke up eager to find him in hopes he'd repeat the verses. He had the lines in his head. All he needed was a good march to roll them out. He let me sleep late while he went to town. A loud creak came from the back porch. I knew the sound. Someone opened the basement.

According to Grandpa, he made the basement door out of heavy wood planks to keep out animals, tornados and curious little girls, the trickiest being little girls. He needn't have worried about me. As much as I loved to hide in his closet, I hated the damp musty dungeon. Cobwebs hung from the ceiling and walls like ragged lace curtains and black widow spiders scurried across the floor. I tiptoed outside barefoot. Someone had parked a dusty green car by the steps and left open both back doors. Cardboard boxes stamped with the words *One dozen Atlas Quart Jars* were piled high in the backseat and trunk.

Rag's voice echoed off the rough-hewn rock walls of the basement. "Man, you're jumpier than a frog on a skillet. I'll leave enough upstairs there won't be any reason for him to come down here. Any tight place spooks him, especially if it's dark. You'd probably have to beat him to get him down here."

Rag meant my father. The entrance to the basement was a gaping rectangular hole in the porch floor. I peered over the edge as Rag's friend, Earl, sprinted up the stairs. He saw me, sputtered a curse and grabbed my arm before I could get away.

"Look what I found," he yelled.

I kicked his shin and was reminded my feet were bare. I yelped.

"Watch her. She can kick like a mule," Rag said.

"This mule ain't got no shoes."

A dribble of tobacco juice ran down Earl's chin, which he smeared with the back of his hand. He used the same grimy hand to drag me below. Rag was a silhouette against the wooden shelves where Grandpa kept his canning jars. The packed dirt floor felt damp and cold under my feet when he set me down. I imagined spiders sneaking from beneath the shelves in search of my naked toes.

"What'd you bring her down here for?" Rag asked.

I hopped from one foot to the other in a silly dance to avoid spiders. "Where's Daddy?"

Rag picked up a cardboard box from a stack and shoved it onto a shelf. Glass clinked.

"What are we going to do?" Earl asked.

"Keep our mouths shut so as not to put ideas in anyone's head," Rag said. He shook his finger at me. "Just what do you think you're doing down here with no shoes on? Get back in the house. Now!"

It wasn't my idea to come downstairs, but since I was there, my curiosity got the better of me. I sneaked a look past my uncle.

He prodded me on my shoulder. "Go."

I pointed at a box. "Is that—"

Before I could finish the question, he flung me over his shoulder like a bag of feed and hauled me upstairs. He plopped me hard on the kitchen counter and pointed his finger like a gun at the place between my eyes.

"You're going to get somebody shot if you're not careful," he whispered.

His usual hint of teasing wasn't there. I swallowed hard. He owned a gun.

"Have you ever shot somebody?" I asked.

"Not so as to kill them," he said. "About what you saw. Don't tell your daddy because he don't care too much for Earl."

"Me neither."

"Hush. See, Earl's been doing a little canning and needs a place to store the jars for a while."

"It *is* moonshine." I'd caught my uncle in a lie. "Daddy says it's too early to plant green beans and corn. Where is he?"

Rag moaned. "We couldn't get his truck started this morning. So after we milked, I took the milk can to town, and he grabbed his tools and headed back across the orchard. Probably there yet." He put his hands on top of his head and scowled. "I'm serious, cross my heart. You, me and your daddy could get in a lot of trouble if you don't keep your mouth shut."

"What if Daddy reads my mind? Miss Redding does all the time. She learned how in teacher's school."

"I wish she could read mine."

"Maybe she does."

"No, she'd be blushing."

"How come?"

"Would a bag of candy corn help you forget what you saw?"

We sealed the bargain with a handshake. He left me on the counter while he buttered two slices of bread. They were my dinner if Daddy wasn't home by noon.

"How come you and Daddy talked nice, yesterday," I asked. "This morning, you helped him with the milking." No doubt tomorrow, they'd be back to fighting.

Rag put the bread and butter sandwich on a plate. "Don't believe in kicking a man when he's down. Even somebody like your daddy."

"Is Daddy down?"

"Couldn't be lower. Didn't realize it until yesterday. The war."

With Daddy, it always came back to "the war."

"Is that why he burned down that house?" I asked. "Or 'cause of the Parkers?"

"No. You're too short to understand. I want you to stay inside until he comes home. Hear me?"

"Somebody'll shoot me if I don't?"

My uncle rolled his good eye at the ceiling. "No. You're a worry wart."

"Then who are they gonna shoot?"

The teasing disappeared from his voice. "Hopefully, not me."

It was true. I was a worry wart. Grandpa often worried I had too active an imagination to be left alone, which did little to assure me a man with a gun wasn't lurking somewhere near. Despite my uncle's telling me not to fret, I coaxed Beau inside when Rag and Earl were in the basement. We spent most of the day in Grandpa's closet along with my Raggedy Ann.

Daddy came home at milking time. He parked his wheezing pickup by the windmill and tramped to the barn. I left him alone. I'd learned from watching the muscles in his face when he wanted it that way. Besides, there was Rag's secret balanced on the tip of my tongue.

At the supper table, Daddy sank into his chair. Beside his plate were two pencils, a pocket knife and a Big Chief tablet with a page half full of scribbles. Cursive wasn't taught until the third grade, but for two years, I'd stared at the penmanship examples above the blackboard at school and knew the letters. It was only when Miss Redding tied them together with curls and loops I became confused.

Once Daddy finished supper, he shoved his plate away to sharpen one of the pencils with his knife. "I asked Rag to keep an eye on you. Did he fix you something to eat?"

"A bread and butter sandwich," I said. "Beau ate it."

Daddy swept the pencil shavings onto his empty plate, then bent over his ruled tablet. He wrote in fits and starts, three or four words at a time. If the poem was so hard to remember, why didn't he copy it out of his book?

I recognized a capital. "You write funny. What's that word?" I asked.

"*The*. What was Beau doing in here?"

Why was my father in such a chatty mood? Didn't he know I had a secret to keep? He stopped writing to look up at me.

I shrugged. "Guess he got lonely."

"Sorry. I didn't think it'd take that long to get the truck running."

"What's that word?"

"*Flower*. That's the title of the poem."

"The cowboy rose? Where's my name?"

"I haven't got to it yet."

"Are you gonna read it to me when you're done?"

"You're too young."

"You told it to me last night. I liked it."

He made a funny noise in his throat that sounded halfway between a laugh and a snort and sent me off to bed.

By the time I dragged my leftover sleep to the kitchen Monday morning, Daddy had left for town. I examined the cowboy rose I planned to take to Miss Redding. After days of floating in a bowl of water, it'd turned to slime. I tossed the blossom outside and returned to the table. As I ate my oatmeal, I studied my father's scrawl in the tablet. He'd written more words, scratched them out, started again and doodled a flower next to my name.

"The Flower," I said as if I were Miss Redding reciting a poem in class.

She often read to us. We put our books in our desks, then waited, chins propped on hands, for her to put words together like a puzzle and turn them into a picture of a place or thing we'd never seen. I hesitated only a moment before stuffing the paper into my pocket.

Miss Redding seemed to hover over my desk all day. Her presence flustered me to the point I fell behind in my work. Not that I ever sped through arithmetic. I hated the subject, but I wanted to finish in time to ask her about the poem.

"Class," she said. "Almost time to go home."

She was talking to me. Everyone else had put their assignments in her basket and were reading library books. I wrote numbers down as fast as I could make them up.

"I'm done," I said, shuffling to her desk with my arithmetic paper hid behind me.

She opened her mouth to say something, then changed her mind when nothing came out. She motioned me around to the side of her desk.

"Your father, how's he. . ."

I understood her problem. He had a way of mixing me up, too. While she made another attempt at speaking, I slipped my arithmetic paper, neatest side up, into her basket.

She caught my deceit out of the corner of her eye. "Did you take your time and check your answers?"

"Yes, ma'am." I wished I had.

She reached for my paper. "Let's see."

"I got something for you," I said to keep her hand from the basket.

"Oh?" She knew what I was up to.

"It's a poem. Will you read it to the class? It has my name in it."

"It does? Bring me the book, and I'll see."

"It's on a piece of paper," I said, pulling it from my pocket. "It's in longhand. That's why I can't read it."

She read silently, her lips tight. Once finished, she stared at the paper a long time before she asked me where I found the poem. My classmates stopped reading to stare at us.

"Don't you like it?" I asked. "Did you see my name?"

"Where did you find it?"

"On the kitchen table."

"Does your father know you took it?"

Was she accusing me of theft? Everyone leaned forward in their desks, waiting for my answer. She cleared her throat. Heads ducked and pages turned. She reread the poem again. This time when she finished, she tapped her pen on her desk. She was going to read it aloud.

"Class dismissed."

Along with everybody else, I gaped at her. She was letting us out five minutes early. At first, no one moved. Then one of the big boys in the back of the room whooped and slapped his book shut. That was the starter's signal for the race to the cloakroom.

Miss Redding whispered, "You need to put this back where you found it."

"I didn't steal it." I doubted she understood me through the hiccups I caught whenever I tried to talk and cry at the same time.

"I don't think your father would like my reading this."

She wiped at her eyes as if the poem made her sad. About that time, the chatter in the room ended as suddenly as it began. I looked up to see my father. His presence released a flurry of butterflies in my stomach. He knew I'd taken the poem. Why else would he be at school instead of at home milking?

My classmates hugged either side of the double doors as if he were a huge rock parting the waters of a stream. They left quietly, eyes down, except Billy Pogue, the school pest, who darted past twirling his finger around his ear.

"Billy!" Miss Redding stammered over the laughter of those watching. The scrawny boy disappeared among the children. "I'm sorry. I'll get Billy and bring him back to apologize."

She half rose, then sat down. Billy was scrawny, but fast. She had no way of catching him. My eyes stung with embarrassment. My classmates made fun of Daddy the same way they had with Wilma Rose. He let them. He stood at attention as if he were a soldier again, staring past them the same way he stared past so many things when he should have grabbed Billy by the collar and given him a good shake before the pipsqueak got away.

"Mr. Timmons?" Miss Redding said. "I'll speak with Billy tomorrow."

Daddy licked his lips and blinked. "I. . . I need to ask you for a favor."

"Please come in."

Despite her smile, a deep red crept up her face. As my father crossed the room in gigantic strides, she folded the poem into a neat square and slipped it into my pocket. I hadn't noticed until then that my father wore a new shirt and jeans. He'd shaved his straggly whiskers and combed his hair as if he had gone to the county seat on business. Whatever the purpose for the clothes, he seemed uncomfortable and tugged at the shirt. When he reached the desk, he put his hand on the back of my head. I ducked.

"Why don't you wait in the truck," he said.

Instead, I ran around the corner of the building to watch him through a window and see if he'd come about his poem. He mumbled and paced. The corners of his mouth twitched a smile. He followed Miss Redding over to the library shelves where she searched through the books. She gave him a dark green one, which he thumbed through and nodded. Whatever he was up to, it wasn't about his verse, though just as bad. On the way past her desk, Miss Redding reached into her assignment basket for my arithmetic paper, and I fled.

My father had parked the pickup outside the gate. For some reason, he'd done his chores early. The milk can sat in back, the egg basket on the floor of the cab. He was only a minute behind me getting into the truck. He didn't start the engine. He sat tapping a disjointed rhythm on the steering wheel.

"I'm sorry I'm not much to be proud of," he said.

True, he disappointed me. It was one thing to let Rag or the sheriff make fun of him, but Billy Pogue? Though Billy was a year older, a good kick from me, and he'd be running home, bawling. I shrugged off Daddy's attempt at conversation. Between my uncle's moonshine in the basement, my arithmetic and the poem, I had other worries.

The moment Daddy turned onto the river road, I forgave him for his lack of retaliation against Billy. We passed the Parker shack. My father gave it and the two dogs on the sofa a glance and expressed his belief the Parkers would be the ruination of the place. Looked to me, his prediction was already fact.

Across the bridge, he surprised me by stopping in the middle of the road beside the Cottonwood Flats. Strings of smoke rose from the Gypsy campfires, but no one stirred outside the trailers.

"Where are they?" I asked. There was always someone about.

He squinted through his glasses. "Probably heard us coming."

He surprised me again when he got out and walked to the edge of the campground.

"Hello?" he called.

I closed the door and locked it in case the same men who threatened to turn me into a slave were back.

Daddy didn't have long to wait for an answer. Three dogs tore through the underbrush. He sprinted to the pickup and jerked the door handle to no use. He pounded on the window.

"Unlock the door!"

I yanked the handle. He crawled inside over the top of me and slammed the door closed. Before he could start the engine, a mob of laughing boys and girls swarmed through the gaps in the camp to hop up on our hood. He tried honking the horn to get rid of them, which only brought more children and more dogs. He groaned. Once the crowd covered the truck, they settled down to wait for his next move.

He rolled down his window to whistle at a boy. The boy jumped up on the running board, followed by four others elbowing for better positions.

"Do you know Sam?" Daddy asked.

The boy's expression went blank. I was just as dumbfounded with the question. Why did my father want to see Sam? He didn't care for him in the least. The only thing I came up with was the horse, probably because I held a ridiculous hope he might buy it for me. He reached into his pocket for a nickel and offered it to the boy.

"Go get him."

The boy grabbed the coin and raced back to the camp with half of the children in chase after his prize. The rest fought to stick their wiggling fingers through my father's open window.

"No more money," he shouted. "No more."

"Are we gonna see Sam's horse?" I asked over the chatter.

Daddy raised his window past the highest reaching hands. "Doubt it. All I see is kids and dogs."

"Maybe he has it on the other side of the camp."

"Wouldn't be surprised if that boy doesn't make off with my nickel."

"Then how come we stopped?"

"Because I'm stupid, that's why. Keep your window rolled up."

With their begging closed off, the children formed a circle of dark eyes around the truck. After a few minutes, two men I'd never seen before ambled from the camp. They clapped their hands, and like magic, children and dogs melted into the trees. The older Gypsy filled his smile with golden teeth. He took off his hat to bob his head as if it were disconnected from the rest of his body and introduced himself as Max.

"I sent the boy to get Sam," Daddy said.

"Ah, yes, but there is no one in my camp by that name."

"How about Tom, Dick or Harry or whatever you want to call him."

"That man left yesterday. None of us knows where he went." Max shrugged and grinned.

The other Gypsy curled his upper lip like an angry dog's and spat one word, "*Beng.*"

Daddy ignored it, whatever it meant, but I had a suspicion it wasn't friendly.

"He wouldn't happen to know where Sam is?" Daddy asked.

Max shook his head sadly. "No." He swept his arm toward the other man and ended the gesture with a flick of his wrist. "This is my brother, Bruno," he said in a booming voice that echoed down the river. "My brother, he just ask me to tell you that he feels very honored that one held in such high esteem as you would come to visit our humble Gypsy camp and he asks that you stay so we may drink to your health."

"Quit shoveling it. Tell Sam I'm interested in his horse." He yanked the gearshift into low and crushed the gas pedal to the floor.

"Are you gonna buy Sam's horse?" I asked as we left the two men in the dusty road.

"Only thing that horse's good for is the glue factory."

"Then why are you gonna buy it?"

"I'm not. How many more questions do you have in your head?"

Instead of telling him I had at least twelve or fifteen, maybe more, I shrugged and rode off in a daydream on Sam's horse.

My father didn't talk the rest of the way home nor during supper. He waited until he finished the dishes before he pulled my arithmetic book from his coat pocket and placed it on the table in front of me.

"Explain to me why you got every problem wrong on this page?"

I stared at my hands. The only excuse I had was the poem, and I wasn't about to tell him that. While he'd washed the milk can outside by the windmill, I'd jammed *The Flower* between the pages of his tablet. I never wanted to see it again. Ever.

"There's no reason for you to get a bad grade in arithmetic," Daddy said. "Your mother was good at math. That's why Miss Louise hired her to help at the store."

I looked up at him in wonder. "Mama worked for Miss Louise?" Why hadn't she told me? Most of the memories left of my mother were of her lying on a dirty sofa and coughing, always coughing and crying.

"She did," Daddy said.

"Did she punch the keys on the cash register?" I could imagine myself wearing an apron and standing behind Miss Louise's counter.

Daddy tapped the book on the table. "Miss Redding tells me you aren't trying very hard. She said today you wrote down any old numbers to get through. She wants you to do it over."

He tore a sheet from his tablet. I stopped breathing, praying the poem wouldn't fall out. A tentative knock on the back door startled us. When I jumped up to see who it was, Daddy ordered me to sit. He walked over to the door and switched off the kitchen light. The glow from the single bulb in the hallway made a ghost of him. His hands and arms appeared and disappeared as he moved in and out of the shadows. Despite the darkness, he left the porch light off when he opened the door.

"Evening," Daddy said. "I wasn't sure if you'd get my message."

Chapter 17

Other than Rag, the last person to come by our house was the Watkins salesman peddling his spices and cough syrup. The poor man managed to jabber two sentences of his sales pitch before he gave up and never came back. The problem was Daddy made people uncomfortable. Their attempts to talk to him ended with uneasy smiles as if they realized they'd forgotten to zip their zipper. I was pondering this when I remembered under the feet of our mysterious visitor were jars and jars of moonshine.

"Nothing to worry about. Come in," Daddy said. "I heard my brother leave awhile ago."

But as footsteps shuffled across the porch, Daddy changed his mind and blocked the entrance. He looked over his shoulder searching for me in the shadows.

"Gracie, go to your room."

I had been told too many times that cats died from curiosity for me to dawdle, especially if our visitor happened to be the sheriff. I slid underneath the table and crawled between two chairs and into the hall. Skidding into my room, I slammed the door behind me with the idea of throwing myself onto my bed for a swampy bout of sobbing. After all, it was Rag's fault, and he hadn't bothered to bring me the candy corn he promised.

I wasn't allowed to mope long. Daddy came into my room and marched in a square—four steps, turn, four steps, turn. In the middle of his third lap, he stopped tramping to stand in front of me.

"Is something the matter?" he asked.

"No."

"Then stop banging your shoes together."

It occurred to me then that it was my way of marching. So why didn't he let my feet alone?

He waited until I sat up. "There are all kinds of secrets. Some we should keep and some we shouldn't."

I supposed he was referring to the whiskey in the basement, so I dipped a toe into the cold water of the matter. "You mean Rag's moonshine?"

I didn't bother to say *Uncle* Rag because I was too put out with him. Daddy moaned and squeezed his head between his palms.

"I wish I had never laid eyes on or even heard about that dadratted moonshine," he said.

I double wished it.

I flopped back onto the bed and restarted my toes. He grabbed my feet and mumbled something about unhappiness. Though relieved he'd moved on from anything to do with moonshine or the sheriff, I couldn't quite untangle myself from the knock on our door to listen to him. Once he finished his ramblings, he reached over to comb his rough fingers through my hair.

"Am I making myself clear?" he asked.

He couldn't seem to remember my ears weren't as large as his, and I couldn't catch all the words he threw at me.

He sighed. "Let's just say that I've been doing a lot of thinking the last few days. I asked Sam to come over tonight to—"

I popped up like a jack-in-the-box. "Did he bring the horse?"

"I don't know. He didn't say."

"I'll see."

"Wait a minute." He caught me by the arm. "Listen to me. This is important. We have to keep Sam's being here a secret."

"How come?"

"I told him I'd help him learn to read, and you know how Rag is about Gypsies. I don't want to put up with his griping. Not to mention what others might do."

I supposed he meant the twins. They made trouble for everybody.

Now that I finally understood that my father wanted to use my A-B-C book, I dropped to the floor to pull my suitcase of keepsakes from under the bed. The yarn holding the book together was loose. I tied another bow in the string and raced into the kitchen ahead of Daddy.

Sam looked up at me from a book he was thumbing through. He called me "little one" as usual, which was the reason at first, I didn't notice his jumpiness. His eyes shifted between the windows and the doors the same way my father's did when he feared the dead men were around.

Sam laughed nervously. "A very curious message your papa send. I tell myself he is not interested in my horse. So I must come to find what he wants from me. He is very clever for a *gadžè*."

"I think behind that dim-witted smile of yours is one sharp man," Daddy said.

"Ah, so we agree. We are both smarter than all other men."

For all their agreeing, neither one seemed to believe the other. I slumped in my chair to keep out of the middle of what had become a *Hot Potato* game of words.

"I still do not understand why you do this," Sam said. "What do you want?"

Daddy shook his head. "Nothing."

"Then you are foolish."

"Don't look a gift horse in the mouth."

"Then I am foolish."

I blinked in confusion.

"Let's say we're both foolish and get started," Daddy said. He nodded at the book in Sam's hand. "Hope you don't mind, I borrowed it from Miss Redding."

"Miss Redding is a kind woman with fire in her eyes," Sam said.

"I've only seen the fire. I didn't tell her why I wanted it, but I thought I'd better let Gracie know what's going on. She's pretty inquisitive and has an imagination that won't quit."

Then my father did the strangest thing. He winked at me. My ears grew hot. I slumped in my chair and started chewing on a fingernail. It was true in the last twelve hours alone, I'd used up at least two or three of a curious cat's lives. I set my A-B-C book beside my arithmetic and waved at him to sit beside me.

"I suppose we ought to start with the alphabet," Daddy said. "We'll practice writing by copying letters from Gracie's A-B-C book. Gracie can tell you my writing's all "scribbly." Then we'll work on the sounds of letters. You put sounds together to make a word just like putting two dimes and a nickel together to make a quarter."

He reached for his tablet. Before my heart had time to hop into my throat, the poem slipped from the pages and dropped to the table like a hailstone from the sky.

Before going to bed, I always said my prayers, but the night had a Christmas Eve feeling about it, and I had trouble focusing on blessing this person and that when I'd witnessed a miracle. We were going to teach Sam to read. And other than a quick glance at me, my father simply picked up the poem from the table and stuffed it into his pocket. To keep the day from ending, I never wanted to sleep again. I'd finished with my "Amen" when I heard a creak in the floorboards outside my room.

"While you're at it," Daddy said. "I wouldn't mind you praying for me. I could use all the help I can get."

He'd never asked me before. I had no way of squirming out of his request and nor did I want to.

"And help Daddy be a good teacher. Amen."

He waited until I was snuggled in before he pulled the poem from his pocket and tapped my nose with it. It didn't seem fair of him to ask me to pray for him, then bring up the poem. I felt double crossed.

"How did this get folded up and stuck in my tablet?" he asked.

"I took it to school to show Miss Redding. I wanted her to read it in class so everybody could hear my name in it."

"She didn't read it, did she?"

"No, she told me I stole it and to put it back where I found it. So I did. I didn't mean to steal it."

"She had to have read it or she wouldn't have told you to put it back."

I corrected him. "Not out loud. To herself."

So far he wasn't angry. He switched off the light and his shadow filled my room.

"After she read it, to herself, did she say anything about it?" he asked.

"Just that you wouldn't have wanted her to read it."

"That's all?"

"Uh huh." I didn't want to tell him the poem made her sad.

"Oh. . ." He strung the word out like a sigh of disappointment.

The first few evenings, Sam slid his finger beneath the words as he sounded out the letters. "*Duh-ah-guh.* Dog." By the next week, he read the last page of the primer without a stutter.

"The man got into the airplane.
Tom and Sally got into the airplane.
And Mother and Father got in.
"This is fun!" said Tom and Sally.
Then the little gray airplane flew away.
Up, up, up and up it went."

"Well done!" Daddy said. "You learn fast."

He leaned back in his chair and clapped his hands. I celebrated by jumping up and down until he warned me I was about to go through the floor. My feet froze to the linoleum. In my mind, I imagined him staring down through the hole and into the basement, asking, *What's in those boxes?*

Days had come and gone, and I hadn't forgotten Rag's warning that somebody would get shot if I tattled. That fear quarreled with my conscience about keeping it from my father. All in all, I'd gathered enough worry warts to have turned into a toad. When Sam and Daddy finally noticed me stuck to the floor, I'd collected tears in the corners of my eyes.

"Gracie, I'm teasing," Daddy said. "If this old house stood up under Rag and me, it'll surely hold you." A laugh rumbled out of his chest as naturally as thunder out of a cloud.

It brought to mind the night I found him sitting on the living room floor in a heap of arms and legs. A sloppy chuckle dribbled down his chin, but coming from my father, I'd counted it as a laugh because he had so few. The one tonight sounded real. Where had it come from? In a way, I had grown used to his grumbles, even his bad dreams. Though I couldn't read minds like Miss Redding, sometimes in the night, I woke to find myself already rolled into a ball beneath the covers and fingers poked in my ears. This before the first scream escaped his lungs. Maybe I heard the dead men rattling through the house before he did.

I stared at the dead bugs and cobwebs in the light fixture above my head. My eyelids were heavy with sleep, though I was determined to stay awake as long as Sam was there. They'd forgotten me. While they shook hands as friendly as the preacher and the undertaker after a funeral, they talked of continuing the reading lessons. Which made me wonder when had my father changed? Which night had he ended his game of pitching words at Sam like snowballs from behind an icy fort? Sometime, he must have settled on using Miss Redding's manners. I supposed it was like my growing taller, one bit at a time without realizing it, until one day, Billy Pogue pointed out my knees dangled too far beneath the hem of my dress. I kicked him for his observation.

"The rate you're learning, I'm going to need to get more books," Daddy said.

He seemed pleased with this idea. The corners of his mouth twitched. Sam, on the other hand, had a grin as wide as a clown's.

"Ah. . . perhaps I know why you teach me," Sam said.

Daddy glanced at me. He raised his hand a few inches off the table, a signal adults used to hush one another when kids were around. I came wide awake.

"Gracie, time for bed."

I jumped out of my chair. With it being Saturday night, I wasn't in a hurry to get to bed. But my father would say nothing more until I left the room. Of course once in the hallway, I stopped outside the kitchen door to listen.

"I know what you're thinking," Daddy said barely above a whisper, "and you're barking up the wrong tree."

"I do not understand this barking," Sam said.

I could have told him about Beau. Grandpa's hound barked up the wrong tree all the time because he wasn't much of a squirrel dog. My eyes popped open. For a second I couldn't figure out why I was in the hall, then I heard another of Sam's *ah's.*

Daddy interrupted him. "Besides, she'd never go for the likes of me."

"You go to the *papa.*"

"It doesn't work that way with us crazy *Gadžè.*"

What doesn't work? The question slipped away with another yawn. I hadn't counted on eavesdropping making me so sleepy. I gave up and started down the hall when Sam's voice echoed out of the kitchen.

"When it comes to a beautiful woman, all men are crazy."

My father's laughter followed me to my bedroom, nudging my heart until it warmed. In his laughing, I could almost hear Grandpa's. I tried to find a giggle like that deep inside me. I couldn't. Sometimes, happy memories were just too sad.

My Father's dead men reappeared that night. I sang *There's a Hole in the Bucket,* a song with enough verses to go on to the other side of forever, but forever wasn't sufficient this time. The thin blanket I hid beneath made a skimpy closet when it came to feeling safe. After the nightmare ended, I peeked from under my covers to see a shadow standing in my doorway. I shrieked. A dead man! The light came on. Daddy, panting, stumbled to my bed.

"Sorry, I just wanted to make sure you're okay," he mumbled.

It was a poor excuse for frightening me, considering he hadn't bothered to check on me since the dead men shook him on the shoulder that first night. He must have thought once he told me they weren't real, I wasn't supposed to worry. The way I figured it, if that were so, why'd they scare the breath out of him night after night?

"Want me to leave the light on and sit here a while?" he asked.

I pumped my head up and down. At that moment, I would have accepted the offer from anybody short of George Parker or Sheriff Lundy. Daddy sat at the end of the bed. He wiped his face on the sleeve of his pajamas and closed his eyes. I kept mine open. One of us had to keep guard. Minutes went by and Daddy's breathing slowed, but then all he had to worry about were dead men. I had them, as well as Rag and his moonshine.

Daddy blinked his eyes. "Still awake?"

I nodded my head. "I've got a secret and I don't know if it's a good one or a bad one." Immediately, I wished I hadn't tugged on this ball of yarn.

"Tell me and I'll let you know."

I hem hawed. "I might get in trouble."

"From who?"

"Uncle Rag. He told me I'd get shot if I told."

Daddy's chin snapped up. "He told you *what?*"

"He'd shoot me."

"What kind of secret are you talking about?"

"There's moonshine in the basement," I said.

"Figures. Remember I told you he was a windbag and not to take his threats seriously?"

"He's got lots of moonshine."

"How much? A dozen jars, two dozen?"

"Boxes. A car load. Earl helped him. Are they gonna shoot me?"

"Is that why you've been moping? I was so sure you'd be happy with Sam coming here that I didn't know what to think. I wish you would've told me."

My double wishing didn't erase the disappointment I heard in his voice.

"Don't worry about it anymore. I'll take care of it in the morning," he said.

I snuggled down into my bed, surprised to find telling Rag's secret was like pulling a loose tooth—scary to think about, but once gone, relief filled the gap.

Without being weighed down by quite as many secrets, I felt I could float among the clouds the next morning. For all my father's idiosyncrasies, he hated to change his routine. Sundays were different, special. He cooked pancakes after we delivered the milk, and my stomach always growled the whole way home. It was the only day, he'd settle down to drink another cup of coffee before he read his New Testament. He never took me to Sunday School and church like I was accustomed to with Grandpa and Miss Louise. The time I asked, Daddy told me he *couldn't*. As with the getting rid of the dead men, I was beginning to understand the gauzy difference between couldn't and not wanting to.

He had something else in mind that Sunday. "Go in and fix yourself cornflakes. I've got work to do."

"No pancakes?"

From the way he glared at the milk barn where Rag's car dripped with dew, I knew my ball of yarn from last night was about to unravel in a tangle.

"What are you gonna do?" I asked in alarm. He'd backed the pickup up to the porch.

"Don't worry. Most likely it'd take a cannon to blast Rag out of bed. I was up and milking when he came dragging in."

He heaved open the basement door. Before he disappeared into the spider webs and darkness, he breathed in and out as if he were about to dive into a pool. He ran down the steps. A few seconds later he bounded back up, shaking so hard the jars in the box jingled like a wind chime. He sat on the tailgate until his hands calmed down. On his tenth trip, he no longer took the time to recuperate before he was off again.

Beau curled up in front of the milk barn. Not a cow mooed. I hung my legs over the side of the basement's entry and tapped my toes to Daddy's feet pounding the stairs, his face bubbling with sweat. Twenty-five boxes. Thirty.

"How many more?" I asked.

"Last one," he said, pausing a second to wipe his face with the sleeve of his shirt.

About that time, Beau let loose a howl as loud as a siren.

Rag shot out of the milk barn. "What are you doing?" he bellowed.

Daddy threw the box into the back of the truck. I jumped into the cab. He hopped in after me. For once, the motor started right off. We headed to the pasture with chunks of our yard flying behind us like a covey of startled quail.

"Wait up," Rag yelled. "Wait!"

Daddy gunned the engine. Rag caught up with us when we slowed for the cattle guard. He grabbed the tailgate to leap onto the back bumper the same time the rear wheels bounced off the pipe. He went headfirst into our cargo. Once he recovered, he crawled to the front to bang on the cab.

Daddy glanced at the rearview mirror. "He's going to put a dent in my truck."

"He's awful mad," I said.

"Not half as mad as I am. Hang on."

He aimed for a rock the size of a hubcap. Despite my feet braced against the dashboard, the impact knocked me to the floor. Rag landed in a heap among the boxes and stayed there. A third of the way up the hill, Daddy pulled off the lane and backed up to the gulley that was our trash dump. He was out of the cab and heaved a box into the ditch before Rag could jump from the bed. Glass shattered. The corners of the cardboard turned dark.

"Hey," Rag yelled. "I know I shouldn't have stored the stuff here, but Earl— I'll take care of it." *Crash.* "Just give me time to unload it, and I'll get my car. Aaron, come on. It'll take every last penny I'll earn for a year to pay Earl back." *Crash.* "Doggoneit, listen to me!"

"I can't believe even *you* would threaten a little kid with a gun. You and your whiskey."

"I never told her I'd shoot her. I said *somebody'll* get shot. And right now it's liable to be you." *Crash.* "Or me. Earl ain't gonna like this."

"Tell him to come see me."

"Trust me, you don't want that."

My father heaved another box into the trash. While he had his back to Rag, my uncle raised his fists. I might have been on the fence when it came to choosing between Sam and Daddy, but I had no trouble deciding whom to root for between my father and Rag.

"Daddy," I yelled. "He's gonna hit you."

He ducked in time, then turned around to point his finger at Rag. "One swing and you're going in the dump with the moonshine."

He was a giant compared to Rag. I'd never noticed the difference before. My father was at least a half a head taller. Rag lowered his fists and ran around to the other side where he began stacking boxes beside the pickup. I counted the number thrown in the trash and the number my uncle saved. In the end, I came up with Daddy twenty-two, Rag nine.

Rag's shook his fist at him. "You better watch yourself little brother. People leave you alone cause they don't reckon you're quite right since you got home, the war and all, but some boys I know would take pure pleasure in devilin' you."

Daddy laughed. "If I didn't think I'd get a flat, I'd drive right over your pitiful stack."

We left my uncle standing beside his boxes, hollering. Daddy aimed the pickup downhill.

"You're not saying much," he said.

I gaped at him. "He's awful mad."

Daddy reached over to pat my head. "You're a worrywart. Let's go fix some pancakes."

I nodded. I was a worrywart, all right, nevertheless a smiling one.

Sometime that night, I woke up thirsty. If my tongue hadn't been stuck to the top of my mouth, I would never have crawled out of bed for a drink. In the dark, the hallway always seemed three times longer and inhabited with all things creepy. I slapped the kitchen wall in search of the light switch.

"Leave it off," my father whispered out of nowhere.

I yanked my hand back. "Daddy?"

Moonlight lit his face and bare chest as he leaned against the wall beside the south window. He craned his neck to peek outside. I shuffled over to him, only to have him jerk me away from the opening.

Once my bones stopped rattling, I whispered, "What are you looking for?"

"Nothing."

"Let's play cowboys and Indians." His bare chest gave me the idea. "It's my favorite game," I said in hopes he would go along with me, though I figured like most adults, he'd forgotten how to play.

"Shhh. Indian scouts have to be very quiet."

I sank to my knees. A tale formed: *At the ranch, it was close to the morning milking time. The cows had begun to stir in the corral, and a thin ribbon of pink floated above the eastern horizon. Bow and arrow rested against my leg. I peered over the boulder (what most people considered a window sill.)*

My story fell apart after that. Rag's car was parked beside the barn. Yesterday morning when my uncle fishtailed onto the road, I'd hoped he and his moonshine were gone forever. But there was his old black Chevy, a smudge on our driveway.

"He's back," I said. Apparently, Earl hadn't shot him, after all.

"Came in about a half hour ago." Daddy took another peek out the window.

"Are you watching him to see if he brought his moonshine back?"

Though his eyes remained hidden in the darkness, his head turned toward me. I noticed something in his hand.

"You got a gun?" I asked.

"Don't worry about it."

Worried? I was thrilled. This was *real* cowboys and Indians. He squeezed my shoulder when two men came out of the barn and disappeared into the shadows.

"Who are they?" I asked.

"Don't know. They followed Rag in. Probably a couple of his buddies. Back to bed."

"I'm thirsty."

A car slowly came from behind the barn and rolled down the driveway. Its only sound was the squeak of its springs as it bounced over a rock. Once on the road, it sped away.

"Last time," Daddy said. "Go back to bed."

I wasn't about to let him out of my sight, not with another worrywart popping to the surface. I followed him to his bedroom where he put his gun in the top drawer of his dresser.

I stood on the bed so I could snoop. "You think they come to devil us?"

"They went to a lot of trouble to keep us from knowing they're here. Are you going back to bed?"

I shook my head. "I wanna see."

He stepped aside.

"Your gun doesn't look like a cowboy gun," I said.

"That's because it's my service revolver."

Lying next to the gun was the New Testament. The curious cat in me wondered if the drawer was his treasure box, like the suitcase I kept under my bed with my alphabet book.

"Finished nosing?" he asked.

I shook my head. Behind the New Testament were six little boxes neatly placed in a row. I counted five blue ones and one brown.

"What are those?" I asked.

Daddy picked up the brown box, turned it over in his hand and shrugged. "Coffins." He recited the poem with my name, not the part I liked, but the scary verse.

"In dreams, I wept for headless flowers and legions of headless men
That tramped through night in rank and file beneath the naked moon.
Bound to orders of gentle mercy, they chanted a timeless dirge
And searched for those who would to die and heed their hypnotic tune.

"Dead soldiers. Coffins of dead soldiers," he said.

"Are you teasing me?"

I hoped he was. Why would he keep dead soldiers in his drawer? All this time, I thought they'd come through his open windows.

"Are you done?" Daddy asked. He made it plain he expected only one answer.

I didn't care how much he fussed at me. He wasn't telling me the truth. For one thing, he held the box as carefully as I had seen him hold a baby chick. He set the brown box right side up in the drawer and gently tapped it in line with the others. My arms prickled with goose bumps.

"Promise me you won't go snooping around in my bedroom."

I promised, crossed my heart and hoped to die. Why would I want to look at a dead man?

Chapter 18

By the time Sam finished all the first and second grade readers, the orchard bloomed, turning the hillside into a blanket of pink. People shopping at Sullivan's General Store started to wonder why the Gypsies hadn't left. No one remembered them camping longer than two or three weeks at a time.

Except of course, Miss Louise.

"Not so. Spring of '24, a late season blizzard drifted the roads shut. Nobody went anywhere, including the Gypsies."

I set my eggs on the counter for John Caleb to count as George Parker strolled from the back of the store.

"Ain't no snow out there now." He nudged me out of the way to drop a bag of potatoes on the counter. "Pay for this," he said to John Caleb before he faced the gathering crowd. "They'll hang around until they steal everybody blind. I can smell 'em clear from my house. Ought to run them out."

Old Mr. Tanner laughed. "Bet my bottle of Dr. Pepper if you try, you'll be the one doing the running."

"Shut up, old man!"

"I'd rather you do the shutting up," Miss Louise said. With her broom in hand, she worked her way through the customers. "The rest of you, get back to shopping or I'm going to close up the store right this minute."

As it was late Saturday afternoon and she wouldn't reopen her store until Monday, her threat wasn't something to ignore. There was Sunday dinner to think about.

She shook her broom at Mr. Parker. "You going to leave, or am I going to have to sweep you out with the dirt?"

"Batty old woman."

John Caleb glared at his father as he left. "She ain't batty," he said in a carefully lowered voice. "I hope the Gypsies stay a long time." He turned to me. "Can't run away just yet. Miss Louise needs me. She tells me almost every day."

My father needing me wasn't much to boast about. But Sam? My chest swelled. How I wanted to tell John Caleb, to jump up and down and scream, *We're teaching Sam to read.* But I'd promised Daddy. All I could do was lug my egg basket and slink from the store. As hard as it was to keep quiet about Sam and me, I felt smug knowing something neither Miss Redding, Miss Louise nor anyone else in Iron Mound knew.

"Mr. Parker's saying he's gonna run off the Gypsies," I said to Daddy.

"I doubt it, but I'll let Sam know tomorrow."

"He's not coming tonight?"

"No, I bought a milking machine from a farmer over near Stillwater. Sam's going to help me bring it home and reassemble it. Since he's good with metal, he's the man for the job."

When Rag found out my father hired Sam to help, he drove off and didn't come back. A happy day, though I'd come to realize my uncle was something of a yo-yo. Sam spent several days of hard work getting the milking machine motor to run, hanging pipes and connecting them to a tank. It was almost as if he belonged with us. The evening they finished, my father invited Sam to stay for a supper of cornbread and beans. He'd asked before, but this was the first time Sam agreed. Even though Sam was in and out of our house, he'd never gotten over being jittery.

We'd sat down to eat when someone banged on the door. Sam jumped up, knocking over his chair.

Daddy nodded toward the dining room. "Take Gracie and go in there."

Sam and I huddled behind the door to listen.

"Where's your brother? We need to talk," Sheriff Lundy said.

I clamped my hands over my ears to shut out his bellowing voice.

Daddy said, "Don't know. Haven't seen him for almost a week."

"I see. You got any moonshine in your basement?"

"Nope."

"Show me."

"You have a warrant?"

"Don't cross me, Timmons. I've been handling complaints about you making threats against a couple of boys. Seeing how you had a tough time over there and haven't hurt anybody—yet, I've been cutting you some slack."

My face turned hot. Everybody knew the twins caused it. I wiggled from Sam's grasp to yell, "Riley and Roland stole my hamburger."

"Little one, no," Sam whispered. I was out of the dining room and in the kitchen before he could grab me. When he caught up with me, though, I was glad he was there.

"What's a Gypsy doing here?" Lundy asked.

"Helping me put up a milking machine."

"I heard you bought one. Pretty big purchase. Little bootlegging on the side to pay for it? Show me the basement."

"No."

"Then you can sit in jail while my deputies tear your house apart."

My father stared at the floor and said something under his breath.

"What'd you say?" the sheriff asked.

Daddy's voice splintered. "Nobody's ever gonna lock me up, again."

"We'll see about that."

Lundy's face swelled into a red blob. He pulled his gun from the holster and pointed it at my father's temple. Sweat poured from Daddy's face as he whimpered through trembling lips. The whites of his eyes shined as bright as the kitchen light. It wasn't right for Lundy to scare him so.

"Daddy," I murmured as much to console myself as him.

He couldn't turn to look at me for the gun held to his head. At my whispering his name, he slowly raised his chin until he was eye to eye with the sheriff. His shoulders straightened a bit.

"I've borne death marches, been beaten and starved. I was forced to sail in the bowels of hell. Seen soldiers and civilians clubbed to death, shot, beheaded." He sighed a lungful of despair. "Ever watch a man give up and die? You can see his life fade from his eyes long before he stops breathing. I know, because I buried more than my fair share of them. All I want is to be left in peace. Go home. There's nothing here."

No one moved.

"Please," Daddy said, ignoring the gun and stumbling back to his chair.

A deputy came to the door. "Sheriff, while y'all was arguing, I took a look-see below. Ain't nothing down there."

"Right," the sheriff said, lowering his gun. "Timmons, don't push me to the edge again."

Daddy rocked in his chair, reciting the sad poem about chickens with arms.
"Look down fair moon and bathe this scene,
Pour softly down night's nimbus floods on faces ghastly, swollen, purple..."

"Crazy man like that ought to be locked up somewhere," the sheriff said. He pointed at Sam. "I expect you won't be staying much longer?"

"On the dead on their backs with arms toss'd wide,
Pour down your unstinted nimbus sacred moon."

Once the deputy closed the door, Daddy stopped rocking. "They gone?"

A flash of silver disappeared into Sam's jacket. He dismissed my puzzled look with a shake of the head and walked over to the window.

"Yes."

"I didn't know if Rag was stupid enough to keep using the basement for his cache. If Lundy found it, he'd just as soon throw me in jail as he would my brother." Daddy buried his head in his hands.

"Is time for bed," Sam whispered to me. He prodded me to the hallway.

"Is Daddy crazy like the sheriff said?" I whispered. The way he'd rocked himself and recited the poem scared me as much as Lundy's gun.

"Your papa would make a good Gypsy. He protects his family from the *beng*. The devil."

Despite Sam's confusing answer, I felt better. "Are you going away like the sheriff told you to? You promised to bring your horse."

"You will see my horse," he said. "Go to bed."

I walked as far as the bathroom before I looked back at the kitchen door. The flash of silver I'd seen was a knife. The poem wasn't about chickens with arms. It was about soldiers. Dead soldiers. The ones who chased Daddy in his dreams.

"Sam's gone," Daddy said the next morning as if he'd misplaced his gloves in the barn or lost his pencil.

He waited to tell me after we came home from delivering the milk. No wonder he'd refused to take the river road.

"Where'd he go?" I asked.

He shrugged.

"Will he be back tomorrow? He promised I could ride his horse," I said, flapping my hands in frustration.

"We talked it over last night and agreed the best thing was for him to move on."

"How come?"

"The sheriff."

"You think he saw Sam's knife?"

"You noticed that?"

I nodded.

"And you're how old?" Daddy asked.

"Almost eight in three weeks. June fourth." I told him in case he didn't remember. When he first came home, he'd been as empty-headed as a balloon about such things.

He repeated his dog-eared lecture of keeping this and that to myself. By now, my head was a closet overstuffed with secrets. One more, and the door would burst.

"We don't know if Lundy saw the knife. Even if he didn't, just seeing Sam here might cause trouble. As it is, people are already suspicious about the Gypsies hanging around here this long." He rattled on about Sam having to take care of his family and friends first.

Of course, I worked the conversation back to the horse. "Maybe he hasn't left yet, and I can ride his horse."

"I heard them go by about four this morning. I'm sorry. I know you'll miss him. So will I. I enjoyed teaching him to read. But just like Sam, we'll have to move on. That's one thing I learned from him."

No one asked me about it. My eyes burned despite my efforts not to cry. Yet as upset as I was at my father, I couldn't stay that way. Apart from one tiny twitch in the corner of his mouth, he looked miserable. I wanted to hug him, but knew better than to try.

"You know," he said, "if you'd go to the corral and put some feed in the trough, I bet you could call Moonie up out of the pasture. When I finish washing up the milk can and buckets, I'll come down and put a bridle on him. Then you can ride around in the corral."

"Moonie?" I couldn't hide my disappointment. "He's not a *real* horse." He was a draft horse. I'd have to ride bareback. We didn't have a saddle big enough to fit him. Worst of all, he plodded—not galloped, not cantered, not trotted—plodded. Not to mention, I had about as much chance calling Moonie in from the pasture as I did calling the man in the moon down from the sky. I figured Moonie thought I was too short to be a *real* person, therefore he was free to ignore me.

"I seem to remember him having four legs, a tail and a mane," Daddy said. "Well?"

"Okay." I tacked on a dramatic sigh. "But he won't come."

"Put some cake cubes in a bucket and rattle them. That'll get his attention."

I shuffled to the feed room in the horse barn, pried the lid off a barrel and dumped a scoopful of cubes into a tin bucket. Moonie was huge, so I doubled the amount. He'd want more before he'd pay any attention to me. Outside, I walked toward the corral in back, banging the bucket on my leg.

"Moo-nee," I called. I heard a whinny close by. "Moonie!" I wouldn't have to spend half the morning looking for the old horse, after all.

"I got him," I yelled with no small amount of pride.

Moonie neighed again. I rounded the corner of the barn and peered wide-eyed through the boards of the corral.

"A horse," I whispered in awe.

On the far side of the pen, a black and white paint trotted back and forth, his muscles rippling, his coat shining in the sun. He was the most beautiful horse I'd ever seen.

"Daddy, a horse!"

I dropped the bucket of cake, raced toward the windmill, only to reverse when a thought popped into my head. I climbed to the top of the fence. The horse trotted over to me, swishing his tail.

"Are you Sam's horse?" He nuzzled my knee. "You're Sam's horse, aren't you? I know you are." I scratched his forehead. "I'll be right back."

I hopped off the fence and sprinted to the windmill. "It's Sam's horse. Come and see. Daddy!"

"You get Moonie?" he asked when I ran up to him.

The question flabbergasted me. Hadn't he heard all my shouting? With a huff, I started over.

"I guess I'd better go see then," he said.

First, he insisted he needed to finish washing the milk buckets. I took over the pump handle and pumped so hard water hit the concrete slab. It splashed on my father's boots and my shoes. He gave me one of his warning looks to let him be.

"He's pretty," I said in my defense. "The prettiest horse in the whole world."

Daddy thought about this a minute before he grinned and went back to swabbing out another bucket. "Just stay outside the corral until we see how pretty his temperament is."

At the corral, I waited for my father until my patience gave up and left, which never took long. I crawled into the pen. When Daddy finally showed up, he was carrying a saddle. It was an ancient thing, older than he was, maybe even his mother. According to him, his grandpa had used it while working on a ranch. He couldn't find one more authentic than that. It had a frayed cinch, green tarnished silver pieces threaded with leather ties and stirrups worn down to the wood. Rats and mice had nibbled off the sheepskin padding on the inside, but he had a thick wool blanket for a substitute.

"I told you not to go in the corral," he said, grabbing the back of my overalls to pull me back to the fence.

"He's a nice horse. I can tell."

He muttered something about hanging around Sam didn't necessarily turn me into a fortune teller. I had to settle for sitting on the top rail while he walked out into the middle of the pen.

"Come here, boy. Got something for you," he said. He tossed a handful of cake cubes on the ground. While the horse ate, Daddy slipped the rope over its head.

"You think this is Sam's horse?" I asked watching him buckle the bridle on the horse's head.

"Appears to be."

"What do you reckon his name is?"

"How about John Greenleaf Whittier." He laughed as he swung the saddle over the horse's back and tightened the cinch. "Got any better ideas?"

It was obvious to me. "Sammy."

"Don't look much like Sam to me, but if you say so."

"He's pretty."

"He's that."

In the months since my father came home, he'd looked out of place, uncomfortable as if he belonged somewhere else. Yet when he mounted Sammy, his back straightened and his shoulders broadened. He raised his chin high. If there had been any clouds about, he would have caught them in his hair. He looked that tall and proud. Every time he and Sammy trotted past me, I clapped and cheered. In turn, he touched the brim of his hat like a rodeo bronc rider to a lady. He dismounted and lifted me onto the saddle. Finally, it was my chance.

The thought struck me he was planning for me to ride atop the horse alone, something I'd never done before. John Caleb always rode with me.

"You aren't scared, are you?" he asked. "Hold onto the saddle horn."

If the saddle horn hadn't been solid metal, I would have crushed it with my grip.

"Scoot forward," he said. He put his foot in the stirrup and swung his leg over the saddle.

With my father's arms encircling me, I settled into the rhythm of the horse's gait. We rode up the lane and into the orchard where the pink blossoms of April had turned brown. He stopped to peel away the shriveled petals of one bloom. A baby peach the size of a pea lay hidden inside like a pearl. He scratched the hard green surface with his thumbnail and held it to my nose. If I sniffed hard enough, I could catch a whiff of a peach, something my father called the scent of hope.

From the orchard, we rode along the eastern fence line until we were on the backside of the hill. A brown and white bird with a broken wing fluttered onto our path.

"It's a killdeer," Daddy whispered.

"What happened to her?"

"Nothing. She's pretending. We must be close to her nest. It's her way of protecting her eggs."

I looked up at him. Now, I understood what Sam tried to tell me. "Like you did last night?"

A smile twitched at the corners of Daddy's mouth. He nudged Sammy toward the bird. It flew a few feet, dropped to the ground and held out her wing. We played our game of catch up another twenty yards when the killdeer in a burst of trilling, soared over the top of our heads.

"How'd she know how to do that?" I asked.

"Instinct. Unlike some folks, she was born knowing how to take care of her family."

He grew quiet, and I wondered if he meant himself.

When we came to the hayfield, he dismounted to open the gate. Back on Sammy, he urged the horse into a bumpy trot. The ride shook me until giggles spewed out of me as if I were a bottle of pop. He started to sing a hiccupping version of *Home on the Range.* I joined in, and soon, we left notes, words and laughter bouncing after us on the trail.

He tucked his arms in close to my sides. "Hang on," he whispered into my ear. He kicked Sammy with his heels.

The horse took to the air. My heart pounded as fast as his feet. The wind swept past us as a hill raced toward us. A half mile away. A quarter mile. The prairie grass blurred. I wasn't afraid. Daddy huddled over me. The thrill of the ride pressed me into him. We became a part of Sammy, and he a part of us.

"Whoo—ee!" Daddy yelled.

"Don't let him stop, Daddy!"

We flew.

We floated in silence on the way home. The leaves and grass would never be any greener nor the air any softer than it was right then.

"How long you reckon we can keep Sammy?" I asked.

"Let's see." Daddy reached around in back for his billfold. "Says here," he read. "I *sell you one piebald gelding for $35.00. You pay now $15.00. When we meet again you pay $20.00.*"

I struggled to turn around without falling off. "Sammy's ours? Really ours?"

Daddy held the paper to my nose, so I could see his and Sam's signatures.

"I only had the fifteen after buying the milking machine and paying Sam for helping me. He agreed to wait for the rest. Because of that he wouldn't give a penny on the price. That man's a horse trader. He knows a sucker when he sees one. At least this way I figure the horse won't keel over until Sam comes for the money."

I had a horse. Who should I tell first. John Caleb? Miss Redding? But if I told Miss Redding first, would Miss Louise be upset? Maybe I'd stand in the middle of the store and shout the news to everybody at once.

In the corral, my father dismounted Sammy to tie the reins to a post before lifting me off.

As he turned around to hold his hands out for me, I fell into them. Hugging his neck was easy. It happened as naturally as yawning when sleepy. He stiffened a bit, then wrapped his arms around me.

"You're my cowgirl," he said, rocking me side to side.

He wasn't afraid of hugs after all.

From then on, I galloped every where I used to walk—to school, the barn, the henhouse. Not on Sammy, of course, but by myself with my right foot always in front, my left playing catch up. In the evenings after we came home from delivering the milk, my father and I rode Sammy until sunset. I always sat between his arms where I could lean against his chest. We talked about the end of school picnic, my promotion to third grade and sometimes, my mother, how much I laughed like her and how she loved strawberry ice cream. Most of the time, we listened to the soft sounds of birds and frogs, to the wind settling down for the night. Daddy said when the world was quiet like that, he could hear God. When the world was quiet like that, I could hear Daddy's heart.

"Here you go," he said as he wrapped my fingers around the reins. "Remember, don't yank."

I guided Sammy home, away from the fiery sky and toward the barn.

"All you need is some cowboy boots," Daddy said. "Would you like a pair for your birthday?"

I nodded. I didn't dare talk for fear of dropping a rein.

"We could eat dinner at Hattie's Café. You can't beat her fried chicken. I don't know about you, but I'm getting tired of my cooking."

I nodded extra hard.

Chapter 19

The morning of my birthday, I put on my only decent dress. All the others were either too short or had suffered under Daddy's attempt to iron. He finally had placed the iron in the back of his closet, saying he hoped he'd forget where he left it. That was right after Christmas, and I hadn't seen it since.

On my way down the hall, I heard the water running. Daddy was in the bathroom, but he had a bowl of cereal and a glass of milk waiting for me. When he hurried into the kitchen, I couldn't help but gawk at him. He was wearing a suit and tie. I'd never seen him dressed up before. He must have had those clothes in the back of the closet along with the iron.

"Mr. Archer won't know you," I said. He'd shaved his straggly chin whiskers. I smelled Grandpa's shaving soap.

Daddy laughed. It bubbled out of him so easily it seemed natural.

"For your birthday, would you like somebody to come with us to celebrate?" he asked. "I've never bought shoes for a little girl before. Maybe there's somebody who can help.

I came up with an answer right away. "Miss Redding! Can she come?"

"That's the best idea I've heard all day."

In a way, it seemed he'd thought of the idea, and I'd only gone along. Not that I cared. On the way to town, we practiced the invitation using what he called his poker game strategy. With my card playing abilities limited to Old Maid, I didn't understand much of it other than it had something to do with playing the hand you're given.

"If she doesn't want to come, don't whine," he said, wagging his finger at me. You don't want to make her."

As a matter of fact, I did and thought deep down, he probably did too.

At Miss Louise's, I thundered up the stairs and threw open the door. "Miss Redding," I yelled.

I raced past the kitchen straight to my room. Since I went to live with my father, I hadn't seen it. I stopped in the doorway. My bed had the same patchwork quilt. The dresser along the south wall hadn't moved an inch. My drawings of Miss Redding, Sam and John Caleb were tucked along the edges of the mirror. I'd have to draw one of Daddy to add to them.

"Miss it?" Miss Redding asked from behind me. She squeezed my shoulder.

"Yes." At the same time, I no longer wanted to live here. I had Daddy, Sammy and Peaches to take care of. I only wanted my room to stay the same, to not forget me.

I looked up at Miss Redding. "It's my birthday."

"I know. I have a present for you."

I followed her into her room. She'd made new curtains for her window and put a new lace doily on her dresser.

I tore the wrapping from my gift. "Daddy's taking me to Guthrie. He's going to buy me a pair of cowboy boots for riding Sammy. Want to come with me?" I didn't give her a chance to say no. "Sammy runs fast. As fast as the wind."

"My, that is fast. You're not riding by yourself are you?"

"Only in the corral. Daddy rides with me when we go in the pasture. I'm his cowgirl." I'd wandered away from what I was to say, but I couldn't stop. "I hugged him. He hugged me back."

Something like a shadow clouded her eyes, which worried me. This had happened before when I went to live with Daddy.

"Can't I be his cowgirl?" I asked.

"Of course you can."

I laughed with relief. "Come with us. He doesn't know how to buy shoes for little girls. He might get the wrong size."

"The salesman will know how to measure your feet."

"But what if he doesn't."

"He will."

The box she gave me was filled with ribbons. She brushed my hair, working a long time in the back where most of my rat's nests were. I moved on to what Daddy called my "next hand."

"He's taking me to a café for my birthday dinner. He said I could ask anybody I wanted to."

"I'd really love to spend your birthday with you, but I'm your teacher. If people saw me with. . ." She didn't finish the sentence, which was unlike her. She rarely muddled words.

"With what?" I asked.

"Never mind. Let's put a ribbon in your hair. Pick a color."

I chose green. "Please."

"I can't. Look at me! My hair's in pins. I'm wearing shorts."

I was wearing her down. Every child knows the louder adults protest, the closer they are to saying yes.

"I don't care," I said.

"There's the end of school reports to finish."

If all other plans failed, Daddy told me to use what he called my "ace in the hole."

I smiled. "We're going to a movie. Daddy said to tell you it's a Gene Kelly movie." I corrected myself. "I mean I said to tell. . ."

That didn't make sense either. I flapped my hands in frustration.

"Did your daddy put you up to this?" She read my mind. How else would she know?

"He said it was like playing cards." I shouldn't have said that, either.

"Well?" Daddy asked when I returned to the pickup. "What'd she say?"

"To tell you that daddies shouldn't let their little girls play poker. It's a man's game."

I wasn't sure what she meant. He obviously did. Red shot up his neck.

"I always was bad at cards," he said. He started the pickup and put it into gear.

"Stop," I said in alarm. "We gotta wait for Miss Redding."

"I thought you said she wasn't coming."

"No. She said she'd be just a few minutes."

The boots my father bought me were made of rich brown leather with tan stitching on the sides and toes. The best part was they smelled like our saddle after Daddy polished it. Despite their genuineness, he rolled his eyes when I refused to take them off. Miss Redding added her fashion advice that little girls' dresses and cowboy boots didn't go together. Why it bothered them so, I didn't know. They eventually gave up and ignored me.

At the theater, my father dropped us off at the door while he parked the pickup. Dark clouds threatened rain. While we waited, I wandered over to the concession stand where a big man with a double chin scooped popcorn. His first chin was a tiny knob. His second was as baggy as the pelican's pouch I'd seen in the encyclopedia at school. Every time he ducked his head to reach the back of the machine, his chin rolled down his chest. He probably could have swallowed a whole fish if he wanted.

I showed him my new boots. When he leaned over the counter to look, I turned my foot to display the wavy tan stitching. He finished his scooping and built a rickety pyramid of popcorn boxes on the back counter.

"Last summer the popcorn man juggled five popcorn boxes at once. Can you?" I asked.

"No."

"What can you do?"

"Sell popcorn. You gonna buy some?"

"Daddy told me I can't have any until intermission 'cause we just finished eating dinner."

"Then run along and find your daddy."

I clomped over to Miss Redding by the entrance where she studied the posters of coming attractions. She loved movies. Last summer, she went to a matinee every week, bringing me along if I promised not to talk or touch the gummy underside of the seats. Her favorite picture shows had lots of kissing. I came for the cartoons and popcorn. Once the popcorn was gone, the cartoon ended and the kissing began, I usually fell asleep and woke with my head in her lap.

"When's Daddy coming?" I asked, plopping on a nearby bench.

"As soon as he finds a parking place. What have you been up to?"

"Showing the popcorn man my boots." I thought it best not to mention he looked like a grumpy pelican.

My father came inside, brushing the rain from his suit. I ran ahead to part the purple velvet curtains separating the lobby from the theater. More velvet drapes with gold trim were drawn across the screen. Along the walls on either side and the back were murals of formal flower gardens and winding rivers through mountains with snow, none of which resembled any place close to Iron Mound. It was as if we'd walked into a palace by mistake.

As the theater began to fill, Miss Redding and Daddy found seats at the end of an aisle and sat me between them. The lights dimmed. In the movie, two sailors danced and sang as they hopped from bed to bed. The only reason I was still watching was Miss Redding promised Gene Kelly would dance with Jerry the cartoon mouse.

She leaned over to me to whisper, "Where did your daddy go?"

I hadn't paid any attention to him. I was waiting for Jerry.

"He's been gone a long time," she said.

"Maybe he went to the bathroom and got lost."

"Don't be silly."

It wasn't silly at all. One time on the way back from the restroom, I had sat next to a lady thinking she was Miss Redding. I was too embarrassed to ask her if she knew where Miss Redding was, so I sat there until the movie ended.

"I'm going to check on him," Miss Redding said as she squeezed past me.

I spun around on my knees to watch her walk up the aisle. As she disappeared into the lobby, I worried she might never find me again.

I scrambled out of the seat. "Miss Redding, wait."

Shhh's came from everywhere. I clomped my new cowboy boots up the aisle toward the exit sign. The curtains had been pulled over the doorway to keep out the light from the lobby, forcing me to bat the heavy velvet in search of the opening between them.

"Miss Redding!" I called.

A big hand reached through the curtains to pull me into the lobby.

"Hush," the popcorn man said, plunking me beside Miss Redding.

Blinded by the lights, I buried my face in her dress.

"He come running out here like he'd seen the devil himself," the popcorn man whispered.

Out of curiosity, I peeked from the folds of Miss Redding's dress. No devil around that I could see. My father sat on a bench at the front of the lobby, mumbling to himself. More than likely he had seen the dead men.

"The intermission's in about fifteen minutes," the popcorn man said. "If you could get your husband to leave."

Miss Redding corrected him, then she directed him away from my father. From where I stood, I couldn't hear much of their conversation, except the explanation, "the war." The popcorn man frowned and shook his head to those words. Put *the war* and Jimmy Lear, the town hero, together, and folks pounded his back and bragged about his medals and how brave he was. Around my father, they edged away to whisper as if he *wasn't right* like Wilma Rose. The injustice of it burned deep in my chest.

"I'll see what I can do," Miss Redding said, walking toward Daddy.

"No!" I yelled. I caught her hand and dug my heels into the carpet. "You can't."

"What?"

She turned to stare at me. I swallowed hard. No kid ever dared to shout at her. I looked over at Daddy. It wasn't hot, yet sweat ran down his face, dripping onto his collar and turning it a pale gray. How could I explain him? I told her of my promise not to sneak up on him, leaving out how he'd knocked me down once, which wasn't his fault. I forgot and grabbed his arm. As for the other place he sometime dwelled in, she could see that, his trembling jaw, his blinking, his mumbling.

Her eyes brimmed with tears as she stroked away mine. I no longer worried she'd forget to love me.

"I have to try," she said.

She sat next to him, close enough they touched. "Mr. Timmons, it's warm in here. Let me loosen your collar."

"Please, don't," I whispered. "He doesn't like—"

She raised her hand to hush me. "Mr. Timmons, let me loosen your collar to make you more comfortable."

She had magic in her fingers. If she could read children's minds, why couldn't her slender fingers loosen Daddy's tie, slip it down a couple of inches, then unbutton his collar? I sat on the floor in front of them, as much under her spell as my father.

"There. Better?" she asked.

His eyes shifted in her direction.

"It's all right," she said.

"I'm sorry. I've embarrassed you," he whispered.

"You haven't."

"Then I've spoiled your movie."

"Mr. Timmons, I should confess. I've seen the movie before."

"What?"

"Last Christmas," she said, "I visited one of my college roommates. You'll think this is silly, but we went three nights in a row."

"Why?"

I thought it a good question, considering how mushy the movie was.

She sighed. "Gene Kelly, the dancing—"

"No, why'd you come today? You weren't fooled by the story of my needing help buying shoes for Gracie."

"You asked me. Didn't you? Granted, I would have preferred you had asked as a poet rather than a poker player. May I call you Aaron?"

It was then Daddy saw me sitting right in front of him. He blurted out my name and fumbled through his pockets until he came up with a quarter.

"Take this," he said. "Go buy you some popcorn, candy, whatever you want."

With that much money, I could buy every box of popcorn behind the counter. I skipped over to the popcorn man and scooted my quarter across the counter so he could see I was there to buy something and not merely to watch him bag popcorn.

"Your daddy send you over here to get rid of you?"

"Nope, he sent me over here to get anything I want."

"So what do you want?"

"Animal crackers." I was hoping to find a pelican in the box.

"Don't have any. Look up there," he said, pointing his thumb over his shoulder at a sign. "That's what I got."

I asked for a Baby Ruth. He slid the candy bar and the change across the counter, but when I reached for it, he pulled it back.

"Not so fast. I think your Daddy'd like to talk to his lady friend alone."

"Lady friend?" I'd never heard those two words put together before.

The popcorn man winked. "You know— girlfriend, boyfriend."

"Are you teasing me?"

I turned around. At school, the older girls made goo goo eyes at the boys and notes were passed. Miss Redding would never do that. She was a teacher, after all.

At supper that night, Rag walked into the kitchen without knocking. Of course, he let the screen door slam behind him. He had a lopsided grin and twirled a stained cowboy hat on one finger.

Daddy let him stand there a minute before giving up and asking, "What are you doing here?"

"Earl was dropping hints I was getting on his nerves."

"So he threw you out, which brings me back to my question. What are you doing *here?*"

Rag winked at me. "I come to bring a birthday present for my favorite niece. Try this on."

He plopped the hat on my head. It fell as far as my nose and smelled worse than Sammy's moth-eaten saddle blanket. I loved it.

"You'll grow into it," Rag said.

I pushed the hat back. "See the boots Daddy got me? Miss Redding went with us to pick them out."

"I heard. And I heard it turned out to be quite a picture show."

Daddy dropped his fork on his plate and moaned.

"Charlie Montgomery's wife finally nagged him into taking her to a movie," Rag said. "He was sitting on the back row and said there was more happening in the lobby than on the screen."

"Shut up, Rag," Daddy said.

"Sheesh. You're back on that old record, and here I am trying to be nice and give you a little advice."

"Then get it over with. I can't stand the anticipation."

"You ought to be more careful who you pull a gun on."

"I didn't pull a gun on anybody. Is that what Charlie said?" Daddy turned to look at the window where we played Indian scouts watching two cowboys. He had a gun then, but how could anyone have known?

Rag snapped his fingers twice in front of Daddy's face. "The sheriff? Remember? He told Charlie and Miss Louise this afternoon, which means about everybody knows now. The only reason he let you get by with it was because of Gracie standing there next to you. That and he knew how unstable you were. Anybody that'd invite a Gypsy to dinner."

"Lundy pulled the gun on me. Not the other way around."

There were too many guns and too many men for me to keep up with. I pulled the hat over my eyes.

"That old tub of lyin' lard," Rag said. "Story's probably all over town by now. Anyway, I came to celebrate Miss Gracie's birthday." He raised the hat from my eyes. "How time flies. You know I was right here in this kitchen when you were born."

"Where was I?"

"In the east bedroom having a birthday party with your mama, grandma and Young Doc MacKay."

"Where was Grandpa?"

"Here with me, waiting for somebody to invite us to the party." Rag pulled the hat down over my eyes and held it there. "We won't go into where your Daddy was."

A chair screeched across the floor. The back door opened and closed. I would have given up my boots if it had been my uncle slamming the door instead of Daddy. As it was, when I yanked the hat off my head, there was Rag. I crawled off of the chair, aimed my boot and landed it squarely on my uncle's shin.

He yelped. I stood my ground, ready to bruise his other shin if he didn't leave us alone.

"Well you little mule," he said, rubbing his leg. "I suppose I deserved that one. But don't let it give you any more ideas."

My head bulged with ideas. So many in fact, I couldn't talk. All I could do was stare a hole in his back as he limped across the kitchen and closed the door behind him, for once, without letting it slam.

After he drove away, I stood at the screen door for a long time, watching the road to the orchard. More than likely, that was where my father went. His pickup was parked beside the windmill, so he was on foot. The sun sank below the peach trees before he climbed the back porch steps. He stood outside, with his hands in his pockets, looking in at me like Grandpa's old hound dog.

"Sorry," he said. "I shouldn't have let Rag get to me. You okay?"

I shook my head. "My toes hurt."

"It's your new boots. I let you wear them too long."

The day I came to live with him, he'd made me swear never to kick anyone, and I didn't see any use in disappointing him. He came inside and set me opposite him to pull off my boots and socks.

"I don't see a blister," he said as he held my foot up to the light.

I pointed at my big toe. "It hurts right here."

I wondered how big a knot Rag had on his shin. Baseball size? A smile sneaked across my face.

"What are you so pleased about?" Daddy asked.

"Nothing." For once, I had a secret of my own, and I planned to keep it. "Is Miss Redding your lady friend?"

Daddy dropped my foot. "What?"

"Is she your lady friend?"

"She's a lady. Definitely a lady." He slapped his pockets, looking for his cigarettes. "And they say you can never have too many friends."

Every woman in the county, including Miss Louise, could fit that definition. I'd hoped for a yes or no. The popcorn man made it seem so simple. My father found his cigarettes, which were in the same pocket as always. He searched for his matches. I pointed at his left pocket and waited. Until he had two or three puffs, he was useless.

"Do you want her to be?" I asked.

"What I want has nothing to do with it." He rubbed his forehead. "You saw what happened this afternoon. Add that to what Rag was saying. That's a pretty wide creek for someone like Miss Redding to cross. Might be best she didn't try."

"Can't you ask her?"

"I don't want to hear another word." He stood me on my feet. "Maybe you better not wear your boots tomorrow."

"My toes feel better."

"You're sure to get blisters if you wear them."

He sat there, lost in thought, his shoulders slumped and chin on his palm. I wondered if he was thinking about Miss Redding, especially when he sighed. When he caught me watching, he left the kitchen, but he returned a few minutes later with a tablet, the one he'd written my poem in. I'd come to think of *The Flower* that way.

He wrote a few words, doodled awhile, no blooms this time but a bridge across a creek.

My curiosity finally got the better of me. "What are you trying to do?"

"Write a poem." He thumbed through his tablet, smiling at some pages, frowning at others.

I'd never supposed he wrote poetry. I assumed he'd memorized my poem from his book, like the one about arms and dead men.

"You wrote my poem?"

"Why, yes. I thought you knew."

I thought poets had to be old men with gray bushy whiskers. I propped my chin on my hands and smiled while he went back to thumping his eraser. Since he first recited my poem, I'd wondered why my name ended up in verse. That question folded itself into what Rag told me earlier, about my father being absent at my birth.

"Did you write my name on purpose?" I asked.

His eyes lost their focus for a moment. "Yes."

"Did you know about me?"

"Yes. While in the camps, I thought about you every day."

His answers swept away the last of the cobwebs between us. I ran around to the other side of the table and pushed an empty chair next to his.

"I'm good at rhyming," I said. "You want me to help?"

Chapter 20

About a week later, I waited in the pickup for Daddy to finish milking. I had the eggs gathered and my boots propped on the dash when he heaved the milk can into the truck bed. From the look of his left cheek and sleeve, a cow had swatted him with her tail while he was milking.

"Boots belong on the floor," he said. "Why don't you change into your canvas shoes instead of your boots when we go to town."

I shrugged. "I like my boots."

"I'm glad, but—" He checked his pocket watch. "I need to make a phone call and change clothes." He trotted to the house. I waited until he went inside before I propped my boots back on the dash. He'd been fussy and mopey since my birthday.

Having the pickup and barnyard to myself, I sang at the top of my voice.

> *"Happy birthday to me.*
> *Happy birthday to me.*
> *Happy birthday to me-ee.*
> *Happy birthday to me."*

I peeked out the window. Nothing could be more embarrassing than to have someone catch me singing *Happy Birthday* to myself. Like Christmas carols, it had special rules about when to sing and to whom, and I'd probably broken every one. I banged my boots together. Since my birthday, I had a sore place inside me that ached for Miss Redding to wrap her arms around.

When the door to the pickup opened, I caught a whiff of soap and Grandpa's shaving cream. I slipped my feet to the floor and tilted my head. Daddy had combed his hair and wore his best boots. He glanced at a paper he'd pulled from his pocket.

"Errands," he said.

"Oh."

"You can stay with Miss Louise until I'm done. She might have something you can help her with."

My curiosity about his behavior turned to dust. Miss Louise's cash register came to mind. Now that I was eight, maybe she'd let me use the big brass machine? All the way to town, I practiced punching imaginary keys on my knees until they were sore.

At the store, he hurried me out of the pickup with a wave of hand.

If it hadn't been for my eagerness to ask Miss Louise about the cash register, I would have pestered him more about what he was up to. I picked up my egg basket and headed to the store's front porch where old Mr. Tanner sat on the top step.

He saluted a passing car with his bottle of Dr. Pepper. "Third time Will Owens' boy been round the block. Gonna wear out his tires if he ain't careful." He wheezed a chuckle from his chest. "Say, heard you got some gen-u-ine cowboy boots."

I turned in a circle so he could admire all four sides. "They used to smell like my saddle, but I stepped in a cow patty. Daddy scraped it off, but they don't smell good anymore."

"Gracie," Daddy called. "Don't bother Mr. Tanner." He had gotten out of the cab and was on the sidewalk.

"I won't. Bye, Mr. Tanner. I gotta go help Miss Louise."

With it being summer, Miss Louise had the windows and the double front doors open to catch any breeze going by. Most of her customers came early in the morning. The old men who played dominoes in the back during the winter had given up the game until cooler weather. I propped my foot against the screen door to keep it from slamming behind me. Overhead, the store's three fans agitated the hot air.

She looked up from her ledger. "How many?"

"Sixteen."

"Set them beside the register."

Instead of scooting them across the counter, I carried the basket around to the other side. It gave me a good excuse to stand in front of the cash register. I fingered the keys, taking care not to touch them too hard and have the cash drawer pop open.

"Daddy has errands to run," I said. "He told me I could help you 'til he gets back."

"He did, did he?"

"I'm eight now. Can I punch the keys on the cash register? Please."

"Not today, sweetheart."

"How old was my mama when she got to punch the keys?"

Miss Louise looked over her glasses at me. "Seventeen, but she didn't have the experience you have."

When Miss Louise was too busy to be bothered with my questions, she'd confuse me with facts.

"Why don't you wait for John Caleb on the front porch while I finish up my books."

Defeated again, I shuffled outside where the hands on the Royal Crown Cola clock hadn't moved. Old Mr. Tanner remained on the step, his pop bottle sweating in his hand. No one could make a Dr. Pepper last longer than Mr. Tanner. I looped my arms around one of the porch columns.

"You looking for your daddy? He went back that way," he said, pointing his bottle at the corner of the store.

I hopped off the porch to see around the building. From where I stood by the spirea bushes, I had a clear view of Miss Louise's garage and the alley behind.

"He's not here," I said.

"That's where he went."

I sniffed the spirea blossoms. In early June, the bushes became a cascade of tiny white flowers. Miss Louise had planted them along the west side of the building from the front to the back. They were her favorite shrub. She liked to put food coloring in a vase to turn the sprigs of blossoms pink. I broke off one of the long skinny branches to give to her.

John Caleb came around the corner. "What you doing?"

"Picking flowers for Miss Louise." I was counting on them to change her mind about the cash register.

"What for? They're hers already."

"Just 'cause."

"Leave your flowers. I got something to show you. I've been working on the tree house."

We headed down the driveway to the backyard. Halfway along the west side, I heard the swing on the back porch squawk like a mad crow. That was how Miss Louise described it. I had never seen nor heard a mad crow to know if she spoke the truth.

I grabbed John Caleb's shirt. "It's Daddy," I whispered.

"How do you know?"

"Old Mr. Tanner said he came this way." But what was he doing on Miss Louise's porch?

"Let's go spy on him."

"What if he catches us?"

"He won't."

The swing screeched, again. It was too much for John Caleb. He dropped to his hands and knees and disappeared beneath the spirea.

"Don't go jiggling the flowers or he'll see us," he whispered over his shoulder.

I left my sprig of flowers beside the opening and followed. We wiggled past two bushes, made a turn to the left and came to the last shrub. It had an area below big enough for us to lie in hiding.

My father sat in the swing. He had his nose buried in his list of errands and was too busy mumbling to himself to have seen us. John Caleb raised up on his elbows, then lowered himself.

"What's he doing?" I asked.

"Nothin'."

The back door opened.

"Hello, Aaron," Miss Redding said.

Daddy jumped up, knocking the swing away only to have it come back and wallop him behind the knees. He spoke Miss Redding's name, then the cat got his tongue. They sat in the swing while he folded and unfolded his sheet of paper until he about wore it out.

"It's for you," he said, shoving it at her.

I stifled a gasp with my hand.

"What's the matter?" John Caleb whispered.

"It's a poem."

"Your pa writes poems?"

"He probably drew a big heart on it."

"What for?"

"The popcorn man said she was Daddy's lady friend."

"No foolin'?"

"This is beautiful," Miss Redding said.

Daddy blushed. "I wanted you to know how I felt about the other day."

John Caleb flapped his hand. "Owww."

I put my finger to my lips.

"Something bit me," he whispered.

My father cocked his head. He'd heard us. His eyes darted from side to side, searching for us the same way he searched for his dead men. I held my breath, crossed my fingers and hoped to die he couldn't see us, because if he could, he'd kill us.

"Did you hear something?" Miss Redding said. She slipped her hand into Daddy's.

We panicked. John Caleb tried to squirm past me, causing a snow storm of blossoms.

"Don't jiggle the flowers," I whispered.

"I can't help it. There isn't room to turn around. We gotta crawl backwards."

"Aaron," Miss Redding said. "I believe I hear crickets, over in those bushes there." She pointed right at us. "I'm positive."

John Caleb and I froze. My father relaxed into the swing, his hands behind his head. A smile tugged at a corner of his mouth. I should have known right then they'd spotted us.

"I believe you're right," he said.

John Caleb elbowed me and mouthed, *Coast is clear.*

Daddy chuckled. I looked at John Caleb in alarm. My father never chuckled.

"If you have a jar," Daddy said, "I'll catch them. They make good fish bait."

We forgot about jiggling the flowers. Once we'd backed out of the shrubs, John Caleb tore past me at full speed. I grabbed the branch of spirea I'd picked for Miss Louise and chased after him.

Old Mr. Tanner still hadn't moved. John Caleb uttered a quick "hello, goodbye" as he pounded up the front porch steps. He opened the screen door and waved at me to hurry.

Mr. Tanner smiled at me. "You find your daddy?"

I stumbled on the bottom step and looked to John Caleb for help. "Ummm" was the only sound that came from my mouth.

Mr. Tanner took the last sip of his Dr. Pepper and set the bottle beside him. "Cat got your tongue?" He raised his eyebrows as if he expected me to answer.

"Ummm."

I liked Mr. Tanner. He was my favorite of all Miss Louise's customers. But at that moment, I wished he'd left his empty bottle and gone home.

John Caleb dashed across the porch. "We didn't see *nobody*, Mr. Tanner."

"You don't say."

John Caleb yanked me to my feet. "The flowers," he whispered in my ear. "Get rid of them."

I shoved them at Mr. Tanner. "These are for you."

"Why thank you. I don't remember the last time a pretty girl gave me flowers."

"Come on, Gracie," John Caleb said.

As he dragged me past Mr. Tanner, my toe caught the empty bottle and spun it across the porch. Such a shame. It would have made a nice flower vase.

We let the screen door slam behind us.

"You were supposed to throw 'em away. Not give 'em to Mr. Tanner," John Caleb whispered. "He's liable to tell your pa."

"I didn't want to waste them," I whined.

"Sorry about the door," John Caleb said to Miss Louise when she gave us one of her looks.

"Me, too," I said.

Miss Louise asked, "What happened to you two?"

John Caleb shrugged. "Nothin'."

I parroted his answer.

"I'm gonna finish cleaning," he said.

"I'm helping him."

We fast walked to the rear of the store where Miss Louise had a closet full of mops, buckets and rags. John Caleb pulled a string hanging from the ceiling. A light came on. I closed the door.

"Do you think they figured us out?" John Caleb asked.

I smiled. "They were holding hands."

John Caleb rolled his eyes as he grabbed a broom and gave me a feather duster. "I told Miss Louise we were gonna clean up. We better get out there 'fore she gets suspicious."

We started cleaning at the meat case. John Caleb's broom was a blur ahead of me. For each of his aisles, I had two rows of shelves to dust. I fell behind. Miss Louise pulled down the window blinds, her informal closed sign. Where was Daddy? Had he left me?

John Caleb met me at the end of the aisle. "I'm done." He grabbed my duster. "What'd you do to it? It looks like you beat the tar out of it."

A feather drifted to the floor. What few remained resembled Spurs' sparse tail more than a duster.

"I was trying to keep up with you," I said.

"You didn't have to. I was gonna help you when I finished the sweeping."

"I didn't know."

Our fussing ended when Daddy said, "Hey, kids. Having fun?" He'd sneaked up on us, another humiliation added to our list of misfortunes. He held out his hand. "Mind if I use your duster, son? You ought to ask Miss Louise for another one. This one's worn out."

"Yessir," John Caleb said, giving me a scornful eye.

My father dusted a box of salt. When he finished, he dusted a box of oatmeal on the other side of the aisle.

"This is kind of fun." He dusted the dirt from our knees. "Yeah, it is." He dusted my head. Four tiny white flowers tumbled to the floor. He grinned at this. "Maybe you ought to sit in the pickup. I need to talk to Miss Louise."

In the truck, I settled low in the seat, eye to eye with the glove box. After Daddy finished tattling to Miss Louise, I'd never get to punch the keys on her cash register. She'd never even let me in the store.

Daddy slipped in behind the steering wheel. "Hey, *cricket*, I'm taking Miss Redding out to dinner tomorrow night. So I had to ask Miss Louise for a favor." He leaned forward to pluck one last flower from my hair.

He didn't seem too angry so I ventured a question.

"Can I wear my cowboy boots?"

I really didn't expect a yes. Nor did I expect him to spew laughter, which seemed a low thing to do, even though I'd spied on him.

Chapter 21

When we came down the hill from the Children's Home the next afternoon, old Mr. Tanner sat in his usual place on the front porch. He raised his eyebrows the same time he raised his bottle of Dr. Pepper to salute us. No doubt my father confused him by turning onto Miss Louise's driveway and parking in back. Daddy didn't want half the county to know he was taking Miss Redding to dinner.

"Don't Miss Louise know?" I asked. She knew everything. Not to mention most of the town's rumors originated at her store.

Until then, he had been in a good mood, if not a little jumpy. "She won't say anything."

"How come?"

"Trust me. She won't."

I left him to his opinion. He proceeded to unfasten his tie, watching himself retie it in the rearview mirror and explaining the rule against having the skinny part longer than the wider part.

"That's quite a feat," he said. "John Caleb do that?"

I looked over at the spirea, wondering if somehow John Caleb put the flowers back on overnight.

My father ran his fingers over his cowlick. "When I was that age, I was doing good just to nail a few boards together."

Now, he had me confused. It wasn't the spirea. He was eyeing the oak in the backyard. John Caleb had rebuilt our tree house with walls, two windows and a tin roof. Apparently, this was what he wanted to show me yesterday before we went off on the tangent of spying. Needless to say, if we'd gone to the tree house, it would have saved us a lot of trouble.

My father carried my egg basket for me. As we walked up the back steps, I lagged behind to study the spirea. He squeezed my hand to hurry me along, stopping long enough to set the basket inside the door.

"That was nice of you to give Mr. Tanner flowers, yesterday."

Had none of my sins gone unnoticed? I ran up the stairs ahead of him.

"Hold on," he called. "We have to knock first."

"How come? Miss Louise never told me to." I looked down at him from the top landing. I must have gone in and out of her door hundreds of times.

He caught up with me. "It's polite, and I'm a man."

He let me knock on the door while he gave his tie one last tug.

When Miss Redding opened the door, I grumbled, "Daddy made me knock." I didn't want her to think I'd do something that silly on my own.

"That's because he's a gentleman," she said.

I rolled my eyes up at him. I was a little mad at him for not letting me go along with them.

"Okay, you've seen how pretty Miss Redding is," he said. "Now, shoo. And don't forget to thank Miss Louise for letting you stay with her. And tell her we'll be back sometime around ten o'clock."

Instead of taking the short cut through the stockroom, I walked the long way around to pick a few sprigs of spirea for old Mr. Tanner. Letting him think I meant to give him Miss Louise's flowers yesterday pinched my conscience.

"Did I see that pretty school teacher leaving with your daddy?" he asked as I came around the corner of the store.

No one must have told him curiosity killed the cat. I nodded and gave him the flowers. My father would have to handle half the county on his own.

I stepped inside, letting my backside soften the screen door. Voices came from the back of the store. Miss Louise wasn't behind the counter, which spoiled my plan of asking about the cash register. John Caleb wasn't around, either.

"Didn't anybody teach you manners?" Sheriff Lundy said from behind me. "Don't stand in the middle of the door."

On hearing his voice, I jerked like a puppet. He always had that effect on me. I stumbled to get out of his way. The problem was he went the same direction and my basket bounced off his belly. I staggered a couple of steps before I plopped seat first on a floor splattered with eggs. Lundy's hound dog face turned a splotchy purple.

"You're as pathetic as your father. I just bought these boots. Where is he?" He hitched up his gun belt.

Was he going to shoot Daddy because I had dropped an egg on his boot? I squeezed my eyes shut and let the sheriff unwind a long string of curses. The screen door opened.

"You leave that little girl alone." Old Mr. Tanner had come to my rescue. He carried nothing but his Dr. Pepper bottle and the flowers I gave him, which didn't seem much of a defense with the sheriff threatening to clean his boots with me.

"I never touched her," the sheriff said.

John Caleb came around the corner of the meat counter and skidded to a stop. "Miss Louise! Come quick!"

She stormed up the aisle from the back room. I was disappointed she came without her shotgun, Old Bluster. She had Mrs. Ponder, though, the preacher's wife who surpassed everyone in town when it came to shaming bad language. By this time the sheriff had nothing left but the air whistling through the gaps in his yellowed teeth. I used the moment to scoot closer to Miss Louise.

She put her wrinkled hands on my shoulder. "Are you all right, sweetheart?"

"I dropped the basket," I said. "I didn't mean to."

"I'm sure it was an accident. Why don't you go outside with John Caleb."

"My eggs all broke."

"Leo will help me clean up."

I chanced a quick look around the store. Other than the sheriff, old Mr. Tanner was the only man in sight.

"Go on, sweetheart," Miss Louise said.

I bolted from the building. There was a spirea bush which had grown flowers overnight that I planned to hide beneath. I kept ahead of John Caleb, but not by much. He grabbed my arm as I set to go down on all fours.

"Hold up," he said. "I got a better place. My tree house."

We raced each other to the backyard. John Caleb gave me one of his ear-to-ear grins as he untied a coil of old lariat he had wrapped around the lowest limb of the tree.

"I didn't know old Mr. Tanner had a first name," he said.

"Me neither." But as long as Miss Louise's spireas bloomed, I promised to take him a sprig of flowers every day.

John Caleb played out the lariat and stood directly beneath the door.

"What do you think?" he asked.

"I saw it. It's a real house."

"Yeah, wait'll you see this. I got just enough rope to stand here," he said. "Can't open the door any way but standing right here where I scratched this X in the dirt."

"How come?"

"You'll see. Better stand clear."

He waved at me backhanded to keep going until I reached the garden fence.

"That'll do. Here she goes." He wrapped the end of the bristled lariat around his wrist and used his full weight to pull down. The trap door fell open with a bang. He dove for the ground when a ladder made from rope and two-by-fours tumbled from the opening, missing him by an inch. Once it quit swinging, he hopped up to dust the dirt from his clothes.

"Whew. That was close," he said, inspecting the rope burn around his wrist. "Miss Louise and Miss Redding have been after me to do something different 'cause they're afraid I'm gonna knock my head off."

Just then his eyes crossed, and he swayed. He might have fooled me if he hadn't laughed.

"You're not supposed to cross your eyes," I said, though I couldn't remember where I'd heard the rule. "They'll get stuck."

"Won't neither. You gotta be born that way like Riley."

I gave into his firsthand knowledge. With the fear of permanently skewed eyeballs gone, I tried crossing mine.

"Listen up," John Caleb said. "This ladder's my secret weapon. I call it the R and R Banger after my brothers, but I betcha it'll knock old Lundy's head off just as good. All we gotta do is lure him back here."

"It'd probably knock his head under the porch."

We whooped and did a war dance.

Despite the lopsided wood rungs, the ladder wasn't hard to climb. The last step needed a jump and a belly flop to land inside. John Caleb forgot to warn me about the kerosene lantern hanging from a rafter. It rang against my forehead. In one corner, there was a crate filled with cans of beans, tuna and soup. He had his old blanket folded to be a bed.

He crawled in after me. "Don't tell Miss Louise, but sometimes I sleep here at night when Pa's gone off somewhere and Riley and Roland are around."

"Where did you get all this stuff?"

"Miss Louise. She wanted her old garden shed torn down. I told her I'd do it if she'd let me fix up our tree house with the boards and tin. I bought nails off of Mr. Caldwell down at the lumberyard. He showed me how to build the rafters." He dug a catalogue page from under the blanket and pointed at a picture of a red bicycle. "I'm gonna buy that one with the money I earned from Miss Louise. She told me she'd help me order it and pay for half of it since I can use it to make deliveries. I'm gonna put a basket on the back. She said the faster I go, the more deliveries I can do, the more money we make. We're partners."

His dreams had always been silly things like thinking he'd been kidnapped by Gypsies or pretending he was an Indian warrior. He was still skinny, still had his freckles, but he'd grown in a way I didn't understand. I wasn't sure if I liked it or his closeness to Miss Louise.

"It's not fair," I said. "We're partners."

"We still are."

"But Miss Louise taught you how to use the cash register, and she's helping you get a bicycle."

"Your pa got you a horse."

I crossed my arms. He crossed his and glared at me. My nose itched, but I couldn't scratch it without losing the staring contest. Finally, John Caleb slapped his legs.

"Shoot, Gracie. We're wasting daylight. How 'bout I teach you to ride my bicycle when I get it, and you let me ride Sammy?"

"You know how to ride a bicycle?" I asked, scratching my nose.

He put his hands behind his head and leaned back against the wall. "Not yet."

"Then we got time to play cowboys and Indians."

I drew back a pretend bow string and let an arrow fly. John Caleb fell to one side. His eyes popped open.

"I got a hatchet from Miss Louise's shed. We can make some real ones out of willow branches."

A tree scratching one of its branches against my window woke me the next morning. The eastern sky was pink. I smelled Daddy's coffee and sat up. Something was out of kilter, as if I had put my clothes on wrong side out and nobody told me. I looked at the pictures on the wall, the dresser and the closet. Everything was where it ought to be, except me. I was in my bedroom at Miss Louise's, not my bedroom at home.

I trotted down the hall to the kitchen. Along the way, I peeked into Miss Redding's bedroom and the parlor, hoping to catch her before she went to the kitchen. If I wanted to weasel out of her what happened last night before Miss Louise did, I had to find her first. Miss Louise disapproved of anyone weaseling except herself.

"Daddy didn't come and get me." I shoved the kitchen stool over to the counter so I could watch Miss Louise mix pancake batter.

"You were fast asleep, so we decided not to wake you."

She let me dip my finger in the batter, then pretended to slap my hand for doing so.

"Would you like to go to Sunday School with me?" she asked.

"I don't have my dress with me."

"Your father will bring it when he comes here in a little bit."

I had that out of kilter feeling again. Before I could ask about it, Miss Louise sent me into the dining room to set the table for four. I gathered the silverware and plates and backed through the swinging door. All this time, I assumed Miss Redding was one room ahead of me and sooner or later, I would find her. She wasn't in the dining room, and I ran out of places to look. I left the dishes on the table and went into the kitchen.

"Where's Miss Redding?" I asked.

Miss Louise grabbed the dishrag to scrub the counter. The little white curls around her face jiggled like the curtains' tassels in a breeze. What I wanted to know was if Miss Redding was going to eat breakfast with us. Sometimes she went early to church for choir practice. My nose caught a whiff of burning bacon. Across the kitchen, the cast iron skillet started to smoke like the incinerator at the Children's Home.

"Miss Louise," I said.

She was too busy scouring germs to look up.

"Miss Louise, the bacon's burning."

She dropped her dishrag. On the way to the stove, she wrapped her apron around her hand for a potholder to slide the skillet off the fire.

"Go open up the living room windows," she said as she flapped a tea towel at the gray fog in the room. "See if we can get a breeze through to blow this smoke out of here."

I ran across the hall to raised the windows. There wasn't enough wind to flutter the curtains, let alone clear the air. I returned to the kitchen where the smoke had grown thicker. Tears dribbled down Miss Louise's cheeks, which she dabbed with her apron. I'd never seen her cry before, especially over bacon. The idea bothered me.

My father barreled into the kitchen, yelling my name and waving at the smoke. I threw my arms around him so hard I knocked him back a step.

"Is there a fire?" he asked.

"Such a fuss," Miss Louise said as she wiped her eyes. "I let the bacon go a little too long is all. No need to make over me."

Miss Redding rushed past him. She wore the same dress as yesterday afternoon. Maybe it was the smoke, but her eyes brimmed with tears as she hugged Miss Louise.

"Let's get this pan outside," Daddy said, "so it'll stop smoking up the kitchen."

He touched the skillet handle lightly before he grabbed it barehanded. I ran ahead of him to open the door.

"How come they're crying?" I asked.

"Miss Louise been upset all morning?"

"Yes. Is it cause the sheriff's still mad at me?"

My father stopped so suddenly I ran into him. From the way he'd complained yesterday about half the county knowing he took Miss Redding to dinner, I assumed he would have heard all about the sheriff and me.

He switched hands holding the skillet. "Why's he mad at you?"

It was too late to wiggle out of telling him everything. He'd only ask Miss Louise. The rest of the way down the stairs, I told him about dropping my basket, the sheriff's new boots and how pathetic we were. On hearing the last bit, his face turned as red as the sheriff's.

"You're not pathetic," he said. "Any grown man that acts that way is the true pathetic one."

Miss Louise had already told me this, but I liked hearing my father repeat it. He opened the back door and guided me through with his free hand.

"Do you think Miss Louise'll still pay me for the eggs?" I asked. "She said it wasn't my fault."

"She buys to sell. She can't sell broken eggs. That's why you have to be careful."

"But I didn't mean to."

Daddy set the skillet on the top step and walked over to the swing. "Doesn't make any difference."

"What if I can't pay Sam?"

"I don't think that'll be a problem unless you're planning on shining the sheriff's boots again." He smiled. "Come over here, cowgirl, and sit down. I've got something to tell you." He searched through his pockets until he pulled out a pack of Juicy Fruit.

"You quitting?" I asked as I sat beside him. Yesterday afternoon when I had seen him last, he hadn't given up the habit.

He nodded and handed me a piece of gum.

"We have to wait down here until things get cleared out upstairs," he said. A lost expression came over his face, as if he had awakened in the wrong bedroom like me.

"How long?"

"Until Kate comes to get us."

I liked how he called Miss Redding by her first name, as if she belonged to us.

He scratched one of his ears. "I'm not sure how to go about this. Kate would know, but she thought it ought to be just you and me."

He explained he'd had a flat tire on the way to the city and how the restaurant he planned to go to had burned down the year before. He thought this was funny but didn't laugh.

"Anyway, if you'd told me yesterday afternoon that I'd be sitting here, a married man."

He shrugged and talked on, while I puzzled over the word *married*. I already knew he was married—to Mama. Grandpa had said so, and underneath my bed, I had a picture of their wedding. But Mama was dead. Did that *unmarry* him?

"Gracie," Daddy said, nudging me. "Are you listening?"

"You're married."

"Yes."

I slumped lower in the swing. "And you had a flat tire."

"No. I mean yes, but not that." He blinked as if I had confused him, instead of the other way around. "I said, Miss Redding and I got married. Last night. She's going to be your mother."

"She is?"

My arms turned into wings. I jumped out of the swing to spin circles.

"Yes. Happy?"

Any happier, I would have burst in the air like a skyrocket.

"You're gonna make yourself dizzy," Daddy said.

"I don't care."

I made one last spin before the floor tilted. Daddy caught me before I fell off the porch. I looked up at him cross-eyed.

"Miss Redding can have my room," I said.

"That's very nice of you. But we decided she'd share mine. It's bigger."

"Can I call her Mama? Instead of Miss Redding?"

"She's not Miss Redding, any longer. She's Mrs. Timmons."

"What if I forget?"

"You're such a worrywart."

"Can we go home and ride Sammy?"

"Not today. You're going to stay with Miss Louise and help her."

This was a blow. Not to go home with Daddy and Miss Redding? "Do I have to?"

"For few days. Miss Louise needs help at the cash register."

I looked at him suspiciously. She hadn't said anything about it. Still, I swallowed his argument whole as if I were a pelican.

While he went to the alley behind the garage to clean the skillet, I bolted up the stairs to find Miss Redding. The smoke had cleared a little, but the odor of scorched bacon hung heavy in the house. With my hands over my mouth and nose, I trotted down the hall to Miss Redding's room where the windows were open but the coolness of the morning had vanished.

Miss Louise sat on the bed next to Miss Redding's open suitcase. She had her back to me while she wiped her nose with her hanky. Miss Redding was slinging hangers back and forth on the closet rod. For the second time that morning, I felt out of place.

"I just hope this isn't another mistake on your part," Miss Louise said.

Mistake? Daddy had asked Miss Redding that once when he took me away from her. The same stony silence filled the room again. I backed against the opposite wall in the hallway.

"You've told him, haven't you?" Miss Louise asked.

"Not yet."

"You can't keep something like this from him."

Miss Redding backed out of the closet with an armful of clothes. She gasped when she saw me. The color drained from her face. "Gracie, how long have you been standing there?"

Miss Louise scooted around to stare at me. "You're supposed to be with your daddy."

A whirlwind went through my head, scattering my flimsy excuses.

Miss Louise put her spidery fingers on Miss Redding's arm. "Kate, never mind me. I'm just an old biddy."

"No, you're not," Miss Redding said. "You're one of my favorite people."

She waited until Miss Louise returned to the kitchen before she took my hand and asked, "All right, sweetheart. How much did you hear?"

"I don't know." How could I put a puzzle together when I only had a few pieces. "Are you in trouble?"

"No."

"I wanted—"

She hugged me before I could finish, which was the very thing I needed, all along.

I followed her downstairs. We stepped out onto the porch as Daddy walked across the yard. He was whistling a hodge-podge of notes that didn't add up to a song but seemed to please him. With all the trouble I was in, I needed a good deed to smooth things over. I walked over to the end of the porch to break off a few sprigs of spirea I planned to tuck into Miss Redding's hair.

"So, how'd it go?" Daddy asked her.

"Better than with my parents. She wished we had waited a little longer."

"I'm tired of dying. I want to start living." He laughed, Grandpa's kind of laugh that half the county could hear.

I turned around to see him put his arms around Miss Redding and kiss her on the lips for a long, long time. Longer than Gene Kelly ever kissed anyone in the movies.

Chapter 22

For all my wishing to have a mother and a father, I never wondered what it would be like to have both at the same time. I peppered Miss Louise with questions. Which one would hear my prayers? Which one would ride Sammy with me? What if I forgot and said Miss Redding instead of Mama? Calling her a different name was as difficult as calling blue, yellow.

Miss Louise told me most questions in people's heads, especially mine, were usually answered in due time. This didn't calm the willies in my stomach, so I asked John Caleb what happened when his pa brought home a new ma.

He shrugged. "Supper started tasting better."

"You ever forget to call her Ma?"

"Pa never told us her name."

He'd been showing me how to figure sales tax. Miss Louise had asked him to teach me and left us in charge of the store while she went to the bank. We were on our own, with no customers except for old Mr. Tanner leaning against the meat case, the coolest place in the room. Miss Louise bought him a Dr. Pepper. I wouldn't get any practice from him.

John Caleb nudged me with his elbow. "You gotta multiply the total by two percent."

My heart sank somewhere below my knees. Learning to use the cash register was harder than I expected.

"I don't know how," I said.

"You'll learn in the third grade."

"You're in the second grade same as me. How'd you learn?"

"I reckon I always knew."

He could barely read the funnies, but for three days, I'd watched him adding and subtracting numbers in his head quicker than I could with a pencil and paper. How he did this irked me to no end, especially when he repeated the story of how he'd been kidnapped from the Gypsies by his pa. Everyone knew Gypsies were good at figures.

"Folks pay their tax with mills," he said. "That's those little paper coins."

"I know. Daddy's got some."

"She made Pa get glass in the broken windows."

"Miss Louise?"

"Nah, the lady Pa brought home to be our ma. She only stayed a month. Pa said the windows weren't worth it."

Mr. Tanner choked on his Dr. Pepper.

"You two better stop yammering and look sharp," he said between coughs. "Customer's coming."

The bell above the screen door jingled. My father stepped inside, carrying the egg basket.

"You all right, Mr. Tanner?" he asked. He slapped Mr. Tanner's back to rid him of his wheezing.

"I'm fine, I'm fine. How's that bride of yours?"

"Getting prettier by the day. Say, you wouldn't happen to need a job gathering eggs. I lost my daughter to the mercantile trade."

"I'll gather them," I said like a silly goose. Seeing Daddy gave me a bad case of homesickness.

John Caleb rolled his eyes.

"Your mama's keeping me busy sweeping roly-polies out of the corners and from underneath the furniture," Daddy said as he set the egg basket on the counter. "She made me move the sofa three times this morning."

While John Caleb counted the eggs, Daddy propped his elbows on the counter.

"I've been so busy I forgot to feed Sammy last night," he said. He brought his hands together in supplication. "Could you possibly give up the cash register and come home to help me?"

It seemed a waste of summer learning multiplication. I dragged my suitcase from under the counter where I'd stored it earlier in the day.

"Good deal!" My father clapped his hands. "Your mama's cooking a special supper for you tonight."

John Caleb leaned over to whisper in my ear, "Told you so."

Miss Louise was right about the answers to my questions coming in due time. That evening, I rode Sammy alone and was proud. Daddy and Miss

Redding trotted beside me on old Moonie. They both listened to my prayers. I fell asleep, contented.

Later in the night, Daddy shrieked. The dead men caught us off guard. With his deciding to "start living," I'd hoped never to hear them again. Perhaps it was because of my happiness his screaming seemed louder and more terrifying than ever before. But this time, we weren't alone. We had Miss Redding. Still, not wanting to take chances, I dove under my sheet and started singing the song John Caleb had taught me while we delivered groceries.

I was down to *Fifty-three bottles of beer on the wall* when the hall light came on, and Mama whispered my name. I poked my head out from under the sheet.

"Mama," I said, throwing my arms around her waist.

"Are you all right?"

I was because she was there.

"I know they're not real."

"Who?"

"The dead men."

In the dim light, I could see her eyes were puffy. She'd been crying. She sat on my bed and ran her fingers through my hair until she found a rat's nest.

"Does your daddy have very many nightmares?"

I shrugged. How many bad dreams was a person supposed to have? I lost count of my own.

"Are they always this bad?" she asked.

I wasn't sure if she meant Daddy's nightmares or the tangles in my hair. Not that it mattered. The answer was the same.

It seemed I'd just closed my eyes when Mama shook me awake. She laid a faded pair of overalls, socks and a shirt on the bed.

"Hurry and get dressed," she said as she set my shoes beside the bed. "Miss Louise called early this morning. Someone broke into her store."

I sat up wide awake, imagining Miss Louise in her nightgown, tiptoeing downstairs with Old Bluster, her shotgun. She crept into the store. Then *kablooey!* Practically the whole town believed Miss Louise wouldn't think twice about turning a thief into a tea strainer. She had as good as promised.

"Did she shoot him?" I asked.

"No, of course not."

I added a lungful of disappointment in my sigh. Mama pulled off my pajama top and stuck one of my arms into my shirt.

"She caught him, didn't she?" I asked.

"Button your blouse. He was gone by the time she got downstairs."

No doubt the shotgun had slowed tiny Miss Louise. I'd never seen it, but with a name like Old Bluster, it had to be as huge as a cannon.

"What'd they steal?" I asked.

"I don't know. You'll have to ask your father. He talked to her when she called." Mama shook open my overalls. "He's loaded the milk can in the truck and is gathering some tools. We're going to help her clean up. Whoever robbed the store made a mess of things."

"Did she call the sheriff?" I asked.

"No, she wants your father to handle it."

If Miss Louise thought he could catch the robber, she was wrong. He couldn't snag the twins even when I pointed him in the right direction. In that way, he and the sheriff were alike. I pulled on one boot and carried the other down the hall after Mama.

And what would my father do if he caught the burglar? Lately, every fight he found himself in, he'd lost.

"What if he hurts Daddy?"

"Sweetheart, Miss Louise thinks John Caleb helped rob the store," she said. "She found his arrowhead. I suppose he dropped it when he was vandalizing the store."

I struggled with what she'd told me. "He wouldn't lose his arrowhead. Will he have to go to jail?"

"That'll be up to Miss Louise."

Daddy came into the kitchen from outside. "I'm thinking we ought to go by the Parker place and get John Caleb. He can help us clean up the mess he made."

Like my grandpa and father, I liked to gather my thoughts on the river road. With all its bumps and holes, ideas shook loose, waiting for me to put them in proper order. The first chug hole, I solved the robbery. The twins took John Caleb's arrowhead and left it at the store to blame him.

My reasoning didn't seem to convince my father. He parked the truck in front of the crumpled woven-wire fence which marked the bare yard. Only a few stunted sunflowers dared to poke their heads through the hard clay.

He wiped his mouth with a shaky hand. "See them?"

He didn't have to tell me what to look for. His left boot carried tooth marks from the stubby-eared dog the last time we were here. I leaned out the window. The air was filled with the whistles and clacking from a flock of blackbirds perched in the dead cedar beside the porch.

Ragged curtains fluttered in and out of the front windows of the house. The door gaped open. Inside was dark. On the porch, the sad-faced hound peeked from behind the rotting sofa. I didn't want my father to catch John Caleb anymore than I wanted the dogs to bite him again. I told him about the hound and felt miserable for it.

"The other one?" he asked.

"Don't see it," I said. "John Caleb wouldn't lose his arrowhead."

"Let the sheriff handle this," Mama said. "Miss Louise would understand."

"He'll throw John Caleb in jail," I said.

Daddy rubbed his forehead. "Gracie, hush. This is hard enough as it is."

"I'm serious, Aaron," Mama said.

"It's the deal I made with Miss Louise." What deal, he didn't say. Instead, he leaned on the horn. "That ought to stir someone up."

It stirred the hound from behind the sofa and started it baying as if it had us treed. The stubby-eared dog crawled from under the house. It hopped up on the porch, probably thinking company had come—there were boots to chew. Despite the commotion, none of the Parkers showed their faces. Daddy tried yelling over the howling.

"Shoot," he grumbled. "Looks like I'll have to be polite and knock." He reached under the seat to pull out his service revolver.

Mama grabbed his arm. "You can't walk up to the door with a gun."

She probably didn't know he was Shawnee. He shook off her hand and unsnapped the leather holster.

"You're going to get shot," she said.

"Not planning on it."

"As if your planning makes any difference to George Parker. Let's go. Miss Louise is waiting."

Daddy shook his head.

"This is crazy," Mama said.

The way she said it put the first doubt in my head, not about the dogs or even John Caleb, but what Mr. Parker or anyone might think of my father waving his gun at them.

"I came to talk to John Caleb. I don't want to get mauled by dogs for doing it," he mumbled. A little of the certainty in his voice had faded.

He got out of the pickup. The dogs waited for him to step over the crushed wire fence before they barreled off the porch, stubby-ears ahead of the hound. Daddy aimed his gun at the sky and shot. Screeching blackbirds exploded out of the tree. Neither dog slowed, so Daddy pointed his gun at Stubby-ears and fired again. Pieces of hard packed dirt exploded in front of the dog. It skidded to a stop, only to have the hound plow into him. Mr. Parker ran out onto the porch with his double barrel shotgun and pointed it at my daddy. Daddy raised his hands. Mama started praying. I was too scared to do anything.

"You shot my dogs," Mr. Parker yelled.

"Sorry," Daddy said. "I witnessed too many of them gnawing my men as I was trying to bury them. You see something like that, it sticks with you."

The hound and stubby-ears sorted out their legs and tails and took off around the house.

"Guess I missed," Daddy said. "I'm laying my gun down, now." He set it on the ground, and then straightened. "I need to talk to John Caleb."

"What?" Mr. Parker said. "You come out here and shoot at my dogs just so you can talk to John Caleb?"

"A little problem at the general store."

"I 'spect the boy's asleep."

"With all this going on? John Caleb! Need to talk to you."

"Leave my boy alone."

"You let a lot of folks down. Come on out here and let's talk."

"You stay where you are, boy," Mr. Parker shouted over his shoulder. "He ain't got nothing on you."

"I'd like to see you make it right, son."

"He's not your son. He's mine and he'll do what I say."

One of the twins ambled outside. "Won't neither."

"Will so," Mr. Parker said, "if he knows what's good for him."

The twin chuckled. "Won't if he ain't here."

"Well, where is he?" Mr. Parker bellowed.

I never heard the answer. My nose caught a whiff of bacon as warm breath tickled my neck. When I peeked over my shoulder, the cross-eyed Riley had his arms propped on my door and was leaning through my open window. I yelped and scrambled over Mama's lap to the other side of the cab.

"Morning, ma'am," Riley said with a brown juicy grin.

He meant his greeting for Mama. I still wasn't old enough to be a ma'am yet.

"Did ya like the picture I drawed for ya?" he asked.

Mama's face turned as red as Christmas. If Riley had any brains at all, he'd have left us alone. Instead he offered to draw Mama another picture if she'd take her clothes off. He was too busy ogling her to see my father storming down on him. He grabbed the twin by the shoulder to spin him around. Riley tried to throw a punch. Daddy checked it with one arm and landed his fist on Riley's nose. Blood went everywhere. Mama screamed. Daddy never had another chance at Riley. The boy took off for the outhouse. I hoped he fell in head first.

Daddy walked back to his gun. "I'm picking up my revolver and leaving."

Mr. Parker, stunned as if hexed by a Gypsy, watched in silence as my daddy got into the pickup.

"Promise me you won't ever use that gun again," Mama said. "Promise me. Please."

"The dogs."

"I don't care about the dogs. You could have gotten yourself or Gracie killed."

Daddy slipped his service revolver into its holster and under the seat. He didn't make any promises about never using it again.

It didn't seem fair Mama scolding him. He couldn't help it if he was afraid of the dogs. Besides, I wondered if he wasn't a lot like Rag in that if he'd wanted to shoot the hound and stubby-ears, they would've been dead. After all, he'd been a sergeant in the army, even if he didn't have any medals to show for it. As for busting Riley's nose, no one, not even Mama, could convince me Riley didn't deserve it.

Daddy backed the pickup out of the Parker's driveway and headed it to town. A lot of fussing went back and forth between their eyes. The river road was rougher than I remembered. If Daddy steered to miss one chug hole, he hit the next one, which was twice as deep. A front hubcap fell off. Daddy saw it in the rearview mirror and stopped to pick it up.

"Does George Parker have any idea where John Caleb is?" Mama asked when he got back into the pickup.

"He said he didn't, for what that's worth."

I knew where John Caleb was. The only place he could be. Maybe it was the washboard road that shook loose the idea. Maybe I'd known all along.

Mama put her hand on my knee. "Stop tapping your feet."

Chapter 23

This new secret burdened me more than the others. No one carried it but myself. Even with John Caleb's cans of food and lantern, he couldn't hide in our tree house forever. If I could figure a way to get him home, I would hide him in the hay barn and sneak him food.

After we delivered the milk, we went to the store. We were early. Main Street was empty of cars and people except Mr. Caldwell, the square-shouldered owner of the lumber yard. He waved his measuring stick at us from Miss Louise's front porch.

"See this?" he called as we got out of the pickup. He tapped his measuring stick on the big front window where jagged pieces of glass hung like witch's teeth. "Threw the rocking chair through it. Whoever did it ought to be horsewhipped."

What Mr. Caldwell couldn't know was John Caleb and I had spent part of one afternoon cleaning that window until it shined. If he wanted to break glass, it would have been something he hadn't taken so much pride in like a jar of cod liver oil.

I headed for the backyard to find him.

"Gracie, where are you going?" Mama asked. "I don't want you near that tree house. It's too dangerous."

I flapped my hands in frustration. Another foot and I would have slipped around the corner of the building. Like most children, I believed in the rule of once out of sight I no longer had to listen to adults. Caught, I dragged myself back to help her with the buckets and the mop she brought.

Mr. Caldwell stood in the middle of the steps. "Pure meanness, it was. Mean as lopping off a dog's hind leg for the fun of it."

Daddy hopped from the sidewalk onto the porch and hurried inside the store. No doubt, he'd had his fill of dogs for one morning.

"Sorry. Got a little carried away," Mr. Caldwell said. "But wait 'til you see inside."

He folded his measuring stick and stepped aside. With him out of the way, Mama raced up the steps. I followed with the mop. Inside the store, I stopped cold. Glass was everywhere—not just from the window, but from the meat case and from the broken jars of pickles and ketchup on the floor. In the middle of it, Miss Louise sat in the rocking chair the robber had thrown through the front window. Mama picked her way across the floor to squeeze Miss Louise's hand.

Daddy picked up a ball peen hammer in front of the case and threw it so hard out the window I flinched. He stalked to the back of the store.

I called after him, "John Caleb wouldn't break Miss Louise's meat case."

"His arrowhead and quarter are there on the counter by the cash register," Miss Louise said. "They're right where I found them."

I crunched through the broken glass to see for myself.

"Are they his?" Mama asked.

A sadness as sharp as his arrowhead stuck in my throat. Most of the cash register keys were bent. The *Sale* key was gone. The money drawer lay smashed on the floor with a jar of mustard dumped in it.

"For the life of me," Miss Louise said. "I don't understand why he broke into the cash register. He knows I don't keep money there overnight."

"Do you have any idea of what's missing?" Mama asked.

"There's no way of telling with it all piled on the floor like it is. Meat's gone is all I know. Yesterday afternoon, I took delivery of two hams, eight pounds of chops and a dozen slabs of bacon."

"Riley was eating bacon," I shouted. Hot tears ran down my face. My idea the twins robbed the store was right after all, but no one listened to me. "He stole John Caleb's arrowhead. You should've shot him with Old Bluster, like you said you would, instead of blaming John Caleb."

It would have kept Riley's stinky breath off my neck, saved Daddy's sore knuckles and his and Mama's arguing about the gun on the way to town.

"Sweetheart, come here," Miss Louise said.

"No, it's not fair. John Caleb's gonna have to go to jail."

"Gracie," Mama said. "It's not Miss Louise's fault."

"It wasn't my fault I dropped the eggs."

"I don't want John Caleb to go to reform school," Miss Louise said. "Neither does your mama or daddy."

"But you told Daddy to catch him."

"No, I asked your father to find him."

Mama quarreled with a strand of hair that kept falling across her eyes. "He wasn't home when we stopped by there this morning."

"That don't mean he robbed Miss Louise," I said.

"Shhh," Miss Louise said, scooting over in the rocker for a place beside her.

I plopped next to her. "He wouldn't—"

"I need to clear something up."

My father came back with a buttered slice of bread folded in two for me. The only reason I took it was because I hadn't had any breakfast.

"Old Bluster," Miss Louise said, "hasn't seen the light of day since my papa took his little shotgun rabbit hunting the winter he died. That being oh. . . some sixty years ago."

"Old Bluster's a rabbit gun?" I asked.

She might as well have claimed it a cap gun. It wouldn't have been any more unbelievable. A little of the twinkle in her eye came back.

"Single shot, if I remember right. Wouldn't folks just die if they knew?" She slapped her leg and laughed.

I gasped. "You made it up? Just like you made up the young men peeking in your bedroom window?" I clapped my hand over my mouth.

"Miss Louise!" Mama said.

"I was only heckling Lundy in hopes he'd quit and move on," Miss Louise said.

"But Miss Louise."

"I'll admit it didn't exactly work out as planned. He hung up on me this morning when I called to report the robbery."

"No wonder."

Miss Louise snorted. "If I'd dropped the burglar off at the front door of the jail, Lundy couldn't catch him." She smoothed her dress. "I was saying, when Papa died, I was away at school, worrying about important things such as balls and pretty dresses and beaus. I had to leave it all behind."

"How come?" I asked.

"Papa spent most of his money sending me to boarding school. He felt bad about my not having a mother and having a right upbringing. After he died, all that was left was the store. That's when my real education began. I was seventeen and had so much to learn about people. I was terrified of being robbed. Afraid someone would cheat me. So I made up Old Bluster when the only blustering came from me."

"But that don't mean John Caleb robbed you."

"No, it means I didn't confront the thieves, but I recognized their voices. They frightened me." Her eyes reddened. "And one voice broke my heart."

Miss Louise put her hand on my shoulder. "I suppose they tore up the store when they found no money to steal. Maybe they would've anyway. All I know is John Caleb was with them."

I squirmed out of the chair. "I gotta go to the bathroom." It was the truth, but if I sat next to Miss Louise any longer, I might start believing her.

"Gracie, wait," Mama said.

"Let her be," Daddy said. He headed for the front door as if that was what he wanted for himself.

On the way back from the bathroom, I slipped outside to find John Caleb, my plan all along.

"John Caleb. It's me, Gracie," I called, though my heart whispered he was gone. I stood on the *X* he had carved into the bare place beneath the oak. The tree house creaked, but only because the wind had picked up. The trap door hung open. The ladder swayed in my hands.

Everything was out of sorts—Mama and Daddy fussing at each other, the twins, the dogs. It'd begun with Daddy's dead men, and Mama's wanting to know if he had lots of nightmares, along with a disagreeable thought that maybe, I shouldn't have told her. I climbed the rungs and belly-flopped through the trap door. The lantern I'd banged my head on was gone. So were the cans of food, the blanket and the bows and arrows we'd made. I sat Indian style, feeling more and more peeved with John Caleb and everyone else. He'd run away. The only thing he left was a broken pencil and the page from the Sears catalogue, the one with the bicycle he wanted more than anything. He'd tacked the paper to the wall. I leaned forward to squint at the faint scribbling.

Gracie. Tell Miss Louis sory. I was skerd. Fix stuff I bust wit my bike monie. Gon luk for Sam. John Caleb

He'd robbed the store and was sorry? I yanked the page from the wall. At school, Miss Redding taught us sorry comes easy once you're caught. John Caleb wasn't yet, but he knew it was coming. Why else would he have run away? I folded the paper and rolled it tight so it would fit in my hand as I climbed down the ladder. I was almost to the ground when I saw the sheriff and one of his deputies walking toward me.

"You think she knows where the Parker kid's at?" the deputy asked.

I scrambled up a couple of rungs and looped my arms and legs around the ropes on either side to keep Lundy from pulling me off.

"What have we got here?" the sheriff said as he tried to pluck the page from my hand.

I refused to be pathetic and cry like a baby so I clenched the paper until my fingernails dug into my palm and yelled for Daddy.

The deputy laughed. "Come on sheriff, she can't be that much to handle."

"Shut up and help me."

My father ran out of the store shouting at the sheriff as the deputy grasped the ladder like a tablecloth and shook it. After a couple of flourishes, my breakfast landed on the sheriff's new boots. He cursed. A big boom split the air, and Daddy screamed. It happened so fast I turned loose of the ladder. The sheriff was so surprised, he dropped me.

Young Doc MacKay propped me up against the tree trunk and told me to watch his finger go left, right and up and down. It was a hard thing to do while bawling at the top of my lungs. But when he finished, he told Mama I'd have nothing but a goose egg to show for the day and sent her off to take care of my father.

"Where is he?" I asked Dr. MacKay.

"He's fine."

That wasn't what I'd asked, and I doubted the truth of his answer. I'd seen my father claw his own face, the blood. A crowd of people had gathered in the backyard.

"Leave us alone," Mama said. "Please."

Enough people moved I could see my father face down on the ground. The deputy had his knee on his back, and Jimmy Lear, the town hero, had his shoulders pinned. Reverend Ponder knelt next to them. The sight made my chest ache as if I'd had my breath knocked out of me.

"Is he dead?" I asked Dr. MacKay. I worried the sheriff may have shot him and that was the boom I heard.

"No, I believe a truck backfired and startled him."

It didn't seem fair to have the town hero sitting on top of my father as though he had won a fight with him. The sheriff stood beside them, lecturing Mama how he ought to take Daddy in for his own good.

At this, Jimmy spat on the ground. "All Timmons did was call you a horse's rear end. That's no reason to throw a man in jail."

"You seen him, slobbering and clawing at himself that way."

"He's just jittery," Jimmy said, "like most of us boys are when we hear something that sounds like artillery going off. I ducked myself when I heard that truck backfire. You would've too, if you'd been what he's been through." Jimmy leaned over to Daddy's ear. "You okay, now, Sarge?" Daddy nodded his head, and Jimmy stood. "Folks, it'd be real respectful if y'all would move on out and leave us alone."

I was so grateful for Jimmy's request I never envied his medals, again. The rest of the crowd I hated and told Dr. MacKay so.

"Never hate," Dr. MacKay said. "It wears out the soul."

"They laugh at Daddy like there's something the matter with him."

"How about we go over to my office and have a sucker?"

"I want my daddy."

"When he comes to get you, we'll give him a sucker, too. Let's go."

I grabbed John Caleb's note by the ladder as Dr. MacKay hurried me to his office. We sat next to each other in his waiting room. Occasionally, he pointed a little flashlight at my eyes to blind me. I was on my third cherry sucker before Mama and Miss Louise came to get me. Daddy was the last to arrive.

My face warmed when I saw him. Scratches scored his cheeks and neck worse than if he'd jumped into a patch of greenbriers face first. I turned away so no one would catch me staring at him. His overalls were dry but not his. The ones he wore to town were old and faded. These were new as if they had come right from the store. This time, he'd peed himself in front of half the county, which explained Dr. MacKay dragging me to his office and why Mama and Jimmy Lear asked everyone to leave.

"Sorry, cowgirl," Daddy said.

He knew why I didn't want to look at him. I unrolled the catalog page.

"It's from John Caleb," I whispered. "He's not in the tree house."

"I know. I checked there first thing."

How silly of me to think I could have hidden John Caleb. My head throbbed. I rested it against Daddy's shoulder and confessed my secret.

"I'm glad you told me," he said.

With those words, some of the morning's weight lifted. I looked up him. The welts on his face were swelling, making them uglier. When he finished the note, he folded it and stuck it into the bib of his overalls.

"Never let anybody rob your ability to see good in a person," he said. "It's awfully hard to get it back once it's gone. I'm sorry I said those things about John Caleb."

"Dr. MacKay, is there anything you can do for him?" Mama asked.

Dr. MacKay tilted his head to one side as if he had a crick in his neck. "Something medically?"

"What she's asking is, am I crazy?" Daddy said, raising his head.

"Stop it!" Mama's reply was as sharp as a slap.

There was a soreness in the room that made me want to hide, something I hadn't thought about in a long time. There weren't any closets, but two seats over, I saw a shiny penny. I hoped the finders keepers rule was the same in Dr. MacKay's waiting room as elsewhere.

"I thought you knew what you were getting into," Daddy said. "You got what you wanted—Gracie."

Hearing my name, I sat up and bumped my head on the bottom of the chair. Now, I'd have two goose eggs to rub, but they hurt less than listening to my parents quarrel. I put my hands over my ears as a whirlwind of ugly voices blew through the room.

"There's a big difference between nightmares and what you did this morning at the Parkers," Mama said.

"You left a few things out about yourself. I'm not a school boy who's never seen a woman's body."

Mama turned as pale as eggshells. Her hands went to her face as she turned her back to us.

Miss Louise put her hand on Mama's arm. "Now's not the time."

My father bolted for the door. Something awful had happened, and to think about it made my head hurt. Dr. MacKay fished his little flashlight from his pocket. I felt Mama's touch.

"Does he have these episodes often?" Dr. MacKay asked.

"It's the dead men," I said. "They chase him."

Lately, I was letting secrets slip, and I wondered if that's how secrets were— let one loose, and the rest scatter like kids escaping from school. I walked over to the window to look across the street. My father's pickup was gone. A crowd had gathered on the store's front porch and sidewalk. He wouldn't come back with that many people hanging about. Though I'd bawled and not smiled at him once all morning, Dr. MacKay brought me another cherry sucker.

He peered out through the curtains with me. "Bad news is the only thing I know that travels faster than the flu." He unwrapped an orange lollipop and stuck it in his mouth.

"Jeffrey," Miss Louise said. "You're going to ruin that child's teeth."

"Sometimes, the best medicine's candy," he said, winking at me. He used his sucker to point at mine. "Better save that one for tomorrow."

Before he let us go, he told Mama that I was supposed to rest and not do anything fun. With advice that cruel, no wonder I was leery of him. She set up a cot for me in the stockroom away from the noise in the store.

"Aren't you going to help Miss Louise clean up?" I asked. It was her reason for waking me before the birds started singing that morning.

Her eyes were still puffy and red, but she managed a smile. "There's a whole store full of people offering to help. I'd rather sit with you."

"Can't we sit at home?"

"Not without borrowing Miss Louise's car."

She finally gave up on me. Before she left, she smoothed her blouse and skirt, and dabbed her eyes with a hanky.

"I must look awful," she said.

She was too pretty to ever look awful, and I told her so. My opinion earned me a hug. She raised her chin and marched into the store, as brave a thing anyone could do with half the county, curious as cats, waiting on the other side of the door.

In the stockroom, I had no clock to keep me company. After what seemed like hours, I peeked over the side of the cot to see if my bones had poked holes in the canvas beneath me. If John Caleb had been there, he would have rolled his eyes at the idea. The only thing that kept me from bawling was Mama's bringing me my favorite ketchup sandwich and the promise I could help her when I finished eating.

My father returned in time to gobble the second half of my sandwich as if he hadn't eaten in a week.

"Where've you been?" I asked.

"Looking for John Caleb. I drove every road that led out of town and everything in between. Couldn't find him anywhere."

"I wish I could've gone."

"I know for a fact it's not much fun laying on a cot staring at the ceiling." He pulled John Caleb's note from his overalls. "Take this to Miss Louise and stay with her awhile. Your mama and I need to talk."

I whispered my father's message to Mama. Her eyes immediately brimmed both with worry and relief. I found Miss Louise in the back corner of the store where the old men played dominoes on winter days. Someone had moved the rocking chair for her. When she saw me, she scooted over so I could sit next to her.

"Daddy's back," I said, giving her the page from the catalogue. "He went looking for John Caleb and couldn't find him."

While she read the note, she rocked the chair with her matchstick legs.

"I want John Caleb back. He's a good boy," she said when she finished reading. "To think, he wants me to have the money he saved for a bicycle."

One didn't seem to cancel the other. The two things Miss Louise loved more than anything were her meat case and her cash register. I couldn't imagine her riding a bicycle.

"This has been a tough day for us girls, hasn't it?" she asked.

A long time had passed since she was a girl, probably, a hundred or so years. Further back than I could imagine. Last night alone, she had added another dozen or so wrinkles to her face.

"Must be hard sometimes with your daddy," she said. "I worry about it. Especially today him laying on the ground screaming, tearing at his face the way he was."

"Why'd he do it?"

"The war."

The same answer for everything my father did.

"Did he mean to?" I asked.

"No, he didn't know what he was doing. That was why Jimmy and the deputy were holding him down. They were trying to keep him from hurting himself."

"Everybody says he's crazy."

Miss Louise's eyes flashed with anger. She tapped my nose with her finger. It made me cross-eyed.

"You get that out of your little head right now. True, he's been scarred by the war, but I'll tell you something about your daddy. You have to keep it a secret. He didn't want anybody to know. You promise?"

I nodded. A new secret to replace the ones I let slip.

"Your daddy asked me to give John Caleb a job. He bought him the clothes he needed. He thought there was something special about him and worried nobody was taking care of him. He said John Caleb was too skinny, and no child should go hungry. Your daddy knows a thing or two about going hungry. When his POW camp was liberated he weighed less than a hundred pounds. Look at me." She stood. "Imagine your daddy weighing as much as me and more than a head taller. See how skinny I am?"

"Uh huh."

"That's the way he was. Nothing but skin and bones. They darn near starved him to death over there. Remember, don't tell him I told you."

"I won't."

Miss Louise had given me a gift, something to hold onto when my courage failed. I'd never thought about some secrets being more sacred than others. This one was. She sat down, leaving enough room I could curl up beside her and rest my head on her lap. While stroking my hair, she began to rock.

"Your daddy's a good man, a fine man," she whispered. "Don't let other people tell you different."

Chapter 24

With the robbery of the store and all that followed, those first few bright days of summer turned. Misery settled over us like road dust. Mama usually found something to cry about before noon. Daddy's response to her tears was to draw back inside himself and to march in a square—four steps each side. He wore a path beneath the elm tree.

Every afternoon, I'd set my egg basket on Miss Louise's counter and frown. She hadn't replaced her cash register because she thought it pure foolishness to buy a new one at her age. She used a dented metal box instead. That didn't stop her from speaking her mind about things. At the slightest sigh from me, she'd scold me for believing I was big enough to set things right when I hadn't even learned to multiply.

"It's not your fault, neither is it John Caleb's that your mama and daddy are fussing," she said. "It's their own doing, and that's that."

I wouldn't have called it fussing, not when they refused to say more than a half a dozen words to each other on any given day.

Miss Louise was struggling herself. Mama helped her at the store a few afternoons a week, but the floors grew dirty, the air musty. Cans of green beans got mixed in with the cans of tomatoes. The wrong change was given out.

Even the weather turned disagreeable. It didn't rain the rest of June and all of July. The temperature rose above a hundred and stayed there every day. In the orchard, the peaches shriveled and fell from the tree. Those left were small and wormy. No amount of wishing or praying could puff up a cloud, bring John Caleb home or make any of us happy.

In early August, my father and I rode Sammy and Moonie to the hayfield one evening and back through the orchard. Grandpa once promised that spring came after winter, but what happened when the drought-stricken trees dropped their leaves too early? Could they survive without them that long?

"Maybe your grandpa was wrong," Daddy said when I asked him. He pulled a small wormy peach from a branch and peeled it with his knife. "Maybe spring only comes for other folks." He handed me small chunks of a peach dewy with juice. The pieces tasted as sweet as candy corn.

"On the way home this afternoon, I came the river road," he said. "There were a couple of Gypsies camping at the Cottonwood Flats."

"Sam?"

"No."

"Are you sure?"

"I talked to one of them. They were passing through. He claimed he never heard of Sam, but you know how that goes. I asked him to keep an eye out for John Caleb. I don't know what else to do."

He said this despite the fact he could multiply and divide. I sighed.

"What's that about?" he asked.

I told him what Miss Louise said about making things right. He smiled, something I hadn't seen all summer long.

The last of October, it finally rained five month's worth in two days. We'd sat down to a late supper when someone knocked on our door. It was dark out. Daddy looked up at the clock. It was the time of year and the time of night.

"With the river coming out, no place to camp," he said.

Despite his pessimism, I galloped across the kitchen and flung open the door, expecting to see Sam on the porch, his little black hat set off-center. Instead, it was a dead man with his hair plastered to his head and his face bruised and puffy. I stepped back.

"Gracie, who is it?" Mama asked.

"Uncle Rag."

"Tell him to come in," Daddy grumbled.

Rag didn't wait for the invitation. He staggered past me and fell into a chair.

Mama jumped up. "I'll call Dr. MacKay."

"No!" Rag said, wincing. A dribble of blood had dried on his chin.

"They might be watching his office."

"What've you done now, and who's they?" Daddy asked.

"A couple of agents from the State Crime Bureau made me an offer I couldn't refuse. Find out who's heading up the moonshine ring or go to jail. Trouble is I don't know, so I've been snooping around."

"You're telling me you don't know who you've been working for all this time?" Daddy asked.

"You think anybody around here would trust me with that kind of information?"

"I suppose not."

"I got caught. Earl and Parker rearranged my face over it." Rag grabbed his hair on either side of his head and pulled. "Oh, man, I should've let those agents throw me in jail."

"Obviously, you got away."

"Barely."

"And you've led Earl and Parker here."

Rag shook his head. "No, I took them on a long foot chase. They were a couple of miles away from their car when I lost them. I figure they'd bumble around awhile looking for me before they'd give up and walk back. River's out. They'll have to go to town and around."

"You swam the river?" I asked.

"No, shinnied up a tree and jumped from limb to limb like a monkey."

He hopped two fingers across the table and scowled as if I were a cow pile he'd stepped into. He turned back to Daddy.

"We've got a little time before they get here," he said.

"Great!" Daddy said. "We've got time. For what?"

"There's a place here I can hide."

"No! You got yourself in this. Get yourself out. I have to take care of Kate and Gracie. Or did you even think about them?"

"Dadgummit, Aaron, my foot's killing me. I fell in a gully. I think it's broke."

Daddy walked over to the doorway into the hall.

"Where are you going?" Mama asked.

"To get my gun. He *thinks* it may take Parker and Earl awhile to catch up with him."

"They're gonna come," Rag said. "Won't make any difference if I'm here or not. Trust me, they're not gonna believe you when you tell them you haven't seen me."

"Then maybe you better skedaddle before I hand you over to them."

"I don't blame you for hating me. I lied to you about getting Annie pregnant."

"I know."

Mama interrupted to send me to my room. I stood, but made it no further.

"She didn't love me. She asked me to marry her, but wanted us to leave right then and go to Dallas. Heck, I didn't care. I loved her. But I had this one last load to deliver, you see."

"I know," Daddy said, his voice breaking.

"How?"

"From the man who helped her get away when you didn't come back that night."

"Get away?"

"I know why she wanted to leave, but I don't know who—" He glanced in my direction and never finished the sentence. "She was too afraid of whoever it was to tell Sam's wife."

"Sam?" I asked.

"Yes, Sam."

I sat down with a plop. The conversation continued to tiptoe around me, but neither Mama nor dynamite would dislodge me from the room.

The last of the color drained from Rag's face. He lowered his head into his hands and moaned. "How stupid could I have been? Why didn't I see?"

"As a family, we're downright blind," Daddy said, stepping into the hall.

"Aaron, listen to me. I would have raised Gracie as my own. I swear I would've. And I wouldn't have left her with the moonshiners if I'd known she was there. I did what Dad asked that night and left right after he did."

Daddy kept walking. The thought of Rag wanting to raise me made me tear out of the kitchen after my father. I found him in his bedroom rummaging through his closet. The excitement of what I'd learned about Sam helping my mother had to go somewhere. I spun in a circle until Daddy backed out with his hunting rifle. The sight sobered me.

"Are the bootleggers going to come here?" I asked.

"Hope not." He loaded the gun with the bullets he kept on the highest shelf. "Better be safe than sorry."

I hopped on the bed to watch him unlock the top drawer of his dresser.

"Can I see?" I asked.

He stepped to one side. His New Testament, revolver and the coffins of dead soldiers were still in the drawer.

I pointed to the boxes. "They're out of line."

"They are." As he tapped them back in place, he whispered,

"In dreams, I wept for headless flowers and legions of headless men
That tramped through night in rank and file beneath the naked moon.
Bound to orders of gentle mercy, they chanted a timeless dirge
And searched for those who would to die and heed their hypnotic tune."

For months, I had tried to get him to recite the poem to me. So why did he pick the scariest part? He took his pistol from its holster, which did nothing to reassure me.

"They're coming, aren't they? Are they gonna catch Rag?"

Daddy stuffed the pistol in his waistband. He kissed my forehead.

"Though I wished to follow them, to leave this hell behind
I woke to find the stalk revived; its leaf tipped with dew
And while I watched in wonder, a fragile bud burst forth
To beckon me to carry it with life and faith anew.

"You're my flower," he said. "When I was in the POW camps, I was starving. We all were. We'd eat anything, the weevils in what little rice we got, maggots, a rat if we could find one."

I cringed and stuck out my tongue.

He smoothed my hair. "There's worse things than carrots."

I agreed with him, but had no plans to start eating them.

"I found a flower by the barracks," he said. "I'd never seen one there the whole time I'd been at that camp. I ate it without a thought. It was the worst day of my life. I was sick. Really sick. My buddy'd been executed. I wanted to die. Just curl up and die right then and there. Then I remembered you. And that little flower. How beautiful it was, how fragile. The only green living thing in that whole barren camp. Until then I'd always figured God was like thunder and lightning. But that night, He came as quietly as a cloud slipping across the moon. The Bible says he never forgets a sparrow. He never forgot me. He forgave me."

I stared at him speechless. All this time, I thought his favorite verse was *Let the dead bury the dead.* He blinked away tears. Behind those dark eyes, he had been waiting for spring to come. For the orchard to bloom. To love me.

He closed the drawer, then changed his mind and reopened it. "I need to talk something over with your mother. Mind keeping an eye on this stuff for me." He nodded at the dresser.

"Okay," I said like the fox to the farmer. Despite the warmth in my heart, I shoved the poem, the maggots and guns from my head once he left the room. First thing, I went for the dead soldiers, not that I believed Daddy's claim, at least not fully. I figured it was only a way to keep me from snooping, like Grandpa's warning of creepy crawlies in the basement. Still, just in case, I cautiously pried the lid from a box.

"Oh. . .," I breathed.

It wasn't a dead soldier. It was a medal—a star with a red, white and blue ribbon. In awe, I picked up the box for a closer look. Why hadn't he told me? Unless it didn't belong to him any more than the little Army New Testament did.

Outside the door, the floorboards creaked. I ditched the box in the drawer, dropped onto the chair and clasped my hands together on my lap as innocent as could be. The footsteps faded. I hopped up. Having gotten away with the snooping, I felt braver and picked up the medal. The star had my father's name on back and the inscription *HEROIC OR MERITORIOUS ACHIEVEMENT*.

Daddy was a hero.

I yanked the lid from the second box which had a heart of purple and gold. His name was on the back of that one too. I went for the next box, then the next. Each one had medals and small rectangular ribbons, more than Jimmy Lear, the town hero, could pin on his chest. I wanted to whoop and do a war dance.

"Gracie," Daddy called from the kitchen. "Come in here."

In my excitement, I'd tossed the lids all over the bed. I gathered them and shoved them onto the boxes the best I could and lined the soldiers' coffins back into a row. He called me again.

"Coming," I shouted, slamming the drawer closed.

I raced into the kitchen and skidded to a stop. My grim-faced father stood by the back door, his hunting rifle resting in the crook of his elbow. Mama had her coat and rain bonnet on and held my jacket in her hand.

"Where are we going?" I asked, hoping the question covered up the combination of pride and guilt beaming from my face.

"Your mama's worried about Miss Louise," Daddy said. "She wants to go check on her. You're going too. With this rain, I think it best to stay all night."

"What's the matter with Miss Louise?"

"Her roof is a little leaky," Mama said. "She might need a good mopper."

Her glance at Daddy made me suspicious. We had our own leak above the stove with a pot to catch the water. Furthermore, my uncle was gone.

"Where's Uncle Rag?" I asked.

Daddy cocked one eyebrow. "I told him to go to hell."

I wondered if he meant the real place or if he was only wishful thinking.

Mama opened the door, then turned back to throw her arms around Daddy. "Be careful. I don't want to lose you. I love you."

"Kate." His voice broke.

My mother's eyes brimmed with tears, something I'd grown used to, except this time my father didn't march off. They held each other like they had those first days after their marriage before John Caleb robbed the store and the sheriff dropped me on my head.

I heard a car.

"That Rag?" I asked as part question and part warning. My uncle was capable of car theft. He still owed me a bag of candy corn, which I had little hope of collecting.

Daddy pulled back the curtain. "Sheriff's car."

"Thank goodness," Mama said.

"Maybe."

"Just don't pick a fight with him."

My father nodded grimly, then jabbed his finger at me as if it were my fault. "Gracie, you'll do whatever I tell you. No questions. If I say down, you drop to the floor like a rock. Do it. You'll have to trust me. No matter what. Promise." He squeezed my shoulder. "Promise!"

More than anything that evening, his insistence I obey him without question, trust him no matter what, frightened me. Understanding crept into my heart like winter cold under a door. He told me the story of the flower for a reason. He wanted me to see his medals, knew my curiosity would get the better of me. He was afraid. Afraid for all of us. I crossed my heart and promised, leaving out the hope to die part.

He opened the door.

Lundy stood on the porch, eyeing Daddy's rifle. "Too big for frog hunting. Too early for deer."

"Been cleaning it," Daddy said. "Learned in the service to always keep it ready."

"Good lesson. Mind if I see it?"

"I do." Daddy pressed his lips together in a show of determination.

That determination slipped when a hand with a pistol appeared just above the sheriff's shoulder.

George Parker stepped out of the darkness. "He owns a revolver, too."

Chapter 25

Daddy's face and shoulders sagged. He surrendered his rifle and let Mr. Parker search him.

"Where is it?" Lundy asked when the pistol wasn't found.

"My wife made me sell it. She didn't trust me with it."

It was an out and out lie—that much I knew, but I had no idea where it had gone unless to Rag.

The sheriff turned his hard eyes to me. "Where's your uncle?"

The frozen expression on my parent's faces gave me little help. "Daddy told him to go to hell." If he hadn't put it that way, I would never have remembered what to say.

"If we find Rag here, I'll shoot your mama and daddy, then I'll shoot you."

To prove his point, he aimed his gun at me. I shook with dread.

A shot rang from the basement. Mama put her hand over her mouth to stifle a scream. The bootleggers had killed Rag. We were next. My knees buckled. I sank to the floor as a warmness spread through the seat of my overalls. I was pathetic.

Lundy smirked over my head at Daddy.

"Your men shouldn't be shooting in the basement. Bullet's liable to ricochet off the rock walls and kill somebody," Daddy said. He stood tall, his brown eyes alert. I had little time for pride. A lantern lit the back door.

"He ain't down in the cellar." The voice belonged to Earl.

"What was the shot for?" the sheriff asked.

"Thought I saw something move. Turned out to be a rat."

"Check in here."

Earl came inside. The sheriff stopped the Parker twins, but not before they snickered at the soggy seat of my overalls.

"You keep watch outside," Lundy said to the boys. "I don't want Rag sneaking off while we're in here."

Mr. Parker and Earl searched the house for Rag and couldn't find him. Neither Mama nor Daddy seemed surprised. Lundy sent Earl to search the other buildings. This was too much for my stomach. I wrapped my arms around my middle. The action reminded him of my presence.

He yanked me to my feet. "You're not gonna throw up." As if he had any say so.

I clamped my hand over my mouth, though I doubted it would keep everything in place.

"Get out of here," Lundy said as I started to gag, "Parker, get her out of my sight."

Mr. Parker dragged me from the kitchen to the bathroom where he plopped me in front of the toilet. While he waited for me to do something, he pulled out a dirty handkerchief to blow his nose.

"You gonna throw up or not?" he asked through his hanky.

I took a deep breath and shrugged. Just being out of sight of the sheriff helped my stomach.

"Where's your bedroom?"

I pointed down the hall.

"Best you keep as far away from Lundy as you can," he said.

He flipped on my bedroom light and kicked my A-B-C book out of his way. I tried to grab the book and put it in my suitcase of keepsakes sitting by the dresser. They were supposed to be under my bed. It was one of Mama's rules. Mr. Parker pulled me away as my fingertips touched the pages.

"In bed," he said. "I'm doing you a favor. You better stay there."

Whimpering, I crawled under the patchwork quilt. If it worked for keeping the dead men away, maybe it would work for Mr. Parker. He moved about for awhile. The floor moaned under his feet. I peeked once and saw him looking beneath my bed. He caught me spying, and I pulled my head back until I heard his footsteps fade down the hall.

As I sat up, a floorboard creaked again below me. I used the last bit of courage left in me to slide my head and arms over the side to look under the bed when I heard someone jiggle the window.

"Little one, open up."

It was Sam. I couldn't see him in the darkness, but I unlocked the window and helped him open it. He had the screen propped up with his shoulder.

"How many men inside?" he asked.

"The sheriff and Mr. Parker."

"Outside?"

"The twins?"

"We have them."

He said *we* as if there were more Gypsies with him. The more the better.

"And there's Earl," I said.

"Good. Come with me. I will take you to my friend."

"What about Mama and Daddy?"

"First, I must help you."

He flicked his gaze over my shoulder and lowered the screen. Puzzled, I pushed it open to see where he went. I heard a sneeze behind me.

"Where do you think you're going?" Mr. Parker asked from the doorway. "I should have known better than try to help."

There wasn't much I could say with my head poking out the window. Sam had disappeared. I was alone. Mr. Parker's fingernails dug into my wrist as he dragged me down the hall and into the kitchen.

"Caught her trying to sneak out," he said, shoving me in front of the sheriff.

Mama and Daddy stared at me with wide eyes. I wanted to shout Sam's name, to let them know like always, he'd come to help us.

"Maybe you're not as pathetic as I thought," Lundy said.

I had the opposite idea. Getting caught was pretty pathetic in my mind.

"Your Daddy and I were having a talk about your mother," he said.

I glanced at Mama's tear-streaked face.

"Not her," he said. "Though I think I'll have as much fun with her as Annie. You probably don't remember me, do you? Your mama usually had you hid in the closet while I was there, as if I didn't know."

"You knew my mama?"

A coarse laugh rumbled from his chest. "Out of the mouth of babes." With all his jiggling, his gun belt slid over his belly. "What's keeping those idiots? If Rag isn't here, we'll have lost his trail."

I glanced over my shoulder at the window in hopes of seeing Sam. What happened to him? There was nothing but the reflection of my father slumping in his chair.

Mr. Parker nodded at me. "What are we going to do with them?"

"Aaron Timmons, disturbed veteran, sets fire to house. All are lost. A tragedy."

I wasn't sure what he meant until Mr. Parker said, "Want no part of killing anybody, 'specially a kid."

"Earl won't have any problem with it."

"It'll get us the chair."

"Shut up. Where's Earl?"

"Let Gracie go," Mama said. "Please."

Daddy remained silent, his head bowed. The door to the dining room wiggled. Daddy glanced in that direction and back. He had seen it. He raised his head to lock his attention on me. Seconds passed.

"No one will believe Aaron would do something like that," Mama said.

"He burned one house already. What's not to believe," the sheriff said.

"You won't get by with it," Mama said.

My mouth had gone dry. Mr. Parker honked his nose until the sheriff gave him a look of disgust.

"Down," Daddy yelled.

I dropped to the floor as if my bones were disconnected. He sprang from the chair to leap over me. At the same time, the dining room door banged open. Rag ran into the kitchen, screaming curses at Lundy.

Mama dragged me under the table as a gun blast cracked the air. Daddy staggered. Two more shots echoed. Plaster rained down on the floor. Hiccupping, I fought against Mama's iron hold of my arms. Mr. Parker sank to his knees less than two feet from us. He grabbed at a knife in his shoulder, pain and surprise contorting his face as Sam raced across the room to knock Mr. Parker's gun away from him.

Despite Sam's appearance, I couldn't stop the hiccups and sobs of fear. A chilling quiet settled on the room. Mama whispered Daddy's name and scrambled from under the table.

Sam whipped a piece of cord around Mr. Parker's wrists before he pulled his knife free.

"Little one," he said, dragging me from beneath the table, "you must be brave. Your papa is."

Rag, holding Daddy's pistol, stood over the body of the sheriff. Daddy lay a few feet away, his face a sickly white.

A frightening thought grew inside my heart as slowly and as conspicuously as the red stain on Daddy's shirt. He was going to die. Being brave had nothing to do with medals. I understood that now and no longer cared if he ever pinned one on his chest. I didn't want him to fade away like my mother and my grandfather. I wanted him to ride Sammy with me. To listen for those rare laughs of his that warmed my heart.

Without saying a word, my uncle glanced at Daddy and hobbled out the door, taking with him whatever he was thinking behind that one good eye of his.

"Gracie? Where's Gracie?" Daddy asked.

Mama held his hand. "She's all right. She's safe."

Sam used his bloody knife to slit Daddy's shirt. "Little one, get me clean cloths. John Caleb, go with her. Hurry."

I whirled around. John Caleb stood beside his pa. He was sucking on his bottom lip trying to keep it in place. Mr. Parker refused to meet his gaze. At Sam's order, John Caleb grabbed my hand and dragged me to the bathroom to get towels. When we returned, Mama was gone.

"Little one," Sam said sharply, "give me the cloth."

He pressed one of our towels against the bloody place in Daddy's side. The screen door slammed. I dove under the table, but it turned out Rag hadn't abandoned us after all. I felt his hand on my back as I crawled over to Daddy, a strange comfort from someone I thought I hated.

He said one word when Sam looked over at him. "Thanks."

Sam nodded in reply.

Mama came from the dining room. "Stop the bleeding the best we can. Dr. MacKay will meet us at the highway. We'll go to the hospital from there."

"I got the truck backed up to the porch," Rag said," but I can't drive far with this foot. Can you?" He'd never seen her fishtail onto the road.

"I can," she said. "John Caleb, we'll need some blankets and pillows. Spread them out in the pickup bed."

Rag leaned over Daddy. "Stay with us, little brother. Don't want you on my conscience."

Daddy's eyes fluttered open. "Didn't know you had one."

"Neither did I."

"We move you to the truck, my friend," Sam said, grabbing my daddy's shoulders.

My father gave him a weak smile. Rag and Mama each held one leg. They carried him outside and laid him in the back of the pickup. The engine was running. Once Sam and Rag were out of the way, Mama tucked the pillows around Daddy.

"John Caleb, you must go with them," Sam said as he hopped off the tailgate.

John Caleb stood on the edge of the porch where the yard light reflected in his tears.

"You are not a Gypsy, nor are you your papa's son," Sam said. "You are a man and you are needed here."

John Caleb hugged Sam, then bolted for the pickup.

"Gracie, you too," Rag shouted as he knelt next to Daddy. "In the cab with your mother."

I hesitated. I wasn't brave. I didn't want to go with them. The old memories of hiding in Grandpa's closet tugged at me. All this time I had it wrong. My father belonged to me every bit as much as I belonged to him. With that thought, I crawled into the bed of the pickup to sit beside him. His hand found mine.

Yet as Mama eased the truck away from the porch, a sense of loss drifted over me. I looked back at the house, at the basement door flung open. Beau huddled on the back step where he would be when we came home. The windmill creaked in the crisp fall air.

Sam stood alone.

The grimness of the night showed on his face. I raised my hand to wave. In acknowledgement, he smiled and settled his hat on his head. Then he turned and was gone, disappearing into the shadows beyond the glow of the yard light and our lives.

<h1 style="text-align:center">Epilogue
1975</h1>

On the night of the shooting, Daddy hadn't sent my Uncle Rag to hell after all. While I was distracted with the discovery of Daddy's medals, Rag was hidden beneath the floor of my bedroom in a secret compartment he built to conceal his moonshine. Only after Mr. Parker dragged me back into the kitchen could my uncle sneak through the house to help. He rushed into the kitchen with Daddy's revolver and killed the sheriff before Lundy could get a second shot off at my father. My uncle swore he only did it for Annie, then with that irritating habit of his, he winked.

My Uncle Rag wandered the fifty states, much like the Gypsies he once despised. He was in and out of our lives, a loose thread that could neither be tied nor cut.

John Caleb never would have left the Gypsies, except for the scribbled letter Daddy sent with the Gypsy he happened to find camping in the Cottonwood Flats. It simply read, *Come home. Miss Louise needs you.* John Caleb still has it, along with his precious arrowhead he wore on a chain around his neck through two tours of duty in Vietnam.

Miss Louise died the summer after the shooting. John Caleb was at her side. After her death, he moved in with us where he belonged and became my real brother.

The first years of Daddy and Mama's marriage were as wild as the ride to the hospital with her driving. I believed their faith in God and the poetry in their hearts kept them together, along with Miss Louise's philosophy that the past can't be undone, only forgiven. One day when I was no longer "too short" to understand, Mama told me about the baby she gave up for adoption in her senior year of college. The father was a young man killed in the war. She'd named the baby Grace, not knowing one day she would meet a little girl by the same name who needed a mother. In a way, my father's belief that Mama married him because she wanted me was partly true, but she had plenty of love for the both of us and her daughter. She prayed for her every day. I never saw Sam again. In the spring and fall, I waited for him. He inhabited my dreams and nightmares, but gradually he faded away like my other childhood losses.

I became a teacher like Mama. One spring afternoon after a trying day at school, I opened the mail to find a college graduation announcement from a stranger named Aaron Miller. Inside was a photograph of a handsome young man who reminded me of the Gypsy who came in and out of my life when I was a little girl. I turned over the photo and read, *My grandson. Thank you. Sven Miller.* I laughed. Sven, Sam, Stefan—Grandpa said Gypsies had more names than Carter had pills.

I called Mama.

"Oh, my," she said at first. Her fluttering reminded me of Miss Louise.

My father and Mama were in the garden when I arrived.

"Gracie!" Daddy called. He refused to call me Grace, just as I refused to call him anything other than Daddy. "Come here and look at this."

I picked my way along the edge of the garden.

"How come you aren't wearing your boots?" he asked looking down at my high heels.

"I came straight from work," I said.

Mama chided him.

Daddy grinned at us. "Look at this, would you?" He scraped a small pink bud with his thumbnail. "The peach tree's about to bloom. I believe spring is finally here."

I loved him so.

He studied the note Sam had written and chuckled. "Funny, he told me his name was Tamàs. I never said anything because I didn't want you disappointed."

At the moment when everyone finished dinner and before we lapsed into the trivial things of clearing the table and washing the dishes, I noticed the old sadness in my father's eyes. Mama told me his claustrophobia and nightmares had returned after years of peace.

"Do you still have that Army Bible?" I had asked before, but he always shrugged off the question.

He rubbed his chin and nodded.

"I'll get it. I know where it is," Mama said.

She returned in a few minutes and handed him the khaki-covered New Testament. He opened it. From his expression, I knew where the pages fell. Inside my shoes, I wiggled my toes. Part of that old habit never went away.

"Let the dead bury the dead," he read.

The memories tumbled from him. Stories bound by the horror of man's inhumanity were released. He had survived the march to Bataan, the constant hunger, the disease, the hell ships and the mines. In a broken voice, he told us of Corporal Lowell, the man executed for stealing the quinine that kept my father alive.

Mama arranged a row of small boxes on the table.

"The dead soldiers," I said. Among the medals was the bronze star and a purple heart.

Daddy frowned. "Those are for trying to keep myself and my men alive. Most of them died. Then I came home and faced my daughter for the first time. I wanted to turn around and never come back. I am no hero."

"But you stayed. You're my hero."

"I almost left. The night of your Christmas program."

"I was afraid you had," I said. "I asked Mama if grownups ever ran away."

"I would have, except you asked me if I was going to come with you. I couldn't go inside, so I stood outside the window, looking in at the flower God had given me."

Tears ran down his face as he recited the poem.

"So I marched along with death across the desert of my soul
Where neither thistle nor the thorn endure the sun's embrace
I prayed the blossom would guide me home, but should this soldier fall
I've smelled the fragrant flower of hope, the flower God christened Grace."

Author's Note

My mother had dementia, a cruel disease. Her childhood memories of farm life and Gypsies camping by the river became the setting for this novel. In the end, the dementia stripped her of all memories except those of picking peaches in her family's orchard and sitting by the silo with her beloved father as he taught her the cardinal directions.

Acknowledgements

Thank you to the City Island Writer's Group. Without your encouragement and generous tearing apart of the story and putting it back together again, it would have remained a lump of pretty words.

Thank you to my friends, Lois Gerber and Veronica H. Hart, who are always available to talk plotting and characters.

A special thank you to my husband for putting up with my dream. I love you.

About the Author

Joan King was raised on the family farm southwest of Guthrie, Oklahoma. Her parents, grandparents and two generations of aunts and uncles fed her stories—tales of love, hardships, history and a few secrets. During the summers, she worked with her parents in the fields, spending long days on a tractor driving round and round. To keep herself entertained, she told herself stories.

She earned her bachelor's and master's degree in music education from the University of Central Oklahoma and taught band in the Oklahoma public schools for fourteen years. In 1990, she moved to Florida with her husband.

She travels back to the farm several times a year and enjoys climbing on the tractor to brush-hog along the creek, all the while telling herself stories.

www.ingramcontent.com/pod-product-compliance
Lightning Source LLC
Chambersburg PA
CBHW050350190726
48284CB00007BB/2222

9781940761299